Everything to Everyone

Sherryl D. Hancock

Published by Vulpine Press in the United Kingdom in 2017

ISBN 978-1-910780-82-4

Cover by Claire Wood
Cover photo credit: Tirzah D. Hancock

www.vulpine-press.com

Growing up my mom always called me a "whirling dervish," teachers called me high strung, and said I wasn't working up to my "potential." We used to call my son the "Tasmanian Devil" because he was always going at top speed. We also have called my daughter our "cute little odd duck" because she never did things like anyone else and was hard to figure out. I have ADHD, my son has ADHD, and my daughter has ADD.

So this book is dedicated to everyone, like us, who has an attention disorder. You are AMAZING, you are BEAUTIFUL, you are AWESOME and you can do ANYTHING. Never forget that!

Chapter 1

Harley Marie Davidson climbed out of her black Nissan 370Z, lighting a cigarette as she did. She walked to the back of the car, popped the trunk, and pulled out her black canvas and leather messenger bag that contained one of her most prized possessions: a customized Alienware 18 laptop. It was the tool she used to do her work, and she'd done everything to make it the fastest processor she could get her hands on.

She finished her cigarette and stubbed it out with a booted foot. She wore faded jeans and a blue tank top that said "Harley Davidson" down one side and had the Harley Davidson logo on top. Along with her Harley Davidson leather boots. At her belt was a gold shield badge and at her hip was a gun. Walking into the building, she waved at the security guard at the front door.

"Harley?" someone queried from her right.

Harley stopped in her tracks and looked over and thought she recognized the woman, but wasn't sure for a long moment.

"Shiloh?" Harley queried, her look speculative.

This didn't look like the Shiloh Styles she remembered. The one she remembered was highly polished and dressed to the nines. The woman who sat in the outer lobby of the Department of Justice building looked like she needed a good hairdresser and a serious session with a stylist.

1

"Yeah," the woman said, nodding. "I thought I recognized you. You look… Well you look different, but the same," she said, smiling.

Harley nodded, her blue eyes looking amused, knowing she looked very different from high school. In high school, she'd tried to fit in, even though she never would. Now she didn't care what anyone thought about her.

"So what are you doing here?" Harley asked evenly.

"I have an interview," Shiloh replied. "Do you work here?"

"For now," Harley said, quirking a grin.

Shiloh nodded, looking very hesitant and shy at that moment. Regardless of what Harley knew about Shiloh Styles, she felt her heart tug. She'd never been good at being a bitch, though Harley remembered that was actually something Shiloh had been extremely good at.

"What are you applying for?" Harley asked then. She took a drink of the Java Monster in her hand, her many silver rings sparkling in the sunlight filtering through the windows.

"It's an office assistant job, with the… CPU. You know what that is?" Shiloh asked hesitantly.

Harley grinned. "Shouldn't you know what that is if you're applying for it?" she couldn't help but ask.

Shiloh looked embarrassed and nodded. "Yeah, you're right I should. I just don't really have computer access right now so I really couldn't research it."

Harley narrowed her eyes. "How is that even possible in this day and age?" she asked, her tone ridiculing.

"When you don't have money to pay for internet access, it's possible, trust me," Shiloh said sharply in her acute embarrassment.

2

Harley closed her eyes, blowing her breath out through her nose and shaking her head.

"I'm sorry," she said, realizing that although she hadn't meant to be a bitch, she'd become one rather quickly. "That was a shitty thing to say."

Shiloh bit the inside of her cheek and nodded. "I get it. I was shitty to you back in high school. It's your turn now."

Harley blew her breath out loudly this time, dropping her head in self-frustration as she sat down next to Shiloh.

"No, that's not actually where that came from," Harley said. "I'm in IT, so to me the concept of not being able to utilize the Internet is completely foreign."

Shiloh pressed her lips together, grimacing slightly. "So I guess that would just be me projecting then, huh?"

Harley gave her a pointed look. "Maybe a little bit," she said, grinning.

"I'm sorry," Shiloh said, shaking her head. "I'm just really nervous about this interview and I have no idea what I'm going to say. I really need this job."

Harley nodded, her look understanding, but a bit perplexed. Shiloh's parents had money like money was going out of style, so why was she so obviously destitute?

Shiloh saw the confusion on Harley's face, and she knew exactly what she was thinking. Once again, she felt completely embarrassed at her situation. This was the kind of thing that nightmares were made of, like showing up at work naked, or suddenly being back in high school and realizing you didn't do the homework or study for the big test. Or, in this case, running into someone from high school that you treated like shit and who now had a job at a place where you were begging for one. Shiloh thought of one word: karma.

"Okay, look," Harley said. "The unit you're applying for is called the Crime Prevention Unit. The position they're hiring for is for the hi-tech crime task force called CHTTCF. What they need is someone organized who can keep very unorganized people on track, and is able to multi-task like there's no tomorrow."

"And you just happen to know this why?" Shiloh asked, looking dumbfounded.

"'Cause they're trying to find someone that can put up with my ADHD ass," Harley said, grinning.

"You?" Shiloh asked.

Harley nodded. "Me."

Shiloh looked back at her, her moss-green eyes reflecting surprise.

"Well, if that don't beat all…" she muttered.

Harley raised her eyebrows at her comment, grinning as she did.

"So are you on the panel?" Shiloh asked.

"Oh, hell no," Harley replied, looking horrified at the very thought.

Shiloh couldn't help but laugh at the look on Harley's face. Then she looked crestfallen. "So should I just go ahead and leave now?"

"Why?" Harley asked, shocked by the question.

Shiloh shrugged, shaking her head.

"Thought you said you really need the job," Harley said then.

"I do," Shiloh said, "but I figure there's no way you want me working for you, so…"

"Why?" Harley asked her tone matter of fact. "Because you were mean to me in high school?" Her look indicated how ridiculous she thought that reason was. "That was what… fifteen years ago… I think I've gotten over it by now."

Shiloh pressed her lips together in mortification. "I guess I need to get over it too, huh?"

"Probably be a good idea," Harley said, grinning as she winked at her.

Shiloh blew her breath out, nodding her head. "Okay, I'll just go in there and do my best, and what happens happens, right?"

"Sure," Harley said, grinning again.

An hour later Shiloh was informed that she'd been hired.

"You should know," the woman said in a condescending tone, "that although your qualifications were, at best, minimal, your success was due to a direct request from the person you're being hired to work for."

Shiloh's eyes widened, not only because of the woman's attitude, but because apparently Harley had just done a very nice thing for her and it shocked her. In truth, she had figured that she'd just hear that she'd not been selected, that even though Harley had acted like their past didn't matter, it really had. Shiloh realized again that she was apparently the only one holding on to that past and she needed to let it go, especially if she was now going to be working for Harley.

Downstairs in the lobby, she asked the security guard if there was any way she could see Harley Davidson. The guard looked back at her for a long moment, and then nodded, picking up the phone. When he put the phone down, he gave her directions to Harley's office.

Shiloh wandered around, getting slightly lost, but then found the door that was marked "Harley Davidson – Consultant." She knocked on the door. She could hear music playing behind the door and it was loud. She could also hear the quick clicking of a computer keyboard. She had to knock a second time.

She heard a short, "Yeah?"

"Harley?" Shiloh queried, opening the door slowly.

"Yeah?" Harley answered as she reached over to turn her music down. "Come on in," she said smiling.

Shiloh walked into the office and looked around. There were a number of posters, with various quotes on them, obviously pertaining to computers. One had a picture of a computer and a cup of Starbuck's coffee, and it said, "Programmers are tools for converting caffeine to code." Another poster had a Windows logo on it, and it said "Difference between a virus and Windows? Viruses rarely fail!" The one just above Harley's computer had a picture of a computer and a woman working at it. The caption said, "The Internet: Where men are men, women are men and children are FBI agents!"

Harley watched Shiloh's eyes go to the posters in her office.

"Some of my friends have extra time on their hands," Harley said, grinning.

"So you're a programmer?" Shiloh asked.

"Sort of," Harley said, reaching over to remove her messenger bag from the other chair. "Do you want to sit down?"

"Sure," Shiloh said, nodding.

She continued to look around the office as she sat down. Then she stared at something over Harley's left shoulder. She stared at it dumbstruck for the longest time, so long that Harley had to turn around to see what she was looking at. Shiloh was staring at the degree on the wall.

"You have a doctorate from MIT?" Shiloh asked, sounding stunned.

Harley nodded. "That's how I justify my outrageous paycheck," she said with a sardonic grin. "Well, that and a fuck-ton of experience with alphabet city."

"Alphabet city?" Shiloh asked.

"FBI, DEA, CIA..." Harley rattled off.

Shiloh looked back at her, blinking a couple of times. "You've worked all those places?"

"Yeah," Harley said, her tone completely nonchalant.

Shiloh nodded, thinking that Harley had gone a lot farther in life than she had.

"I guess you really didn't need Mount Sinai that badly, did you?" Shiloh asked, referring to the Christian college preparatory school they'd attended.

Harley chuckled, her look wry. "No, I guess not."

Shiloh looked uncomfortable suddenly. "Harley, I really should apologize."

7

"No," Harley said, shaking her head, "you don't need to apologize. We were kids; you were doing what your father told you to do."

Shiloh shook her head. "I should have told him no."

Harley shook her head again. "Why? He would have done what he did anyway."

"Yeah, you're right, he would have," Shiloh said. "But he wouldn't have made me into a villain in the process."

Harley held Shiloh's gaze, her look telling Shiloh she wanted to say something, but was hesitant. Part of Shiloh wanted to ask what Harley wanted to say, but the other part said to just keep her mouth shut. This was her new boss.

"So," Harley said, "when did they say you could start?"

"Um," Shiloh stammered, "they said I needed to get fingerprinted and get a background check done."

"Oh, yeah," Harley said, nodding, "I always forget about that part."

"They didn't do one on you?"

"They just had to do a quick update on mine. I have like clearance for miles," she said, grinning.

"Alphabet city and all, right?" Shiloh said, with a wink.

"Damned skippy," Harley replied.

"Anyway, I really wanted to thank you for this," Shiloh said sincerely.

"Don't thank me yet," Harley said, with a rakish wink. "You haven't seen what a pain in the ass I'm gonna be to work for."

"Either way," Shiloh said, maintaining her serious tone. "This was really nice of you. The lady that did the hiring made it very clear to me that I was highly underqualified."

"Eh," Harley said, waving her hand airily. "She's highly underqualified to be a human being with a heart, so I wouldn't take anything she has to say too seriously."

"Will you just let me thank you?" Shiloh asked, her tone strident.

Harley held her hands up in surrender. "Okay, okay. Thank away."

Shiloh laughed, shaking her head. "I think I'm beginning to see the pain in the ass part…"

"Ohhhh…" Harley uttered, her eyes sparkling mischievously. "I see how it is!" Then her look grew serious. "Can I ask you a question?"

"Okay," Shiloh said, nodding.

"Why aren't your parents helping you out?" Harley asked gently.

Shiloh took a deep breath, blowing it out in a sigh. "Because they kicked me out and cut me off."

Harley looked surprised by that information, but didn't ask any other questions, simply nodding.

"Well, hopefully this job will help you out," she said after a couple of long moments.

"It will, you have no idea," Shiloh said, smiling. "Well, I better get out of here and leave you alone so you can work. Again, thank you so much."

Harley nodded. "You're welcome," she answered seriously.

***

"Now, who is this girl again?" Devin asked that night at the bar. Some of the group was sitting out on the patio at The Club.

Harley sighed, leaning back in her chair. "She's the daughter of the headmaster of the school I got myself kicked out of."

"Do we want to know what you did to get yourself kicked out?" Jet asked raising a black eyebrow.

Harley grinned. "Well, let's just say I was doing a little early experimentation in the lesbian field."

"Wait, I thought Devin was your first," Skyler said, looking at her wife.

Harley started laughing looking up at the night sky. "Sweet file not found of the Puget Sound!" she said. Then she looked at Devin. "You told your wife?"

"Wait, what the hell was that?" Quinn asked.

"What?" Harley asked.

"File not found…" Quinn repeated.

"Just my way of saying holy shit," Harley said, grinning.

Quinn blinked a couple of times. "Alright then," she said simply, causing everyone to laugh.

"Harley doesn't do anything like everyone else," Devin said, grinning at Harley.

"Broke the mold," Harley said, grinning.

"While you were still in it," Devin replied, winking.

Harley laughed, nodding. It was obviously something they'd said to each other a few times.

"So you two were in college together?" Xandy asked.

"Yeah, at MIT," Harley said, nodding.

"Are you a doctor too?" Dakota asked, winking at Cody.

Harley laughed. "I have a doctorate, yeah."

"Too many fuckin' doctors round here these days…" Quinn muttered good-naturedly.

"You say that now…" Xandy said, shaking her head with a smile on her face.

"But when I need one," Quinn said, giving her girlfriend an openmouthed glare. "Is that what you're saying?"

"I don't think we'll be very useful," Devin put in, gesturing to herself and Harley. "Especially not with the kind of trouble you get up to," she added, waggling her finger at Quinn.

"Wot?" Quinn asked, sounding very Irish and looking very guilty at the same time.

The group laughed.

"So, wait, wait, wait!" Devin said, holding up her hand and pinning Harley with a look. "So what exactly did you do to get kicked out?" she asked, repeating Jet's question.

Harley rolled her eyes heavenward, putting her tongue between her teeth. "I kind of made out with the headmaster's daughter."

"Wait, that's the girl that you just got hired?" Skyler asked.

Harley shrugged, nodding.

"Was she that good of a kisser?" Dakota asked, her eyes sparkling with amusement.

Harley laughed aloud. "No, she really wasn't, but I just felt bad for her today."

"Why?" Quinn asked.

"Because her parents have all this friggin' money and they've apparently cut her off completely. She said she couldn't even afford to get Internet."

"That's criminal," Devin said seriously.

"Right?" Harley replied.

"Why'd they cut her off?" Skyler asked.

Harley shook her head. "I don't know. I didn't want to pry too much. Regardless, she needed the job, and I figure I know her."

"You mean you *knew* her," Devin said. Just because she knew her from high school, it didn't mean she still knew the girl.

Harley looked back at Devin. "Yeah, you're right."

"Well, hopefully it works out okay," Jet said.

Later that night, Dakota climbed into bed beside her girlfriend. She held her from behind, sliding her arm under her neck and putting one hand on her waist.

Jazmine turned her head. "Is that room making you crazy again?" she asked tiredly.

Dakota grinned. "Uh-huh," she murmured.

Dakota was working on their house, wanting to make changes to one of the rooms to open it up, but it was driving her insane. The previous owners had done all kinds of crazy half-assed repairs and renovations. Dakota constantly had to undo something that had been done and make it right before she could change it.

Jazmine turned over, looking at Dakota.

"Favorite movie line," Jazmine said.

It was something Jazmine did to help Dakota get her brain to let something go for a bit.

Dakota grinned. "Uh…" she stammered, "has to be 'I think we need a bigger boat.' "

"Jaws!" Jazmine exclaimed.

Dakota smiled, nodding.

"Okay what's yours?" Dakota asked.

"Gotta be 'He didn't eat me! That's 'cause he just ate a cow, stupid!' "

Dakota looked back at her for a long moment, then shook her head. "Nope, don't know it."

"Lake Placid!" Jazmine said, grinning.

Dakota blew her breath out, shaking her head.

"Well we'll have to watch it sometime. Okay, favorite season?"

"Fall," Dakota answered.

"Me too!" Jazmine said. "There are tons of cute boots and I look better in warm colors and layers!"

"You look better in nothing, babe," Dakota said, smiling.

Jazmine laughed. "Okay, you win."

"Cool, what's my prize?" Dakota asked, her eyes sparkling in the semi-darkness of the room.

"Me?" Jazmine said.

"Ohhh, best prize ever," Dakota said, leaning in to kiss Jazmine's lips.

They kissed for a few minutes, and then Dakota stopped and looked contemplative.

"You just figured it out, didn't you?" Jazmine surmised.

"Yup," Dakota said, nodding. "Thanks babe," she said, getting out of bed.

Jazmine sighed, shaking her head, even as she grinned. Her relationship with Dakota only seemed to get better with time. For someone who was formerly completely against any true commitment, Dakota was very single-minded when it came to Jazmine. Women came on to Dakota all the time, easily sensing her sexual prowess in the confidence that oozed from every pore. Dakota rarely even looked for long; she was perfectly happy and settled with Jazmine. For Jazmine it was a balm to her ego that had been seriously damaged by Rayden Black Wolf's rebuff of committing to her not once but twice.

A half an hour later, Dakota returned to bed, sliding her hands over Jazmine's skin skillfully. Jazmine awoke to her body alive with sensations. Dakota spent the next hour making love to her and bringing her to multiple orgasms before finally allowing Jazmine bring her to her release. Afterwards they lay together, Dakota next to her, lying on her stomach with an arm and leg thrown over Jazmine's body possessively.

"Have I mentioned how much I love it when you lie like this?" Jazmine said, looking up at the ceiling, her hand stroking Dakota's arm that lay across her torso.

"Once or twice," Dakota said, her tone sated.

"I really love it," Jazmine said. Then she turned her head to look at Dakota. "And I really love you."

Dakota nuzzled Jazmine's shoulder, kissing it softly. "I love you too," she said softly.

Jazmine had been the first woman Dakota had ever allowed herself to be completely open with. That was because Jazmine had been the first woman who'd been willing to see past Dakota's tough exterior and off-putting behavior. She'd seen the side of Dakota that she'd kept well hidden from everyone except for a very small handful of people.

Dakota felt extremely fortunate to be with the beautiful, very sexy, and talented dancer. Jazmine frequently danced in music videos and was the dancer artists would use when they wanted a woman that was extremely eye catching and stood out from the crowd. With her long rich red hair, perfect body and curves, sweetheart-shaped face, and bright emerald-green eyes, Jazmine was definitely a stand out. Dakota found her endlessly appealing. Jazmine was also an incredibly caring, sweet, and warm woman who took care of Dakota and supported her every step toward independence.

It was really good relationship for each of them.

***

It was three weeks before Shiloh's background check was completed and another week after that before she was able to start working. The day she finally started, the security officer told her that she was scheduled to meet with Special Agent in Charge, Rayden Black Wolf, first thing. Shiloh was surprised by this information, but did as the security officer instructed and went to the second floor. In Rayden Black Wolf's outer office she was greeted by a secretary who told her to go on in.

"Special Agent in Charge Black Wolf?" Shiloh queried timidly.

"Yes," Rayden said, smiling. "You must be Shiloh," she said, standing from her desk and extending her hand to Shiloh.

Shiloh was surprised by Rayden's height and build. She looked very much like the Indian warrior depicted in the statue on her desk, down to the long black braid down her back. A black wolf stood next to the warrior.

Rayden glanced down at the statue, smiling fondly.

"My wife found that," she said, grinning. "Unfortunately it depicts a Plains Indian, so not really my people, but the idea is there."

"And your people are?" Shiloh asked.

"Cherokee," Rayden said, grinning.

"Oh," Shiloh said, nodding. "Okay, so mountain people are really yours."

Rayden grinned, her eyes reflecting surprise as she nodded.

"I love Native American history," Shiloh said. "I studied it a lot when I was younger."

"I see," Rayden said, smiling. "Well we'll need to talk some time; I'd love to see how accurate your information is."

Shiloh inclined her head. "I'm sure you could tell me a lot of things I don't know about your culture," she said. "So, you wanted to see me?"

"Yes, please have a seat," Rayden said, nodding.

Shiloh sat down, folding her hands in her lap, trying not to appear as nervous as she felt for some reason.

"As you may or may not know, I'm technically Harley's boss," Rayden said.

Shiloh nodded, blinking a couple of times.

"I wanted to meet with you because I wanted to tell you what your job is really going to be about."

Shiloh's eyes widened slightly. "I'm sorry, ma'am?"

"Well, my understanding is that you know Harley, is that true?"

"We went to high school together, but I don't really know her that well now."

Rayden grinned. "Well, she asked me to hire you, so I'm guessing she feels like you'd be someone she can work with,"

"She was doing me a favor, ma'am," Shiloh said. "We ran into each other the morning that I had my interview and I told her how I really needed the job. I guess she felt sorry for me."

Rayden's grinned widened. "Well, we'll see how grateful you are when you have to deal with her for a while," she said, her tone amused.

Shiloh looked back at Rayden, her face reflecting hesitation. "Harley said she was a pain in the ass too... Now I'm starting to worry..." she said, her moss-green eyes wide.

Rayden laughed a deep rumbling sound that was rather contagious.

"Harley is… Well, she's the best damned programmer out there is my understanding," Rayden said. "And according to Devin Boché, who's apparently known her for years, she is absolutely frenzied when it comes to her programming. So, that's exactly why I needed to hire an assistant for her. You are basically going to be Harley's handler."

"Handler?" Shiloh repeated, a little shocked.

"Basically," Rayden said, "Harley is not only ADHD, but she is also extremely intelligent, which unfortunately lends itself to her being rather manic about her work."

"Okay…" Shiloh said, her tone leading as she tried to figure out where the *handling* was going to come in.

"The ADHD tends to make her hyper-focused at times," Rayden said. "Workwise it causes her to miss meetings, conference calls, and it also sometimes means she doesn't go home for one or two days at a time, which management, namely me, really frowns upon."

"A lot of overtime?" Shiloh said.

"And with as much as she makes, that's murder on my budget," Rayden said, rolling her eyes. "But it isn't just that, because I really like the kid. She literally forgets to eat, sleep, and just plain relax sometimes. And then there's that damned jet that she drives."

"Huh?" Shiloh asked trying to catch up.

Rayden grinned, thinking the poor girl was really going to have a fun time dealing with Harley.

"The car that Harley drives is some kind of supercharged something or other," Rayden said, grinning. "You'd have to get Harley to explain, or better yet, when you meet Skyler Boché ask her, she'll more likely make sense and she knows all about the kind of car it is."

"Skyler Boché?" Shiloh asked. "Married to Devin Boché?"

"Exactly," Rayden said, nodding. "Skyler has the same model of car, but apparently Harley's is way faster, and believe me, if you get in that car with her, you better buckle up and hold on."

"It's that fast?" Shiloh asked.

"She handed everyone their asses on a run a few months back," Rayden said grinning. "Except for Quinn; she still needs to have a rematch."

Shiloh looked confused.

"Next time you're in the parking lot, take a look at the cars out there. Anything that looks remotely fast probably belongs to one of the group."

"The group?" Shiloh repeated.

"A group of women that hang out together. If you're around Harley long enough, I'm sure you'll meet them at some point."

Shiloh nodded, trying to take in everything she was being told. "So you need me to keep track of things for Harley and remind her of things," she surmised.

"Yeah, but believe me it's not going to be as easy as it sounds," Rayden said, chuckling. "And I would really consider it a favor if you'd kind of keep an eye on her with regards to things like eating and when she's overdoing it."

Shiloh nodded, thinking it was crazy that someone needed to be reminded to eat, but she didn't figure Rayden was telling her this for no reason.

"How will I know when she's overdoing it?" Shiloh asked, looking worried.

"Trust me, you'll be able to tell," Rayden said. "About a month and a half ago, she had apparently been up for days working on a program to detect some kind of signal computer voodoo stuff. She literally passed out in the café upstairs, scared the crap out of the owner."

"Yikes!" Shiloh said, her eyes wide.

"Yeah," Rayden said, nodding. "The way I see it, she wasn't behind the wheel of her car, but that's when I knew I needed to get someone in here to assist me in keeping an eye on her."

Shiloh nodded again. "I will do everything I can."

"That's all I can ask," Rayden said. She stood and extended her hand to Shiloh again. "If she gives you too much shit about anything, just let me know, I'll chew on her. Or if worse comes to worse, I'll call her dad."

"Her dad?" Shiloh repeated surprised. "The biker guy?"

Rayden grinned. "I guess that was his cover, yeah."

"Cover?" Shiloh queried.

She remembered how much grief Harley had gotten in high school, not only about her name, but about her father being some 'dirty biker.'

Rayden looked at Shiloh for a long moment. "Her dad was one of the best undercover narcs in the city," she said.

"He was a police officer?"

Rayden nodded, grinning as she did. "And I guess even Harley kept that a secret."

"Yes, she did. Everyone really thought he was a biker when we were in high school."

Rayden pressed her lips together. Shiloh had a lot to learn about this world that she was now a part of.

Shiloh knew she was never going to pass her algebra class without help. Every boy that said he'd "tutor" her had that lascivious look in his eyes when he said it. The instructor had told her that she should ask Harley Davidson, and she had practically laughed in his face. Now she was desperate, because if she failed the next test, the instructor said he had to tell her father. She reconsidered.

She found Harley at lunchtime sitting on the lawn alone, for once not with all the other degenerates she hung out with regularly. The girl just didn't have any style at all. Her blond hair was a mess, and she wore tattered jeans and a black t-shirt that had the name of some random band on it. Her shoes were beat up Vans. Shiloh looked at her in her Jimmy Choo slides, rolling her eyes that she was standing on the grass in them.

"Excuse me?" she queried, her tone condescending.

"Yeah?" Harley asked, looking up at her, her hand shading her eyes.

"I was wondering if you could tutor me in algebra," Shiloh said more than asked, her tone far from entreating.

"I could," Harley said wryly. "But didn't you have like twenty other offers?"

"I need help with algebra, not to be felt up by some guy," Shiloh replied snidely.

Harley half laughed, half coughed. "Okay."

"So will you tutor me or not?" Shiloh asked impatiently.

Harley shrugged. "Yeah, I guess."

"Your generosity is only exceeded by your overwhelming enthusiasm," Shiloh said sharply.

Harley looked up at her, her look blank.

Shiloh sighed. "When can we start?"

Again, Harley shrugged. "Whenever," she said, picking at a thread on her jeans.

Shiloh stood staring at the other girl for a full three minutes. Harley continued to pull at the string on her jeans, succeeding in unraveling a full section of thread. She wondered if the other girl had actually forgotten she was standing there.

"Hello?" Shiloh queried.

Harley looked back sharply. "What?"

"Oh my Lord!" Shiloh exclaimed her voice strident. "When can we start? And if you say whenever one more time..." she warned.

"When do you want to start?" Harley asked, her look inscrutable.

"Tonight?" Shiloh queried.

"Sure," Harley said, her tone amiable.

"You are impossible!" Shiloh exclaimed. "Seven o'clock at my house. Don't be late."

"Where do you live?" Harley asked.

"Everyone knows where I live!" Shiloh said, rolling her eyes.

"Except apparently me," Harley said, her tone wry.

"Fine!" Shiloh said, sure that Harley was just giving her trouble.

She pulled a pad of paper out of her notebook, wrote the address on the paper, and ripped it out handing it to Harley.

Harley arrived twenty minutes late, and Shiloh was livid, right up until Harley was the first person to ever explain algebra to her in a way that made sense. It was like a miracle.

Shiloh left the meeting with Rayden and went back down to Harley's office. She knocked on Harley's office door. Once again, she could hear loud music and was certain that Harley hadn't heard her knock. Something she was going to need to get used to she imagined. She opened the door and peered in. Harley was tapping away at the keyboard. She was wearing jeans, boots, and this time a tank top that had a picture of a light bulb on it. Above the picture it said, "How many programmers does it take the change a light bulb?" Below it, the wording said, "None: It's a hardware problem." Shiloh grinned at the shirt. She noted Harley's white-blond hair was up in a ponytail, except for two long rainbow-colored braids that extended halfway down her chest.

As she walked into the office, Shiloh waved her hand at Harley who finally looked up. Harley immediately reached out to turn her music down.

"Hey," Harley said, smiling at her.

"Hi," Shiloh said, smiling back.

"So you're here now?"

"Yep," Shiloh said, nodding.

23

Shiloh looked around Harley's office, trying to get a feel for how Harley organized things. Harley watched her, grinning as she did.

"What?" Shiloh asked.

"What're you doing?"

"Um, trying to figure out how you organize."

"I really don't," Harley said, shaking her head. "I think that's what bugs most people."

Shiloh smiled. "Okay, so will you be okay if I work on organizing you?"

Harley shrugged. "Sure."

Shiloh nodded, looking around the office. "Do you mind if I look at things? Is there anything I'm not allowed to look at?"

"You can look at anything you want. I'm betting you don't read code, so I'm betting I'll be safe there," Harley said, winking at her.

Shiloh laughed, nodding. "You are definitely safe there."

Another couple of days and a number of questions later, Shiloh had a simple system for keeping Harley's files organized. She'd made her project folders and color coded them according to their priority. She set up an iPhone and synchronized it to Harley's calendar, and met with various other staff that Harley was doing projects for. She'd also found Harley's major weakness: she almost never said "no." Even if a new project would completely overwhelm her, and put her behind on other projects, she always agreed to do it.

After one such meeting, Shiloh knew she needed to try to help in this area as well. She met with Rayden for a few minutes, finding more and more that she liked SAC Black Wolf; she was easy to talk to and seemed to be very supportive of everything she suggested.

"I'll give you a list of her priority projects," Rayden told her. "She can take smaller projects, but you're going to need to talk to her about timing on things. I'm not sure if she's fully aware that there are only twenty-four hours in a day and that she has to sleep at some point." Rayden said the last winking at Shiloh.

"I'll make sure I remind her of that often," Shiloh said, grinning.

"Good plan," Rayden said, laughing.

Chapter 2

Shiloh began going to meetings with Harley. During the meetings she'd take notes and ask whatever questions she needed to in order to have a conversation with Harley afterwards. She noticed that Harley looked surprised when she asked questions in the meetings.

In one meeting, she inserted herself into the conversation by stopping Harley from saying she could take on the project. Shiloh instead told the manager that they'd get back to her about whether or not Harley had time in her schedule for this particular project. Once again, Harley looked surprised by Shiloh's statement, but said nothing.

"Okay, so what kind of time will this project take?" Shiloh asked as she sat down opposite Harley's desk back in her office.

Harley looked back at her surprised by the question, then looked like she was calculating the time. Finally, she shook her head.

"Not sure, I need to look at what all is involved."

"Okay, what does that entail?" Shiloh asked.

"Well, I need to see what they are using right now," Harley said, still looking befuddled by all the questions Shiloh was asking.

"What do you need to know about what they're using?" Shiloh asked then, undaunted.

"I need to see what operating system it is, what the program is, what language it's written in..." Harley said, seeing that Shiloh was writing it all down and nodding.

"And I should be able to find that out, right?" Shiloh said.

Harley looked back at her for a long moment. "I said *I* need to..."

"I know, and I'm saying that I can check it out and tell you," Shiloh said.

"What do you know about code language?" Harley asked.

"Well, I know there are a number of them, but I know that some of the more in demand languages are SQL, Java, Javascript, C Hashtag—"

"C Sharp," Harley corrected, with a grin.

"Oh, is that how you say that one? Okay. And then there's Python and, um, C++?" She queried the last one.

"Right," Harley said, smiling, finding it endearing that Shiloh had apparently done some research on coding to try to be helpful.

"And the other ones I read about were PHP, IOS, and Ruby on Rails."

Harley grinned, nodding. "Okay, and how are you going to know what the program is written in?"

"Google?" Shiloh replied, smiling.

Harley pressed her lips together, finding it endlessly amusing that Shiloh was trying so hard to help her.

"We'll talk about how much it's not that easy later," Harley said her blue eyes dancing amusement. "But I suppose what you can do is sit down with them and get their business process for what they're doing now and how they do it and why it's not working for them."

"What will that tell you?" Shiloh asked.

"It'll tell me if I need to create a whole new program, or if I can just fix what they've got by adding some coding."

"So one takes a long time, the other not as much," Shiloh clarified.

"Exactly," Harley said nodding. "Then I need to help them test it and verify, and then go forward."

"Okay, but can I do that part?" Shiloh asked.

"Which part?" Harley asked, her mind already racing with everything she needed to do that day.

Shiloh could see she was losing Harley's attention. Harley was reaching over to plug in her phone, which meant her music would start soon, and it would be impossible to get her back. Reaching out, Shiloh put her hand on Harley's arm, feeling Harley jump slightly when she did.

"Just stay with me for one more minute, okay?" Shiloh said her look serious. "Can I work on the testing stuff with the program? They just need to test out your changes to their program and see if it works, right?"

"Right," Harley said, grinning. "And yeah I guess you could do that part... Getting them to test stuff is always the hardest part, they don't understand it."

"Okay," Shiloh said, nodding her head. "I'm going to read up on that part. You go ahead and get to whatever you were doing. I'll leave you alone for a couple of hours."

"Okay," Harley said, nodding, already starting to open programs on her computer.

Shiloh shook her head. The woman was singularly minded.

Shiloh had found out quickly that Harley's tendency to forget things interfered greatly with her personal life. She forgot dates, birthdays, holidays, and her tendency to stay at the office all hours of the night didn't help either. Shiloh was finding that lesbians tended to get paranoid when their girlfriend didn't come home at night.

She had this graphically illustrated to her a soon after she started working for Harley.

The woman Harley was dating at that time came storming into the office. She barely slowed at Shiloh's desk, so Shiloh had to jump up to follow her as she threw the door open to Harley's office. She walked into the woman screaming at Harley.

"Who the fuck is it, Harley!" the woman, a diminutive blond, yelled.

Harley, who'd obviously just been dragged out of some kind of programmers trance, looked back at the woman like she couldn't comprehend what she was asking.

"Who is what?" Harley asked, looking completely baffled.

"Whoever you're fucking behind my back!" the woman yelled.

Shiloh quickly closed Harley's door behind her, staying in the office in the event that she needed to call security.

Harley looked back at the blond for a long moment her mouth open, then she shook her head. "I have no idea what you're talking about."

The woman put her hands on her hips, her look accusatory. "You didn't come home last night!"

Harley's eyes widened. "I was here last night," she said, holding up her hand in futility.

"Right, sure you were," the woman said, looking unconvinced. "If you want to break it off Harley, just tell me." She said the last with a sigh.

Harley's mouth dropped open, then she closed it, still looking baffled. Then a look of defeat crossed her face as she shrugged.

"If that's what you want, fine," Harley said, her tone dispirited.

"Fine!" the woman yelled, and then turned to storm out of the office.

Shiloh, who was leaning against the door trying to remain inconspicuous, scrambled to open the door and get out of the way. The woman threw her a nasty look as she stormed past. Shiloh looked back over at Harley, who sat looking rather stunned.

"Are you okay?" Shiloh asked.

Harley looked back at her for a long moment, and Shiloh knew she wasn't really seeing her at all. Finally, Harley blinked slowly, swallowing convulsively and then nodded, turning back to her computer and turning her music back up. Shiloh bit her lip in concern, but knew she needed to leave Harley alone.

Shiloh got the opportunity to ask questions of someone who knew Harley a day or two later. She met Devin Boché when she came to the office and stopped in to say hi to Harley. Devin walked up to Shiloh's desk, smiling, her bright green eyes sparkling.

"So, you're the poor soul they hired for Harley?" Devin asked, grinning.

Shiloh looked up at the woman standing at her desk. She was beautiful, but also a bit quirky looking with purple streaks in her black hair and multiple piercings in her ears. She was dressed very stylishly with her makeup matching her mint-green shirt and jewelry.

"I'm Shiloh," Shiloh told the woman.

"I'm Devin Boché," Devin said, extending her hand to Shiloh.

"You're the one who recommended Harley to SAC Black Wolf," Shiloh remembered, as she took Devin's hand and shook it.

Devin nodded. "Yeah, she and I went to MIT together. I knew she was the best programmer out there, who was willing to work for the light side of the force." She said the last with a wink.

Shiloh chuckled, nodding. "Well I'm trying to make sure she can keep doing that without killing herself."

"And I appreciate that," Devin said, smiling. "So if there's anything I can do to help, let me know."

"Actually there is," Shiloh said holding up her finger. "Would you have time to grab some coffee sometime?"

Devin looked at her watch, a very expensive looking Movado. "I have time after I say a quick hi to Harley. Can you break away?"

Shiloh took a quick look at Harley's calendar. "Yeah, she's got another two hours of programming time before I drive her insane about eating lunch," she said, smiling widely.

Devin laughed at that, nodding. "Okay, I'll be right back."

Devin walked into Harley's office without bothering to knock, and left the door open so Shiloh could see what she did next. She walked over to stand behind Harley who didn't even seem to have noticed Devin's entrance. She put her hands on each of Harley's shoulders and leaned down, kissing her on the cheek. Harley immediately stopped typing and turned her head to the side, glancing up and back at Devin, smiling.

"What're you doin' here?" Harley asked, as Devin moved to lean on Harley's work surface next to her.

"Had to come talk to Jericho about a case they're looking at having me consult on."

Harley nodded. "Cool."

"Okay, well, I don't want to bug you, I know you're busy," Devin said, leaning down to kiss Harley on the head. "I'm stealing your assistant for a little bit though."

"Okay," Harley said, grinning.

Devin walked out of the office and heard the music go right back up. She just grinned and shook her head.

"Come on," Devin said, nodding her head to Shiloh.

Twenty minutes later, they were settled with coffee in a corner of the cafeteria upstairs.

"So what do you need to know?" Devin asked.

"How well do you know Harley?" Shiloh asked, unsure if she should really ask all the questions she had.

Devin shrugged slightly. "Probably better than anyone else here, why?"

"Does her... I don't know what to call it..."

"ADHD, insanity, one-track mind..." Devin supplied.

"Right, all that," Shiloh said, waving her hand around in a circle to encompass all that Devin had just said. "Does all of that cause her relationship problems?"

Devin looked back at her, narrowing her eyes slightly. "Always," she said simply.

"Does she even understand why?" Shiloh asked. "I mean, I know how that sounds, but I don't mean it to be mean... You know?"

Devin grinned as she took a sip of her coffee. "The answer is that, no she doesn't get it at all," she said. "She goes along being her, she draws women in, unintentionally most of the time; she just has that cool, aloof vibe. The problem is that once they're with her, they expect her to pay attention to them. That's where the problems start."

"She doesn't pay attention to them?" Shiloh asked.

"She does when she's there, but then she's... well, here or home on the computer, or in her head at The Club... And they get sick of it... That's when the games start."

"The games?" Shiloh asked.

"Yeah, the pay-attention-to-me games," Devin said, her green eyes sparkling in malice. "Some of them just blow her phone up, others get dramatic, others pull stunts to get her attention, and it's really bad sometimes."

"Like what kind of stunts?" Shiloh asked, sounding concerned.

"One chick got really drunk and got herself into a huge fight with a butch that had Harley getting in the middle of it," Devin said, shaking her head. "She ended up in the emergency room when the other chick pulled a knife on her. Harley can fight, but she's not equipped to handle crazy."

"So this girl just got into a fight to get Harley to pay attention to her?" Shiloh asked, shocked.

"Unfortunately," Devin said. "But that was before she was hanging with the group. Now we keep an eye on her, at least at The Club."

"The group," Shiloh murmured. "I've heard of them a few times."

Devin grinned. "Well, it's just a group of us that have ended up connected in one way or another. We do stuff together; Harley was an easy addition."

Shiloh nodded. "I'm glad she has that at least," she said. "Some girl walked into her office the other day screaming at her about not coming home."

Devin rolled her eyes. "That would have been Sheri. She was a bit psychotic, afraid that Harley was cheating on her all the time."

"Yeah, that's what she thought. At least that's what she screamed at Harley, anyway."

Devin nodded. "How'd Harley take it?"

Shiloh shook her head, looking frustrated. "She just gave up and let the woman break up with her."

Devin shook her head slowly. "Yeah, Harley's not about confrontation."

"I can see that," Shiloh said. "I just felt so bad for her."

Devin looked at Shiloh, wondering. "So can I ask you something?"

"Sure," Shiloh said.

"What happened between you and Harley back in high school?"

Shiloh was taken aback, she wasn't aware that anyone knew about that.

"Why? What did Harley say?" she asked, worried suddenly.

"She just said that you were the headmaster's daughter and that she got kicked out of school for making out with you."

"Did she say what school it was?"

"No, what difference does that make?"

"Because it was a private Christian high school," Shiloh said. "And what happened between Harley and me was a huge violation of the school's honor code."

"And what happened?" Devin asked, her eyes sparkling with curiosity.

Shiloh bit her lip, looking hesitant.

"Would it help if I tell you that I was her first in college?" Devin asked.

Shiloh's mouth dropped open in shock. "You were?"

"Yeah, and she was mine," Devin said, smiling fondly.

"Wow," Shiloh said, truly surprised. "I don't know if it helps, but I guess maybe you understand how easy it is to get drawn into her."

Devin nodded. "Yes, I do. Like I said, she draws women to her all the time, even when she doesn't try. She never seems to get what she did."

Shiloh laughed softly. "That would actually kind of explain our encounter," she said, smiling as she shook her head.

They were in Shiloh's room at her parents' house. Harley was trying to help her study for the final exam. Shiloh was beyond nervous. Over the last few months, she and Harley had come to a kind of a friendly relationship, not that she ever acknowledged Harley at school. Her friends would never understand that at all! Harley never seemed to care. It was apparent from Harley's appearance that she hadn't slept the night before. It was for that reason that Shiloh wasn't surprised when she asked a question and Harley didn't answer. She looked over and saw that Harley was asleep on her bed. Harley was lying across the bed with her legs dangling at over the edge.

Shiloh got up and walked around to look down at Harley. She saw that Harley was really a pretty girl, and could be so much prettier with makeup and better clothes. Sometimes Shiloh felt bad that she had so much when kids like Harley didn't have anything it seemed. Well, her father was a biker, what kind of job would that mean he had? Shiloh heard that the guy was never home and when he did come home, he was a drunk.

She was still looking down at Harley when the girl opened her blue eyes. Shiloh was struck by how blue they were. She found herself smiling down at Harley.

"You have such pretty blue eyes," she said, her tone wondrous.

"I like yours better," Harley said, smiling wistfully.

"Why?" Shiloh asked, moving to sit on the floor next to where Harley's head lay.

Harley turned over on her side, looking at her.

"They're just really different," Harley said, smiling tiredly. "So, do you think you're ready for the test tomorrow?"

36

"I don't know. I'm not sure if I'm going to be able to remember everything I need to remember the formulas and all that," Shiloh said, shaking her head.

"You can, you just have to know that," Harley said, smiling, her blue eyes sparkling.

"You really think so?" Shiloh asked, looking doubtful.

"Yeah I do," Harley said, her look sincere.

Shiloh looked back at Harley and their eyes connected for that long moment. Shiloh felt something shift in her heart; she didn't understand it, but suddenly she was focused on Harley's lips. Harley's look flickered and, as if in slow motion, she reached her hand out to touch Shiloh's cheek, sliding to the back of her head and pulling her slightly forward. Shiloh shifted forward, trembling as she did. Their lips were so close; Shiloh could feel Harley's breath on her cheek. Their eyes connected and they paused, Harley's eyes searched Shiloh's. Shiloh closed the slight distance between them, pressing her lips to Harley's.

They both jolted slightly as their lips connected and Harley's hand at the back of Shiloh's head tightened slightly. Shiloh moaned softly and Harley immediately deepened the kiss, moving her other hand to caress Shiloh's cheek. Shiloh reached up her shaking hand and touched Harley's cheek as they continued to kiss.

Suddenly Shiloh realized what she was doing and she thought about what her father would say. She quickly pulled away.

"I can't, I'm sorry, I can't," Shiloh said, moving back.

Harley looked shocked for a moment, but then started to nod as she sat up, looking a bit shell-shocked.

"I'm really sorry, I'm just... I'm not gay," Shiloh said.

Harley wouldn't look at her, she just nodded her head and stood up.

"I'm gonna go," Harley mumbled.

"Harley, wait," Shiloh said. She went to stand up even as Harley walked past her to leave the room.

Harley was gone before she even managed to get to her feet. She sat on her bed and thought about what had just happened. She didn't understand all this feeling going on in her head. Her body had reacted to the kiss, but she didn't understand that either. She wasn't gay, she wasn't. It was all so confusing! Putting her fingers to her lips she could still feel them tingling from the kiss.

The next day she talked to her best friend, Kim.

"So, she kissed you?" Kim said looking horrified.

"Yeah, but I wanted her to," Shiloh said, her look wistful.

"Why?" Kim asked looking shocked.

"I don't know," Shiloh said, shaking her head. "I just did and when she did it was... I just didn't know it would feel like that..."

"Shiloh, you aren't some sick lesbo," Kim said snidely. "That dirty little piece of white trash needs to be kicked out of this school. She's never belonged here anyway."

"Kim, if it wasn't for her I'd be failing algebra right now," Shiloh said. "And she's not trash, she's really smart."

"She's some sick lesbo, she shouldn't be around decent people," Kim said, disgusted. "Look what she did to you, who knows who else she's attacked like that."

"She didn't attack me, for God's sake!" Shiloh said.

38

Kim put her hand to her throat, her eyes wide, shaking her head, her brown curls bouncing around at she did.

"I cannot believe you just took the Lord's name in vein!" she said, sounding very much like Shiloh's mother.

"I need to get to class," Shiloh said, wishing now that she hadn't said anything to Kim.

In her algebra class, Shiloh saw Harley but she still wouldn't look at her. She sat down and pulled out her calculator and pencil in preparation for the test. Harley finished her final before Shiloh and left class before Shiloh could talk to her.

The next day everything went to Hell.

"So after that my dad heard about it and he went on a campaign to get Harley kicked out of his pristine school," Shiloh said, after telling Devin what had happened. "It was awful, I felt so bad for her."

"She didn't tell your dad that you had initiated the kiss?" Devin asked.

Shiloh shook her head. "No, she never said a word about it. I could never figure out why."

Devin grinned. "'Cause that's Harley," she said. "She's not about revenge. I'm not even sure she has a mean bone in her body."

Shiloh laughed softly. "Yeah, that sounds about right."

Devin canted her head. "So did you ever experiment with any other girl?"

"Oh no," Shiloh said, shaking her head. "My father condemned everything about that lifestyle and he just said such awful things I was too afraid for the longest time. And then I just didn't, too much turmoil. I worked for my father you see, in the church and all, so starting something like that would have just been bad news."

Devin nodded. "So can I be really nosey and ask why your parents cut you off?"

Shiloh chewed on the inside of her cheek for a long few moments, looking hesitant. "I was dating a guy that my parents fully approved of, and let's just say I was way too honest with him one night, about Harley in fact. When he became a complete pig about it, I saw his true nature and was done dating him. And once again, word made it back to my father and he decided I wasn't the kind of daughter he wanted."

"Wow, he really hates gays huh?" Devin asked.

"Oh yeah," Shiloh said, nodding.

"So he'd really hate that you're now working with Harley, wouldn't he?" Devin said, grinning.

"Yep," Shiloh said, not looking the least bit sorry.

"Good," Devin said, her grin bordering on evil. "Well, I can tell you that I love Harley to death, she's just one of those people that you can't help but like. I'm also really glad that you're helping her out, she worries me sometimes."

Shiloh nodded. "Yeah, I can understand that."

"You need to come out and meet the group sometime soon," Devin said. "I think you'll find that your father's attitude about gays is completely unfounded."

Shiloh smiled, nodding. "Well, I suspected that for a long time, but I definitely would like to meet the group. You all sound like you're pretty interesting."

"We have a few characters, Sky and me notwithstanding," Devin said, grinning.

"Sky is your wife, right?" Shiloh asked looking curious.

"Yes," Devin said, smiling fondly, "and the very love of my life."

"How did you meet her?" Shiloh asked.

"She came to a party at my house," Devin said. "And I pursued her relentlessly until she gave in."

"You pursued her?" Shiloh asked, smiling widely. Then she nodded. "I guess I can see that, you seem like a very upfront person."

"Oh yeah," Devin said, rolling her eyes. "And Sky wanted nothing to do with me at first, but I wore her down." She winked.

Shiloh laughed. "Well it obviously worked if you're now married."

"Yes, it did," Devin said, smiling brightly.

"Well, I should let you get back to your day, and I should get back down there to get Harley to eat lunch," Shiloh said, moving to stand.

She extended her hand to Devin. "Thank you so much for this," she said. "I just wanted to get a better idea of how I can help Harley with everything, you know?"

Devin nodded. "Yeah, I know," she said, smiling. "And feel free to call me anytime. Like I said, I absolutely adore the girl, so if you need my help, you just let me know. Okay?"

"Okay," Shiloh said.

***

Dakota lay on her stomach, her bare back on full display, and her hair still damp from her shower. Jazmine walked into their bedroom and couldn't help but smile. It still made her smile every time she saw Dakota, because the woman just plain made her happy. She couldn't believe how easy their relationship was. They meshed so well, it was almost seamless. She loved the younger woman more than she would have ever have believed possible.

When she'd first met Dakota she was involved with Rayden Black Wolf, a relationship doomed from the start. Rayden was still in love with her dead wife, who hadn't turned out to be dead. Dakota had been the boi toy of a rich socialite, a partner in a dance studio Jazmine and Natalia had been starting. When Jazmine had found out the woman, Cassandra Billings, was also abusing Dakota, she'd discovered her protective streak. In the end, Jazmine had been the one to lead Dakota's best friend, Cody, her mother, Lyric, and Rayden to Cassandra's house to rescue Dakota and then nurse her back to health.

It was during Dakota's recovery that Jazmine had realized that she was in love with her. She'd seen Dakota's vulnerability and had wanted nothing more than to protect her from everything that could hurt her. She'd been thrilled to find out that Dakota had also fallen in love with her as well.

Now, staring down at this wild woman she'd been lucky enough to catch, she couldn't help but smile. Setting her bag on the floor, she climbed onto the bed like a tigress, leaning down to kiss Dakota's back gently.

"Mmmm…" Dakota murmured as she reached her hand up to touch Jazmine's face. She turned her head as Jazmine leaned down to kiss her lips.

"Rough day?" Jazmine asked as she moved to sit next to Dakota, reaching her hands out to smooth them over Dakota's back.

"And then some," Dakota said, sounding as exhausted as she looked.

"Well, rest. I'm going to go make some dinner, okay?" Jazmine said, moving to kiss Dakota again.

"Mmmhmm," Dakota murmured.

An hour later, Jazmine brought a plate of food into the bedroom. She sat down on the bed and slid her hand over Dakota's back.

"Babe?" Jazmine said quietly.

"Mmm?" Dakota murmured.

"Food?" Jazmine queried.

"Yes, please," Dakota said, turning over with a wide smile.

Jazmine smiled back at her girlfriend, picked up a piece of chicken, and held it out to Dakota, grinning. Dakota moved to sit up, taking the chicken from Jazmine's hand with her mouth, kissing Jazmine's fingers as she did. Jazmine handed her the plate and a fork.

"Do you want a beer?" Jazmine asked.

"Sure," Dakota said. She kissed Jazmine who then got up to get her own plate and a beer for Dakota.

When Jazmine walked back in the room, Dakota was eating sitting naked in the middle of the bed. Again, she couldn't stop the smile on her face from widening.

"What?" Dakota asked, grinning at her.

Jazmine sighed. "Just feeling really disgustingly happy today."

"That's a good thing, isn't it?" Dakota asked. She took a drink of the beer and set it aside on the nightstand.

"Yes, yes it is," Jazmine said, sitting down to eat her own dinner.

They ate in companionable silence for a while and Dakota checked emails. At one point, she was reading an email and stopped chewing. She reached her hand out to touch Jazmine's hand, looking shocked.

"Holy hell…" Dakota said, her tone awed

"What?" Jazmine asked.

"There's a client wants a bid to work on a Craftsman…" Dakota said, her voice trailing off as she grinned.

Jazmine looked back at her for a long moment, her look blank.

Dakota shook her head, and pulled up Google. She looked up a picture of a Craftsman-style house and showed it to Jazmine.

"A Craftsman is a style of house," Dakota told her. "They started building them in the late 1800s. I loved this style when I was in school. I've always wanted to work on one, but there aren't a lot of them here in LA so I never really thought I'd get the chance."

Jazmine looked at the pictures. "Wow, these are beautiful…" she said sliding her finger over the iPad to change pictures.

"See all that woodwork?" Dakota said, pointing to one of the pictures. "That's what I want to work with… Restoring it or learning to duplicate the style."

Jazmine could see the excited light in Dakota's eyes.

"So you're going to bid on the job, right?" Jazmine asked.

Dakota looked at the email again, and narrowed her eyes slightly. Then she nodded.

"There's a walk-through of the house in three days. I need to see what kind of work they need done before I know if I'm even qualified to do it."

"Why wouldn't you be qualified?"

"It's pretty specialized. I'm not sure I know the right people I'd need to get the job done, but I'm definitely going to check it out."

"Good," Jazmine said nodding. She didn't like the idea that Dakota wouldn't get this opportunity that she so desperately wanted.

Three nights later, Dakota arrived home and was on her computer for hours. Jazmine made a point of leaving her alone, knowing that she needed the time and the concentration to work on the project. She made dinner and took it the office Dakota had created for the two of them.

Dakota had created a custom office, giving each of them their own workspace. She'd built a desk with file drawers and cabinets that ran from floor to ceiling. She'd used sage greens and plum colors for Jazmine's area. She'd also created filing space for Jazmine for the studio schedules, invoices, and account information. She'd even done some custom work to create an area for them to sit and bounce ideas off each other or for Natalia and Jazmine to work on things together. It was a big room, but Dakota had utilized the space to give it a cozy feel without it feeling crowded.

Dakota's area had custom counter space for her to lay out plans and drawings. She had a drafting table, and had built a drawer setup to lay out plans for her various projects. The colors on her side of the office were caramels, browns, and a rich navy blue; it was very much Dakota. They both had computers and a printer that they shared. Dakota had also invested in a plotter to print out drawing and plans for various projects. It was a true office that worked great for both of them.

Jazmine set the plate of food down next to Dakota's computer, waving a beer in front of the computer screen. Dakota grinned and took the beer, clicking on another screen as she took a drink.

"You need to eat too, babe," Jazmine said smiling.

"Mmmhmm," Dakota murmured.

"Oh Lord, I see I'm going to lose you on this one, huh?" Jazmine said, grinning.

"What?" Dakota asked, glancing over at her. "No, babe, no," she said, smiling and reaching her hand up to touch Jazmine's cheek. "I just want to get my bid in and be done for the time being on it."

"So, is it a lot of work?" Jazmine asked.

Dakota blew her breath out, nodding. "Yeah, it's literally a top to bottom restore. There's a lot to work with, but there's going to be some serious creativity involved."

"Which you totally love," Jazmine said, smiling.

"Which I totally love," Dakota said, smiling too.

"Okay, well, please eat, and I'll leave you alone so you can get your bid in."

"Thanks, babe. You're always taking care of me…" Dakota said, moving to stand to kiss Jazmine's lips.

"Of course," Jazmine said, smiling.

"I love you," Dakota whispered against Jazmine's lips.

"And I love you," Jazmine said, staring back into Dakota's eyes. "Now get back to that bid, so you can beat everyone else out and get that job."

"Yes, ma'am," Dakota said chuckling.

Jazmine left the room and Dakota stared at the door for a full minute. She knew just how lucky she really was to have found Jazmine. Her life had been a series of women who didn't give a crap about her, but they'd been rich and they'd taken care of her financially, so she'd taken care of them sexually. It was the way things were for her for years.

Her mother had been addicted to crack cocaine and had started selling her daughter at the age of two to perverts and men who wanted little girls. At the age of twelve, Dakota had decided she'd had enough of being used by her mother, and ran away. She'd started selling herself and keeping the money she made. Even helping other girls along the way to be smart about how they hooked. She'd met Cody Wyatt, another young runaway living on the streets, and had helped her escape from a man who was trying to be Cody's pimp. Dakota taught Cody to be street smart and how to be safe when hooking. They'd become friends and Dakota had become Cody's first female lover.

Unfortunately a year into their relationship they were squatting in an abandoned house. Dakota had caught a cold and, bound and determined to get Dakota medicine, Cody had gone out to work that night to make enough to buy what Dakota needed. That was the night Cody was arrested for prostitution and since she was only thirteen at the time, she was taken to juvenile hall.

Things sucked without Cody around. Dakota hated being out on the streets without her trusty sidekick to watch her back. She was worried about Cody not making bail, so she knew she really needed to hustle to make enough money to bail her out if they even let her bail out at all. She'd already been with two johns that night when an expensive-looking car pulled up alongside her. The windows were dark so she couldn't see the driver until he opened the passenger window. She leaned down, glancing around the car's interior. It was an import, not an American car, usually a good sign it wasn't a cop.

"Hi," she said casually, "are ya lost?" She knew that was a good way to ask what he wanted, without being overt.

The man smiled at her. He was in his forties and was kind of fat, but not overly so. He was also balding slightly in the front and trying to hide it. Dakota didn't care, he was driving an expensive car, which meant he could afford more.

"I was wondering if you'd want to come hang out with my wife and me," he said. His voice was friendly, like he was just inviting her to a party.

"Sure, I could do that," she said, nodding. "But I'm kind of looking for help to bail a friend of mine out of trouble. Do you think you could help me with that?" she asked, her blue eyes shining with feigned innocence.

"Oh sure," he said, nodding. "How much does your friend need?"

"Well, it really depends on how much trouble she's in, but I'm sure that fifty would go a long way to helping her. If I find out that she's in more trouble than that we can see what else you can help with," she said, thinking fast. She needed to know what she was agreeing to before

she set an actual price, but the guy hadn't even blinked at fifty, so she figured she was good to go.

"That sounds like a good plan," he said, smiling again. "Hop in." He unlocked the passenger door.

Dakota climbed into the car, and looked around again. The man put his hand on her leg, clad in tight shorts. Dakota had to force back her instant revulsion at the look of open lust in his eyes. She wondered if there was a "wife" at all. He put the car in gear again and drove off.

Dakota was really surprised when he drove west on the Sunset Strip and continued past the Beverly Hills Hotel. He then took a right onto a road that took them up into the hills.

'Holy hell,' Dakota thought to herself. 'Is this guy like some totally rich dude?'

When he finally reached his destination, the man clicked a button in the car and a gate opened up. The house he drove up to wasn't huge, but it was definitely nice. Dakota thought she must have been dreaming or something.

They got out of the car and he led her inside. She walked into the foyer of the house looking around and doing her best not to look completely shocked by where she was. This was far from some quick fuck in a back alley in the guy's car.

"Do you want a drink?" he asked. He walked through the foyer into a sunken living room to a bar in front of a whole wall of windows.

"Yeah, sure, Jack if you have it," Dakota said, thinking if she could get a good buzz going she could at least get through this okay.

"And what have you brought home?" asked a blond-haired woman who walked in from another room.

Dakota turned to look at the woman, who was stood staring at her. She was small, shorter than Dakota, but with the silkiest looking blond hair Dakota had ever seen, and very dark eyes. She was dressed in a long shimmering white dress and she had jewels at her neck that sparkled. Dakota was bowled over and it showed. The woman swept over to Dakota, looking the girl over. Dakota was tall and lanky, with dark hair that was somewhat spikey, and her best features were her very blue eyes. She was wearing skin-tight shorts that sat low on her hips and a black tank top with no bra. Her breasts were small, but perky. She wore a black cord around her neck with a tiny pendant peace sign on it. On her feet she wore beat-up black Converse that she'd found in a dumpster a year before.

"Well, aren't you cute?" the woman said, smiling at Dakota with perfectly straight white teeth. "What's your name, sweetie?"

"Dakota," she replied, her voice coming out husky.

"Mmmm..." the woman murmured, moving close to Dakota. "You look like you could use a few good meals and a shower. Come with me."

With that the woman turned around and walked away without looking back, fully expecting Dakota to follow her, which she did. She glanced over her shoulder and saw the man watching lustfully, but he made no move to follow them.

Dakota followed the woman through the house into a huge master suite and then into the master bathroom.

"Leave your clothes there," the woman said, pointing to a spot on the floor. "There are towels here," she said, pointing again. "You look smart. I'm sure you can figure the shower out." She winked, then left the room.

Dakota stood staring at the door thinking, 'What the hell is going on?'

She shrugged to herself, if nothing else she'd get a hot shower out of the deal and finally be truly clean again for a few minutes. It took her five minutes to figure out the odd contraption; it had multiple knobs and settings. She finally got something resembling hot and found soap, and shampoo and conditioner in dispensers. 'Geeze rich people can't pick up a bottle or a bar of soap like the rest of us?' she thought to herself. 'Holy hell I've died and gone to heaven!'

Twenty minutes later, she climbed out of the shower and wrapped herself in a huge soft towel. She toweled off her hair and when she lowered it, she found the blond standing watching her. She now wore a short black Kimono-style bathrobe. Dakota stood and stared at her for a full minute, unsure of what she was supposed to do. This was always the hard part.

"I'm Lily," the woman said, her voice sounding very cultured to Dakota's ears.

Dakota nodded warily. She knew there was a catch here somewhere.

Lily walked toward her, her dark eyes staring into Dakota's. Dakota recognized lust in the woman's eyes, but unlike when she saw lust in a man's eyes, she was not revolted. In fact, she realized she was attracted to the idea of this woman.

As the evening continued, Dakota ended up on autopilot, doing what she knew would please her client. She did her best not to think about what was happening, just doing her best to do her "job." She refused to think beyond that, not wanting to consider what her life could be like if she hadn't had a worthless mother. She'd done that too many times, and it never amounted to anything but blinding anger on her part.

At one point, while Dakota and Lily were being particularly intimate, the husband appeared and pressed his hard on against Dakota's backside. To Dakota's utter shock, however, Lily pulled Dakota away from him.

"Only me, Henry, not her," Lily told him, presenting him with her backside instead, and bending over to allow him access.

Dakota watched as "Henry" did his thing and it was obvious that it wasn't doing a thing for Lily. So Dakota did her best to take Lily's mind away from it. Lily wasn't like her usual clients and Dakota soon realized that she was enjoying her time with her.

Later as Henry slept, Dakota and Lily lay on the other side of the bed. Lily was curled up against Dakota while Dakota's hand stroked her skin.

"You are the first woman I've ever had sex with," Lily told her.

Dakota looked down at her surprised. "Really?" she asked, trying to keep the wonder out of her voice.

"Yes," Lily said, "I always wondered why I found girls so much more attractive than men, but now I know."

"What do you think you know?" Dakota asked, her voice cynical.

"That I like sex with women."

"Girls," Dakota corrected.

Lily sat up. "How old are you?" she asked, looking afraid suddenly.

Dakota looked back at this extremely manicured and refined woman and tried to decide what she wanted to say. She knew she could *get away with telling her she was eighteen. She knew the woman wanted to believe it so she would if Dakota said so.*

Finally, she said. "How old do you want me to be?"

Lily looked back at her and Dakota could see her thought processes. Lily was now afraid that Dakota was going to get her into trouble.

"Look, it's cool, okay?" Dakota said sitting up. "I'm not trying to get anyone into trouble here."

Lily blinked a couple of times and Dakota could see that her conscience was warring with her desires. Apparently, her desires one out and two weeks later, Lily kicked Henry out and kept Dakota with her. It was the beginning of Dakota's life with rich lesbians or would-be lesbians.

Jazmine had been asleep for two hours when Dakota finally crawled into bed behind her. She pulled Jazmine into her arms and snuggling up against her. Jazmine turned over, opening her eyes and looking up at Dakota in the semi-darkness.

"Did you turn in your bid?" she asked softly.

"Yep," Dakota said, smiling. "Now we just wait and see what happens."

"If you're meant to get it, you will," Jazmine said.

"Well, let's hope I'm meant to get it," Dakota said, grinning.

"Of course," Jazmine replied.

Dakota kissed Jazmine's lips. "Thanks."

"For what, babe?" Jazmine asked, looking puzzled.

"Just for… everything," Dakota said. She wasn't sure how to put into words how she was feeling.

"We take care of each other, babe, that's what we do," Jazmine said, sensing that Dakota was feeling really emotional.

She knew it meant that Dakota had been mentally revisiting her previous life and it had put her in a melancholy mood. Dakota still had a hard time expressing herself when it came to emotions, and Jazmine therefore never expected deep explanations of how she felt. The fact that Dakota was with her and only her, and that she seemed perfectly happy was enough to tell Jazmine everything she needed to know.

To help keep Dakota from having to try to respond, Jazmine curled herself up in Dakota's arms, resting her head against Dakota's chest. Jazmine put her hand over Dakota's heart, leaving it there pointedly.

Dakota knew that Jazmine was once again allowing for her inability to communicate when it came to feelings, but Dakota was bound and determined to try and explain what she was feeling. Sliding her finger under Jazmine's chin, she tilted Jazmine's face up to hers.

"I love that you take care of me," Dakota said. "And I love that you understand when something is important to me, and make it feel like it's important to you too."

"If it's something you want, Kota, it *is* important to me," Jazmine said, shortening Dakota's name in a way that Dakota loved. Dakota knew that Jazmine was trying to tell her that it was indeed important to her too.

Dakota smiled warmly. "That's what I mean," she said. "You take what's important to me and make it important for you too."

"Isn't that what you did with the studio?" Jazmine said, her eyes shining. "You knew it was important to me, so you sold that Bugatti that you adored to help Nat and me with the money."

Dakota looked back at her, her eyes reflecting something akin to surprise.

"Did you forget about that?" Jazmine asked.

"No," Dakota said. "But... I mean, the car wasn't even something I paid for, so it was really free money."

"Okay, but you certainly didn't have to invest a million of it with me and Nat in the studio, right?"

"Well, no," Dakota said, her tone reasoning. "But that's what I wanted to do."

"Why?" Jazmine asked simply.

Dakota looked back at her for a long moment, her lips pressed together in thought.

"Because you came for me," she said softly.

"And I would always come for you, no matter what," Jazmine said. "And I told you, you didn't have to give me a million dollars for a studio for that."

"But I wanted to," Dakota repeated.

"Because you love me."

"Yes," Dakota said, nodding.

"And because you knew it was important to me," Jazmine said.

"Yes."

"And that's why things that are important to you are important to me too, babe," Jazmine said, smiling.

Dakota smiled sweetly.

"I get it," she said, grinning.

"Good," Jazmine said, smiling. "Now let's get some sleep, so we can actually function tomorrow."

"Good plan," Dakota said, and she leaned in to kiss her lips again. "I love you."

"I love you," Jazmine replied.

They fell asleep with Jazmine curled in Dakota's arms. Dakota felt like she'd become one of the luckiest people alive when she'd met Jazmine.

Chapter 3

Two weeks after starting to work for Harley, Shiloh had become completely indispensable. She was on top of Harley's schedule constantly; reminding her of appointments, setting up meetings, and monitoring the meetings to ensure that Harley didn't over extend herself.

One afternoon, Harley led the way out to the parking lot and to her car. They were heading to a meeting at the Los Angeles Attorney General's office in downtown Los Angeles.

"So this is the car I've heard about…" Shiloh said, smiling.

Harley grinned. "You've heard about her?"

"I was warned to buckle up and hold on," Shiloh said, grinning too.

Harley opened the passenger door to the sleek black sports car and gestured for Shiloh to get in. She closed the door after her and went around to the driver's side. "That's probably good advice," she said as she pushed the button to start the car.

The vehicle rumbled to life and Shiloh's eyes widened at the feel of power. She glanced at the seat behind her and over at Harley's seat, and noted that the seat belts weren't standard seat belts you'd find in a normal car.

"Are these seats… um…?" Shiloh began, and Harley started to chuckle.

"They're racing seats," Harley said, with a wink. "And before you ask, yes those are racing harnesses and you should definitely put yours on."

"Oh my…" Shiloh said, smiling despite her grave tone.

Harley backed out of her parking space and glanced over to make sure that Shiloh was buckled up. She turned on the radio, and it sprang to life with a rock rap song. The song was Saliva's "Click Click Boom." As it began with heavy guitars and drums, Harley accelerated out of the parking lot. Harley sang the words as she drove, zipping quickly around cars. Shiloh found herself watching in fascination.

"I take it you drive like this all the time?" Shiloh asked as a quieter song started.

Harley grinned, nodding. "Yeah, kind of like my brain, I need to drive fast."

"How many speeding tickets do you have?" Shiloh asked.

"None," Harley said, her grin widening. "Fortunately cops don't usually give other cops tickets."

"How do they know you're a cop?" Shiloh asked. "Or do you tell them when they stop you?"

"Most of the time I don't have to. If they don't recognize the car by now, which most of the locals do, they run the plate and see the UC registration."

"What's that?" Shiloh asked.

"Police officers can register their cars to have the plate come back to the department, rather than their personal address. When a cop sees that they know that they're dealing with law enforcement."

"They recognize your car?" Shiloh asked. Then shook her head. "Of course they do. It's pretty nice…"

"Thanks, I love her," Harley said, smiling fondly.

"Her?" Shiloh asked, having heard Harley use the feminine pronoun a few times.

"She's hot, she's fast, and she's powerful, what else would she be?" Harley asked, her blue eyes sparkling. "The best kind of woman I know, that's my Erin."

"Erin?" Shiloh asked.

Harley smiled as she dodged around yet another car on the freeway. "It's short for Erinyes, which is another name for the Furies in Greek mythology. You know the goddesses of vengeance?"

"Oh my…" Shiloh murmured.

Harley waggled her eyebrows at her, smiling as she did.

"So how much does a car like this cost?" Shiloh asked. "If you don't mind me asking, that is."

"Base price," Harley said. "Well, she was about forty thousand to start with, but I've done a lot of things to her since I bought her a year ago."

"Like?" Shiloh asked.

"Like the Stillen Supercharger, the Amuse body kit, custom wheels and paint, the racing seats, the nano ceramic window tint, a hell of a lot of tuning, new exhaust, sway bar, the list goes on and on."

"And I understood about none of that," Shiloh said, laughing. "So after all that what would you say the car cost?"

"I haven't really added it up, but probably a good hundred thou," Harley said, shrugging.

"Holy crap!" Shiloh exclaimed.

Harley laughed.

"That's a lot of money, Harley," Shiloh said.

"That's not counting the Harley I have too." Harley said, grinning.

"You have a Harley too?" Shiloh asked. "Isn't that a little bit ironic?"

"My dad has one, I have one," Harley said, simply.

"I see," Shiloh said. "And I heard that your dad isn't exactly the biker everyone in school thought he was…"

Harley tilted her head slightly. "Who told you? Rayden?"

"Yes," Shiloh said nodding. "You never told anyone at school, did you?"

"No," Harley said, shaking her head. "He was undercover. I wouldn't take that chance."

"But it might have made things easier for you."

Harley glanced over at her, as she once again moved around a slower vehicle. "Seriously? You think those people, or even you, would have been more impressed hearing that my dad was an undercover narc?" She shook her head, looking cynical. "That might have been worse."

"Why?" Shiloh asked, shocked by Harley's statement.

"Well, when they thought he was a biker they were at least half way afraid of him," Harley said, her lips curling with annoyance as she remembered how she used to feel.

"Oh," Shiloh said, nodding, "Yeah, I believe that."

They pulled up to the building a few minutes later. Harley parked in the garage across the street and they walked over. Harley showed her badge to the CHP officers inside and they waved her through. She waited on the other side for Shiloh to get through the security check. Then they headed up to their meeting.

They were meeting with some of the legal staff about a system they already had in place. They wanted enhancements made to it to make it track more information on cases. The meeting involved a number of lawyers, some of whom were fairly rude. Unfortunately, the one lawyer Harley did like, Sierra Youngblood-Marshal wasn't in the meeting. The meeting didn't go well when the lawyers weren't told "yes we can do that" right off the bat. Harley had been strictly instructed by Rayden not to say that in meetings anymore. It often meant that Shiloh had to intercede when she could see that Harley was itching to say yes.

"I don't understand why this is such a difficult request for you people," said one hawk-faced lawyer, his tone condescending.

Shiloh wanted to snap that if he thought it was so easy, why didn't he handle the changes he was requesting. Instead, she folded her hands and said nothing. She glanced over at Harley to see that her blue eyes were unfocused. Her hands were in her lap and fingers moved as if they were on a keyboard. It meant that Harley was already planning the work she would need to do to handle the request. It also meant it was time for Shiloh to step in. She moved her right hand to still

Harley's motions, at the same time putting her left hand in front of her on the table. She leaned forward looking at the lawyer who'd spoken.

"We will be happy to look into the problem and determine whether or not Agent Davidson has the time to handle your request."

"This is a priority for the Attorney General," the man snapped.

Shiloh smiled tightly, like she hadn't heard that one before. "I'm sure it is, sir," she replied. "However, Agent Davidson works for the Division of Law Enforcement and is therefore beholden to her own programs first and foremost." She looked at him with a guileless smile. "Perhaps if our processes aren't up to your rigorous needs and standards, you could ask Chief Deputy Youngblood-Marshal if her budget would allow you to hire an outside contractor for this particular project."

"That would cost far too much!" the man said. "And wouldn't happen nearly fast enough. For all the money Agent Davidson makes, I would think this could be fit into her busy schedule."

Shiloh's eyes narrowed. She glanced at Harley to see how she took what had just been said. Harley merely looked back at her and quirked her lips slightly, her look otherwise serene.

"First of all," Shiloh said, doing her very best to control her temper at that moment, "Agent Davidson has a doctorate from MIT and graduated with honors, and has a resume that would likely put yours to shame. So what she makes is probably not even close to what she's worth as a programmer. Secondly, no matter how much money a person makes, it doesn't create more hours in a day. So your assumption that because she makes a lot of money, she should be able to fit your project into her schedule is not only ridiculous, but also incredibly presumptive of you. You have no idea how many projects she has or how hard she works, so do us all a favor and take what we're willing to give you, or take my other suggestion. The choice is yours."

With that, Shiloh stood up and looked over at Harley, who moved to stand with a grin on her lips and her blue eyes twinkling in subdued humor. They left the room and Shiloh held her tongue admirably all the way out to the car. Once there however, she exploded.

"What an asshole!" she yelled. "Oh my God, he's such a fucking jerk. I could have just stuffed my foot right in his big stupid mouth! Argh!"

Harley leaned against the hood of her car, took out a cigarette, and lit it, watching Shiloh pace back and forth, ranting. It took five full minutes for Shiloh to calm down. When she finally did, she leaned next to Harley.

"I guess I'm probably gonna get yelled at by Rayden," she said, her tone resigned.

"For what?" Harley asked.

"For my insult to that guy, 'cause you know he's going to call her."

"Probably," Harley said, nodding.

"Well, fuck him. It was not okay for him to talk about you that way."

A grin played at Harley's lips. "You do seem a bit incensed about it."

"That didn't piss you off?" Shiloh asked.

Harley shrugged. "Not really."

"Well, it pissed me off!"

"Apparently," Harley said, her eyes dancing with amusement.

Shiloh pressed her lips together in consternation. "Was I really bad?"

Harley considered, but then shrugged. "Not too bad, no."

"Well, I just don't want anyone putting you down like that, it's not okay," Shiloh said, her tone reasoning.

"It's not, huh?" Harley asked looking amused once again.

Shiloh narrowed her eyes at Harley. "Don't make me smack you."

Harley chuckled. "No, ma'am," she said with amusement.

"Let's go back to our office where I can bury this request in the bottom of the pile of requests you have," Shiloh said, smiling.

Harley took one last drag off her cigarette, stubbed it out, and threw it in a trashcan nearby. Then she walked over to open the passenger door of the Z for Shiloh. Shiloh smiled up at Harley, then got into the car.

They were halfway back to the office when Shiloh got a call.

"It's Rayden," Shiloh said, grimacing.

She answered it, and Harley could hear her half of the conversation.

"Hi... Yes we did... Yes, I figured he would... Rayden, he was being a complete asshole... Sorry, I mean jerk..." She listened for a moment, then laughed, nodding. "Yeah he said with as much money as she makes she should be able to fit this in... Exactly! That's what I told him... He was a major windbag... No, Sierra didn't make the meeting... I know, I doubt he would have said that with Sierra there either... He did? Well, good, I'm glad he caught the disrespect I was giving him, because he didn't give Harley any respect at all... I know...

okay. I know, I'm working on a list for you… okay. Thanks… We're headed back now. Okay… thanks again."

She hung up then, looking relieved.

"So you're not in trouble?" Harley surmised.

"No," Shiloh said, grinning. "Rayden said that he tried to pull some kind of rank on her and she basically told him to remember who he was talking to, and that if he wanted one of her people to help him he'd better watch how talked to all of us."

Harley laughed, nodding her head. "Yeah, that sounds like Rayden. She doesn't take much shit from people."

"I love that woman…" Shiloh said with a sigh.

"Careful," Harley said with a wink. "Someone might think you're serious."

"Don't make me smack you," Shiloh said again, narrowing her eyes at Harley.

"Promises, promises," Harley muttered.

They were both silent for a few minutes as music played on the stereo.

"Which song on here would you say is most you?" Shiloh asked curiously.

"Hmmm…" Harley murmured, looking thoughtful. She scrolled through the menu of songs and selected one.

A song began playing called "Everything to Everyone" by Everclear. The words were harsh and very self-critical. It bothered Shiloh that Harley felt like that song was her. The lyrics talked about her putting herself in stupid places and how she ended up making herself the victim. The song went on to talk about how she's selling herself by

65

trying to be everything to everyone. It said a lot about Harley and that she just couldn't ever say no to anyone.

"You really think that song is you?" Shiloh asked as the song ended.

Harley glanced over at her, detecting the concern in Shiloh's voice. She was puzzled.

"Yeah," Harley said her tone guileless as she shrugged. "Pretty much seems like I'm always trying to please someone and never really succeeding totally."

There was no sarcasm or anger in her voice, she wasn't complaining about not being able to make people completely happy. It was like she was just stating a fact.

Shiloh looked over at the other woman for a long moment.

"I don't think that's true, Harley," Shiloh said. "I just think that people always want way more than they should ever expect from one person."

Harley looked over at her again, her look mystified. "You mean work, right?"

"I mean anything," Shiloh said. "People think that you're going to solve all their problems and make life perfect for them. You're just one person."

A slow, befuddled smile spread over Harley's lips. "So you think it's their fault that they don't get what they want?"

"Yeah," Shiloh said, nodding.

Harley nodded, looking unconvinced. "If you say so," she said noncommittally.

"I say so," Shiloh responded her tone inarguable.

Harley simply chuckled and shook her head.

Shiloh remembered what Devin had said about Harley not having a mean bone in her body. After spending the last couple of weeks with her, she thought Devin was definitely right. Harley extended her hand, figuratively speaking, to everyone; Shiloh had seen it time and time again. Most of the time people were very shocked by Harley's ingenuousness; she was hardly the complete geek many of them expected. But she wasn't exactly the slick, frank personality she could be either. With her education and experience, Harley could demand a much larger amount of money for what she did, but she seemed perfectly content doing what she was doing.

Insults and rude behavior most of the time seemed to bounce right off of her. Shiloh tended to think it was because Harley wasn't paying attention, lost in her own mind. She found it endlessly amusing when someone would attempt to put Harley in her place, and instead of a reaction, they received a simple blank stare, or a seemingly serene look. Shiloh had come to find that the serene look always meant that Harley wasn't paying attention; she was instead caught up in some thought in her head. Shiloh had a hard time keeping a straight face when people were taken aback by Harley's reactions or lack thereof. She also had a hard time keeping a civil tongue when they were nasty to this woman who was as guileless as they came.

People at work came at Harley like she was the answer to every computer program problem they had, and that she could fix anything. It never seemed to occur to these people how much time their requests required, and how much work they were truly asking for. Because Harley wanted to help them and make them 'happy,' she would do her best, but sometimes there was just nothing that would help, or a program just couldn't be altered the way they wanted. It was something that hung Harley up constantly and it was something Shiloh was trying to keep from happening.

A text message chimed on Harley's phone a few minutes later. Harley pulled the phone out of her jacket pocket and Shiloh immediately grabbed it.

"Not while you're driving," Shiloh said, her tone chiding.

Harley grinned. "Okay, but my ADHD needs to know what the message was, so can you read it?"

Shiloh laughed. Harley always referred to her cognitive disorder as if were an actual person. She found it funny and cute at that the same time.

"Your phone is locked," Shiloh said.

"Seven six three two," Harley said immediately.

"That desperate for a text message are we?" Shiloh asked as she entered the passcode.

"A… D… H… D," Harley replied, measuring out the letters with a grin.

Shiloh laughed and pulled up Harley's text messages.

"Looks like it's from a Kimberly. She says, 'When are we getting together?' " Shiloh said, glancing at Harley.

"How about never?" Harley replied. "No, don't type that!" she said, laughing as Shiloh started to do just that.

"So you don't want to get together with her?" Shiloh asked.

"No, she's worse than Sheri was with the psychotic over-the-top paranoia. Thanks but no," Harley said, smiling tightly.

"So you can say 'no' sometimes, huh?" Shiloh replied, her eyes sparkling with amusement.

"Well, yeah, it's pretty easy to do in text," Harley said, grinning.

"So do you want me to reply?" Shiloh asked, holding up the phone.

"No," Harley said, shaking her head. "Replying implies interest."

"Even if the reply is, um, 'We're not'?" Shiloh asked, grinning now too.

"For some lesbians, yes, exactly," Harley said, rolling her eyes.

"Wow," Shiloh said, widening her eyes.

She scrolled through the lists of texts Harley had. "You get a lot of text messages…"

"Lately again, yeah," Harley said, nodding. She didn't look the least bit concerned that Shiloh was holding her phone and looking at the list of text senders.

"Why lately?" Shiloh asked.

"I guess 'cause I'm single again," Harley said, her voice holding no ego whatsoever.

"So they're like circling sharks that smell blood in the water?" Shiloh asked.

"Or just desperate women looking for anything," Harley said, her voice unaffected.

"You're not just anything," Shiloh said, once again not liking Harley's self-denigrating.

Harley glanced over at her again, raising an eyebrow at her tone.

"Okay…" Harley said cautiously.

"Don't give me that *smile and nod at the crazy person* tone!" Shiloh said her eyes narrowed at Harley. "I'm just saying that these women are probably interested in you because you're awesome."

"And you know that how?" Harley asked her look cynical.

"I've met you, remember?" Shiloh replied.

"Yeah, I remember," Harley said, grinning. "And you've seen what a pain in the ass I am at work. Imagine that in a personal relationship," she said then, her look wry.

Shiloh pressed her lips together disapprovingly. "I think you've let too many women tell you that there's something wrong with the way you are, and it's complete bullshit."

"It is, huh?" Harley replied, grinning openly now.

"Yes, Harley Marie Davidson, it is."

Harley pressed her lips together, widening her blue eyes comically. "The whole name now…" she said, chuckling.

"Don't make me smack you," Shiloh said, reverting to her usual threat when Harley was being difficult.

"I imagine that one day you'll actually carry out that threat," Harley said, laughing.

"With you, yeah, probably," Shiloh said nodding and grinning at the same time.

She liked the sound of Harley's laugh and it felt good to be able to tease her and be teased by her. It had been years since she'd had a close friend and she really liked Harley's personality. When she wasn't focused on a computer, she could be funny and ironic at the same time. It was great to have this kind of relationship with someone who was really her boss. She loved her job.

Dakota had given up on the Craftsman project, thinking that she'd come in too high. She did her best not to be too depressed about it, knowing that because she was still getting established, she didn't necessarily have the reputation she needed to do this level of work. The bid had been a bit high, because she'd known she'd need to rent equipment that she didn't have, and that it would require a higher level of expertise and consulting that would cost money.

"I'm just not there yet," Dakota told Jazmine one evening as they sat eating dinner.

"You will be," Jazmine said, her tone sure.

Dakota smiled. "Know that for a fact, huh?"

"Yep," Jazmine said, smiling in return. "Hey, Savanna wants us to come to dinner tomorrow," she said then. "She said the baby is getting cuter every second and you haven't seen her in two weeks."

Dakota chuckled. "Yeah, I bet," she said. "I'm betting she wants something else done to the room."

"Well, that's possible," Jazmine said "But you know she loves seeing you too."

Dakota smiled, nodding.

Savanna and Lyric Falco were Dakota's adopted mothers. They were the two women who'd adopted Cody many years before. When she'd met them months earlier, they'd taken her under their wings. At the age of twenty-four they'd done an adult adoption to make Dakota part of their family. Dakota had even taken Lyric's last name of Falco out of respect. It was something she'd never expected to have; a family that loved her. Much like having one woman to love her, it had been an impossible dream.

The truth was, she loved Savanna and Lyric dearly, for all her blustering about changes to the nursery that she'd done. The baby, Anastasia, named after Lyric's mother who'd died giving birth to Lyric, was the product of sperm from Lyric's oldest brother Jacomo and Savanna's DNA. She was an undeniably beautiful baby, with Savanna's rich dark auburn hair and the blue Falco eyes. Dakota loved having a baby sister and was willing to do pretty much anything to make the child smile. It was something Jazmine found incredibly endearing about Dakota.

"What time does she want us there?" Dakota asked as she picked up their finished plates and took them to the sink.

"She said six," Jazmine said.

Dakota nodded, pulling out her phone and checking her calendar. "Yeah, I should be able to make that. I'll have to meet you there though."

"Okay," Jazmine said, nodding.

Dakota clicked back to her email and saw the new email that had just come in.

"Oh Holy hell…" Dakota breathed as she read the email standing in the middle of the kitchen.

"What?" Jazmine asked, moving to stand.

"I got it…" Dakota said, looking stunned.

"Got…" Jazmine started to ask. Then she saw the smile spreading over Dakota's face and knew. "You got the Craftsman job?"

"I got the Craftsman job," Dakota said, nodding as she smiled ecstatically.

"Oh my God!" Jazmine exclaimed and she threw her arms around Dakota.

Dakota hugged Jazmine tightly, her mind racing.

Jazmine stepped back looking up at Dakota, seeing that her mind was already working.

"When do you start it?" she asked.

Dakota shook her head. "I don't know…" she said, looking back at her phone and rereading the email. "I meet the owner on Thursday. I guess that's when we'll talk about start dates… I can't believe this…" Dakota said, her smile bright.

"I'm so happy for you, babe," Jazmine said, ecstatic that Dakota was finally going to get to work on a project she was passionate about.

The next evening they were over at Savanna and Lyric's house. Cody and McKenna were there as well. They were all sitting outside on the patio, Lyric, Cody, and Dakota were all smoking, since the baby was sleeping in the house.

"Get all that out of your systems," Savanna said, motioning to her girls. "'Cause no one will be smoking when Ana wakes up."

"We know, Mom," Cody said, rolling her eyes.

"That's why we're doing it now," Dakota said, grinning.

"Instead of when Ana joins us," Lyric added.

Savanna gave her girls a narrowed look. "You three are starting to finish each other's sentences, and I'm not sure that's a good thing," she said, winking over at McKenna and Jazmine.

The other three Falcos grinned at each other as Savanna shook her head. After the nightmare of the not-too-distant past, when Lyric and Cody had been badly injured, Savanna was happy to have the life they had now. She looked around at the women sitting around the patio table, and smiled warmly. She couldn't imagine their lives being any different. The addition of Dakota and the birth of their daughter seemed to complete the picture. Lyric and she were indeed very blessed. She caught Lyric's look and smiled, she knew that Lyric could sense what she was thinking. She always could. It was one of the many things she loved about her wife.

She and Lyric had been married for almost ten years. They made a good pair. Lyric was a special agent supervisor for the Department of Justice, working on their human trafficking task force and Savanna was a clinical psychologist who worked with runaways. It had been Lyric who'd been willing to help Savanna when she was worried about a fourteen-year-old Cody, one of the girls in the group home she ran at the time. Savanna had been attracted to Lyric instantly, but Lyric hadn't realized she was gay. Eventually Savanna managed to convince Lyric that the reason her numerous relationships with men never seemed right, was because she was gay. They two had been together ever since. Lyric had never even looked at another woman. Savanna was her one and only love. They'd adopted Cody shortly before getting married.

After Lyric had survived being shot three times a year and a half before, they'd decided to have a child together. While they were going through that process, they'd met Dakota, the woman who, as a teenager, had actually taken care of a teenage Cody during her early time on the streets. Savanna and Lyric had felt an immediate need to take Dakota in and care for her as well, even though she was an adult.

Especially when they'd found out what had been happening in Dakota's relationship with Cassandra Billings. Lyric and Cody had both been involved with rescuing Dakota from Cassandra's mansion. It had seemed natural that they add Dakota to their family too.

"So what is a Craftsman?" Lyric asked Dakota.

"Here," Dakota said, pulling out her phone and showing Lyric the pictures she'd shown Jazmine.

"Nice…" Lyric said nodding. "I'm betting the house doesn't look that good right now?"

"No," Dakota said. "It's in a major state of disrepair right now, but that's what's cool about it, I get to bring it back to life." Her blue eyes sparkled with excitement.

Lyric nodded, smiling. "I get it. How much you charge for something like that?"

"A lot," Dakota said, grinning. "But it'll be worth it once it's done."

"Oh, I believe that," Savanna said, smiling. "With the good work you do."

Dakota beamed at the compliment from Savanna, and Lyric winked at Savanna. Savanna and Dakota had a special connection, much like Lyric and Cody did. Whatever Savanna said, Dakota took as law, so Savanna was always careful to choose her words wisely.

"Thanks," Dakota said, her look happy.

Jazmine looked on, smiling. She knew that Dakota absolutely adored Savanna. She was the mother that Dakota had never had. It was a good healthy relationship for Dakota, and Jazmine was grateful that fate had brought Dakota to the Falcos.

"I guess this means you won't have time for a few changes to the baby's room, huh?" Savanna said, sighing.

"No, it doesn't mean that," Dakota said, shocked that Savanna would think that. "Family comes first, you just tell me what you want done, and I'll do it, Mom. You should know that."

Once again, Lyric and Savanna exchanged a look. Dakota was fiercely loyal to her newfound family. It was a wonderful trait.

"I just want to do a couple of things, I promise," Savanna assured Dakota.

"Whatever you want," Dakota said, smiling.

"Okay, we'll talk," Savanna said, winking at Dakota, who smiled in return.

"So what's going on with you two?" Dakota asked, looking at Cody and McKenna. "Are you ever getting married?"

"Yes," Cody said, narrowing her eyes at Dakota. "We're just looking for the right place."

"Uh-huh," Dakota said, her look cynical. "She's stallin'," she said, winking at McKenna.

"Am not," Cody countered.

"Uh-huh," Dakota repeated. "First it's 'oh we can't find the right place', then it's 'oh we can't set a date.' "

"Shut up, Dak," Cody said, grinning. She recognized the mischievous glint in Dakota's eyes.

"See? She's all defensive and shit," Dakota said, chuckling.

"No," McKenna said, her tone chiding. "We just don't know where we want to have the wedding. There are so many options. I heard that Devin and Skyler's wedding was incredible."

"You know that Devin makes bank, right?" Dakota said. "I heard that she doesn't get out of bed for less than a hundred thou... So I'm not sure you should base your choice on what she did for a wedding, sis..."

"Well, I have rich parents who are dying for us to get married," McKenna countered.

"Yeah, so they can have grandkids," Cody said, rolling her eyes.

"Ohhhh...." Dakota said, laughing. "Already? Wow!"

"Hey, I didn't say we were having kids right away," Cody said.

"You didn't?" McKenna queried, her look pointed.

"I said we'd talk about it," Cody said, looking cornered suddenly.

Dakota started laughing.

"Shut up, Dak!" Cody laughed, even as McKenna started grinning.

"Make me," Dakota said.

"Anytime..." Cody said, narrowing her eyes with a grin on her lips.

"Okay you two," Lyric said, giving her daughters a quelling look. "No fighting, you'll wake the baby."

"I want to wake the baby!" Dakota said. "I need my baby fix for the day."

"Maybe you should be talking about having kids instead," Cody said, winking at Jazmine.

"Watch it," Dakota warned.

"Oh, different when it's on the other foot, ain't it?" Cody said gleefully.

"Quit picking on her," McKenna said, poking at Cody.

"She started it," Cody said, sounding like a petulant child.

This had everyone laughing.

"So how's everything with the studio?" Savanna asked Jazmine.

"Great!" Jazmine said. "Natalia's got her entire class over there now. I'm getting more and more of my old contacts back and they're starting to come down too. We're actually thinking about expanding… Which reminds me…" she said, turning to Dakota. "That shop next door is moving out at the end of the month."

Dakota gave her a quizzical look. "You're thinking you want to buy that space?"

Jazmine bit her lip. "Maybe?" she said hesitantly.

Dakota did some quick calculations in her head, then nodded. "With what I'm making on this job, we should be able to swing that."

"Are you sure?" Jazmine asked, not wanting to put too much pressure on their finances.

"I'm sure," Dakota said, grinning. "What are you wanting to add? Do you know yet?"

"Some smaller rooms for more intimate classes like yoga, and maybe mediation or something…" Jazmine said. "And maybe a room for ballet."

"Little people or big people?" Dakota asked, already thinking about what she could do in the space.

"Maybe both?" Jazmine said, her look comically cautious.

"Sure, let's make it harder," Dakota said, grinning.

"I know, I know, but I know you can help with that part," Jazmine said batting her eyelashes at her girlfriend.

"Uh-huh…" Dakota said, narrowing her eyes.

"Pretty girls will get ya every time," Lyric said, winking at Dakota.

"Don't I know it," Dakota replied.

"But you love me…" Jazmine said smiling.

"Yes, yes I do," Dakota said, sighing. "Don't worry, babe, we'll figure it out."

The group was silent for a few minutes then, each away with their own thoughts.

"McKenna is taking her board exams next week," Savanna said.

"Wait, what does that mean?" Dakota asked, looking puzzled.

"It means that if she passes the exams she can apply to become board certified," Cody said. "Which means she'll be able to practice like Mom."

"Aw," Dakota said, nodding. "Very cool. So are you gonna open your own practice, or do a home like Mom?"

"I'm not sure," McKenna said. "I'm thinking about opening my own group home, like Savanna's, but I haven't decided yet."

"Would it be for teens or adults?" Dakota asked.

"Definitely for teens, like you and Cody were," McKenna said softly, knowing that it was still a tender subject for both of them.

"Regular kids or LGBT?" Dakota asked.

McKenna blew her breath out. "I really think I'd do LGBT kids. It's not that I have anything against the straight kids out there, I just think our own need more support, you know?"

"Yeah," Dakota agreed. "Well let me know if you decide to do your own house, I'd be happy to work with you on it. You'll get the family discount."

"And what's the family discount?" McKenna asked, smiling.

"Free," Dakota said, smiling. "I can even help you check out houses if you want."

McKenna looked surprised by both comments. "Wow, that would be great, but I'd have to pay you something…"

"No," Dakota said, shaking her head. "You're family. Family doesn't pay each other money, right Lyric?"

Lyric grinned, loving that Dakota saw it that way. "That's the way I always see it."

"See?" Dakota said, grinning.

McKenna smiled, inclining her head. "Well, it isn't how my family is, but this one does tend to be much more special."

At that moment, a small cry could be heard on the baby monitor. Dakota and Cody immediately stood up.

"Hey, it's my turn," Dakota said. "You had her last time."

"I don't think so," Cody said, shaking her head.

"'Fraid so," Dakota said, walking toward the back door.

"Brat," Cody said, grinning.

"And?" Dakota queried as she walked inside.

"That was it, just stating fact," Cody muttered, even though Dakota had already gone inside.

The rest of the family listened on the baby monitor as Dakota walked into the baby's room.

Dakota smiled down at her baby sister.

"Well there's my beautiful little girl…" she said softly.

Anastasia gurgled happily at seeing Dakota.

"Come here, little one," Dakota said as she leaned down to pick up the baby. "Hello beautiful," she said, smiling as the baby cooed and focused on her necklace. "What… You want this?" she asked as Anastasia's little hand closed over the silver angel wing pendent.

"Wait, wait, wait…" Dakota said, laughing as Anastasia lifted it to her mouth. "No, don't eat that, it's probably dirty… Okay, but don't tell mama Savanna or she'll probably kick my butt." She laughed softly as Anastasia stared up at her with her big blue eyes, chewing on the pendent. "Ready to go see everyone? Or should we just run away together? Hmmm?"

Everyone grinned at what Dakota was saying. It was astounding to hear how fond of she was of the baby, and how happy she sounded when she talked to her. Cody never would have believed it, but Dakota was a really good big sister and definitely had a soft spot for Anastasia.

"We could just sneak out, Ana…. I'm tellin' ya… But then you'd miss everyone wouldn't you?" Dakota sighed loudly. "Okay, okay, you win, we'll stay here. Come on, let's go see everyone."

A couple of minutes later Dakota walked out with Anastasia in her arms.

"There's my girl…" Lyric said, smiling at her daughters.

"Which one?" Savanna queried.

"Both of them," Lyric said, winking at Dakota.

Anastasia was still holding Dakota's necklace in her hands and it was all wet with saliva. Dakota didn't seem to mind at all.

"What have you got?" Savanna asked her baby daughter. "Are you eating sister's necklace?"

"She talked me out of it, what can I say?" Dakota said, grinning.

"She could talk you out of pretty much anything," Jazmine said, smiling.

"Which is astounding since she can't talk yet," Cody added.

"The hell you say," Dakota said, giving Cody a narrowed look. "She talks to me. I dunno why she doesn't talk to you, probably 'cause yer ugly."

"Better ugly than smelly," Cody countered.

"Jaz says I smell good," Dakota said, sticking her tongue out at Cody.

"She loves you, she'll lie to you to keep you happy," Cody replied.

"Does not," Dakota said, her eyes twinkling.

"Does too," Cody replied, grinning.

Jazmine and McKenna exchanged glances, rolling their eyes at their women. It was a wonderful evening.

Chapter 4

"What?" Harley asked as she walked back into her office to a look she now recognized as Shiloh's glowering look.

"Where did you go?" Shiloh asked.

"Uh…" Harley stammered, holding up a can of Java Monster timidly.

"Did you have your phone on you?" Shiloh asked.

"Yeah…" Harley said hesitantly, with a comical grimace. "But I had my headphones plugged in and the ringer off…"

"Harley!" Shiloh gasped, shaking her head. "That's exactly what we talked about last week! You can't turn your ringer off or I can't get ahold of you when you're plugged in!"

Harley grimaced again, closing one eye like she was waiting to be struck.

"Oh, God, stop it," Shiloh said, grinning as she shook her head.

"So what did I miss?" Harley asked.

"Just the conference call with Sierra and Midnight…" Shiloh sighed.

"Oh fuck," Harley said. "Is Rayden on her way down here to kill me?"

Shiloh chuckled. "Fortunately, Rayden is fully aware of your debilitating attention span of a gnat, so no, she's not."

Harley gave a toothy fake *see? All better!* smile.

"Don't even give me that smile Harley Marie Davidson. I had to tap dance for ten minutes while Midnight Chevalier breathed down my neck."

"On the phone?" Harley asked her look comically perplexed.

"That isn't the point!" Shiloh said, trying to keep a straight face in the face of Harley's amused look.

"Shy, I'm really sorry," Harley said, moving to lean against her counter, looking sincerely apologetic suddenly.

Shiloh gave her a narrowed look, but couldn't manage to stay mad at her when she was giving her such a sad look with those big blue eyes.

"You're worse than a puppy dog sometimes, you know that?" Shiloh said.

"At least I'm housebroken," Harley said, grinning.

"There is that," Shiloh said, rolling her eyes. "They are going to call back here in ten minutes. You are not leaving this office during that time, do you understand me? I will handcuff your ass to this chair if I have to."

"Ohhhh…" Harley murmured playfully.

"Don't make me smack you," Shiloh replied predictably.

"Will that be before or after you handcuff me?" Harley asked, grinning.

"Oh my God, you are the worst!" Shiloh said, pushing at Harley's shoulder.

Harley laughed, nodding her head. "I try."

"You win at that," Shiloh said. "And while you were out and about, did you buy yourself lunch, or just more caffeine?" she said, narrowing her eyes.

Harley suddenly looked heavenward.

"And that's my answer, isn't it?" Shiloh said, shaking her head. "I'm going to go upstairs and get you food," she said. She pushed Harley into her chair giving her a pointed look. "You will not leave this office, do you hear me?"

"But..." Harley began.

"No, no buts, Harley. You are going to sit here in this chair and wait for that call."

"You're going to leave me here and hope that I don't wander off again?" Harley asked, a grin starting on her lips.

"That's it, where are your cuffs!" Shiloh said, reaching towards Harley's back pocket.

"Okay, okay, sheesh!" Harley said, holding up her hands in surrender. "I'll sit right here and not move, promise."

Shiloh gave her a pointed look. "I'm only trusting you because you need to eat," she said, "but if you wander off on me again, I swear I'm going to fit you for a shock collar and a homing device."

Harley chuckled. "Yes dear," she said, pressing her lips together comically.

"I'll be right back," Shiloh said.

"I'll be right here," Harley assured her.

Ten minutes later, Shiloh came back with a sandwich and Harley was on the conference call with Midnight Chevalier, the Attorney General for the State of California, and Sierra Youngblood-Marshal, the head of the Criminal Division for the AG's office.

"No, ma'am, it isn't that," Harley was saying as Shiloh walked in. "That program isn't capable of that level of detail… No ma'am, I did evaluate it, and that's what I found."

Shiloh handed Harley half of the sandwich and put a bottle of water down next to her, pointedly moving the can of Java Monster and finding that it was already empty. Harley could consume caffeine at an incredible rate. Shiloh held the can up and shook it, giving Harley a shake of her head as she rolled her eyes. Harley merely grinned as she took a bite of the sandwich, even as she began nodding again.

"Yes, ma'am, I mean Midnight, yes, I can build a program that would do that, but it's going to take time because of my other priorities."

Shiloh stood listening with her hands on her hips.

"It's going to take at least a month of straight programming," Harley said. "And that's if I can find a COTS program that's customizable to that level… COTS means customizable off the shelf, ma'am… Right… And yeah we'd have to pay for that, and then all the time it would take to customize… Sure I can write a program but that'll take even longer."

Shiloh was shaking her head, the last thing Harley had time to do was write a whole new program for the AG's Criminal Division. She pulled out her phone and walked out to her desk so she could call

Rayden to let her know what was happening. Rayden asked for the phone number of the conference call. The next thing Midnight, Sierra, and Harley heard was Rayden and Jericho clicking onto the line. Harley's eyes widened as she looked at Shiloh. She put her hand over the mike on her headset.

"Did you call Rayden?" She whispered.

"Yes," Shiloh said. "They're trying to poach all of your time and I thought Rayden should know about it."

"You do get that Midnight is everyone's boss right?" Harley said with a grin.

"Yes, I get that, but Rayden is your boss."

"And Jericho is hers, and she's on the line now too... And oh boy..." she said, widening her eyes and taking her hand off the mic. "I'm here, ma'am. I... well... yeah... but... I... Last night? Um... like... three hours... Why?" She winced and Shiloh could hear someone's voice raised through the headphones. "Really, ma'am, I don't need that... But I really... I... no... yes... but..." Finally, she blew her breath out loudly as she shook her head and rolled her eyes.

Putting her elbow on her counter, Harley rested her chin on her hand. Apparently, now she was just listening to the rest of the group talking back and forth. She picked up the sandwich and ate it, her eyes wandering over to her computer, then back over to Shiloh and shook her head.

Shiloh watched in amused silence. She was fairly certain that it was Midnight Chevalier's raised voice she'd heard, and she was also fairly sure that they'd asked Harley how much sleep she'd gotten the night before and that had caused the outburst from the AG. Shiloh hoped that Jericho and Rayden were protecting Harley, even from the

Attorney General herself if they needed to. She'd finally met Jericho Tehrani, the Director of the Division of Law Enforcement, in a meeting the week before, and really liked the no-nonsense director.

Jericho seemed to be good about looking after her people and appointing people like Rayden who would do the same. There had been high praise for all of Harley's work from the director, and she'd agreed wholeheartedly with Rayden's contention that Harley's projects should be limited to DLE, and no other units unless time permitted. Shiloh had presented a list of Harley's projects and the time it would take her to complete them. Harley had remained, for the most part, silent during the meeting, not because she was in any way intimidated by the director, but simply because she was mentally still working through a bug in one of the programs she was working on. At one point Jericho had directed a question at Harley and when Harley didn't answer, Shiloh had had to prod her to get her attention.

"What?" Harley had asked, suddenly focusing on the meeting again.

"I asked if you were set for equipment," Jericho repeated, her bright blue eyes sparkling with subdued humor. "But if you don't want another Alienware, I understand…"

"That's not funny, Jerich," Harley had said, her eyes narrowed. "Besides, I have the eighteen, I don't really need that, but a faster server would be great. Actually a dedicated server to compile data and run my executables would be handy."

"What am I looking at cost wise?" Jericho had asked.

"Well, if I get what I want you're looking at around half a mill," Harley had said, grinning.

Jericho looked back at the younger woman, her face impassive, even as she blinked slowly.

"We're talking about a computer server?" Jericho had asked.

Harley had grinned. "Yep, one of the fastest out there right now."

"Does it make French fries?" Jericho had asked, grinning.

"Not that I'm aware," Harley had replied a grin on her lips.

"Half a million?"

"Well, yeah by the time you round up the taxes and all, 'bout that," Harley had replied, undaunted by the disbelieving look on Jericho's face. "You did ask."

Jericho had nodded. "Yes, yes I did."

Shiloh had seen Rayden and Jericho exchange a look, something akin to *holy shit!* but Rayden had just grinned and shrugged.

Now as Shiloh watched Harley listening to the conversation, she could see that Harley's mind was wandering off. Harley opened a window on her computer and started clicking on things; she did a few searches and typed a few lines of code. At one point Shiloh's phone chimed, and she saw that Rayden had texted her.

The text read, "We've lost her, haven't we?"

"Yep," Shiloh texted back. "You can't allow her to sit at a computer and not expect her to play with it."

"LOL, yes, I know," Rayden replied.

"How's Jericho fairing in the battle for Harley's time?" Shiloh asked.

"Oh, she's giving Midnight a good run for her money," Rayden replied.

"She really can't take that project on, Ray," Shiloh tapped out. "She's barely sleeping as it is."

"I know, we made Midnight aware of that. We're trying to convince her to hire Devin to come in and handle the Criminal Division project."

"Does Devin make as much as Harley?" Shiloh asked.

"More," Rayden said. "She's been consulting longer than Harley has, it's always a bidding war for her time."

"Harley's just as good," Shiloh said, even though she really wouldn't know one way or the other.

"I'm sure she is," Rayden assured, "but she hasn't built the reputation that Devin has."

"Maybe I should convince Harley to start working on that…" Shiloh tapped out.

"That's not being a team player, Shiloh," Rayden said.

"I'm on Harley's team, Ray," Shiloh said with a winking emoticon.

"That much is clear," Rayden replied with a winking emoticon too.

"Take care of our girl."

"Working on it."

"Good."

The conference call mercifully ended a few minutes later. Harley never even noticed, she was too busy tapping away at her program. Shiloh reached behind Harley and hung up her phone, carefully removing the headset Harley was wearing. Then she reached over and turned up Harley's music, leaving her office a minute later. She wasn't sure if Harley ever even noticed. Her boss was definitely one of a kind.

***

Jazmine could hear the music playing in the bedroom as she walked into the house. She stood in the foyer and listened for a couple of minutes, recognizing the song as Breaking Benjamin's "Follow." It was loud. It wasn't a good sign, and Jazmine knew it. She set down her gym bag on the table, and walked into the kitchen. She grabbed some Coke from the fridge and a bottle of Jack Daniel's from the liquor cupboard, and poured about three shots worth into a glass with the Coke. She blew her breath out and headed upstairs with the glass in hand.

Walking into their bedroom she saw exactly what she'd expected: Dakota sitting on the bed, wearing a blue t-shirt and faded jeans. She'd kicked off her work boots, and sat with her knees bent, her feet on the bed, and her arms over her knees. Her forehead rested against the back of one hand. An empty glass sat on the nightstand next to her. Jazmine turned the music down some. Dakota's head snapped up immediately, and Jazmine could see the despair in Dakota's blue eyes.

"So, this won't be your first…" Jazmine said. She handed Dakota the drink and sat next to her feet, her eyes searching Dakota's. "What's wrong?"

Dakota drained half the glass, grimacing as the alcohol burned her throat. She leaned back against the headboard looking up at the ceiling, willing the alcohol to do it's magic.

"Dakota, please tell me what's going on…" Jazmine said, feeling afraid suddenly. "Is it your family?" she asked, referring to the Falcos.

91

"No," Dakota said, shaking her head, her voice gravelly.

"Is it the job?" Jazmine asked then, knowing that she had been set to meet the owner of the property that day.

Dakota's eyes dropped to look back at Jazmine, the look in her eyes forlorn.

"What happened?" Jazmine asked, her bright green eyes searching Dakota's.

"The owner…" Dakota said, her lips curled in derision. "The owner is Cassandra Billings."

"What!" Jazmine said, shocked. "Are you fucking kidding me?"

"I wish I was," Dakota said, her tone defeated.

"Did she do this just to fuck with you?" Jazmine asked, her eyes blazing in anger.

"She claims she did it to apologize."

"Then why be sneaky about it?" Jazmine snapped.

Dakota shrugged. "I guess she figured I wouldn't have responded to an email from her. I've ignored every call, text and voicemail… So that was a safe assumption."

Jazmine shook her head, her look glowering. "I'm sorry, babe," she said, putting her hand on Dakota's knee.

Dakota nodded her face a mask of frustration. She scrubbed her face with her hands.

"Now I gotta go back to all my subs and explain that I promised them a job that got fucked up because of my fucking screwed up past life…" she said her tone agonized, banging her head against the

92

headboard over and over in frustration. "People count on me... and I've now screwed them."

"Dakota, stop!" Jazmine exclaimed, putting her hand behind Dakota's head. "You didn't screw them, Cassandra did."

Dakota blew her breath out through her nose in a sound of impatience, her look reflecting disgust.

"You think I'm gonna explain to these professionals that I used to fuck her and because she got a little bit violent during one of our sexual encounters, she decided to apologize by conjuring up a job?" she asked, her tone indicating that if Jazmine thought that she was nuts.

Jazmine looked back at Dakota for a long minute. "A little bit violent, Dakota?" Jazmine queried, her look disbelieving. "She almost killed you! She almost let you bleed to death!"

Dakota shook her head, her look dismissive. "Whatever, either way, I'm not exactly about to jeopardize my business relationships with an overshare from my past, okay?"

Once again, Jazmine stared back at Dakota. She couldn't believe what she was hearing. Had Dakota actually forgotten that Cassandra Billings had cut her repeatedly and then left her in a pool of her own blood for two days? How was that possible?

"Whatever?" Jazmine repeated, her look amazed. "Like it's no big deal?"

"Jaz," Dakota sighed, shaking her head, "I really don't want to get into this, okay? Can I please just sit here and fucking drink myself into oblivion for a bit?"

Jazmine blinked a couple of times, surprised by Dakota's tone of voice as much as she was by her words. She got up and did her best not to feel hurt by Dakota's dismissal. She nodded and walked out of the room.

Dakota watched her go, knowing she was pushing Jazmine away, but unable to stop herself from doing it. Dropping her head against the headboard again, she banged it a few more times, making her ears ring. She picked up the drink and drained it. Getting up she felt slightly dizzy, and she wasn't sure if it was from the alcohol or from hitting her head repeatedly.

In her mind, she was picturing all the people who'd agreed to work with her on this project. All the people she was now going to have to call back and try to think of a reason that she wasn't going to be able to use them. She had to think of something that didn't make her sound like a fucking lunatic.

"Fuck!" she yelled throwing the glass across the room and watching it shatter against the wall.

She strode to the closet, pulled on her leather jacket, and put her boots back on. She picked up her keys and walked out of the bedroom. She didn't see Jazmine as she strode out to the garage, hitting the button to open the door. She got into her 1955 Ferrari 250 GT, and turned the engine over. It started with a throaty growl. She backed out of the garage, hit the button to close the door, and then roared off.

Two hours later, Cody Falco stepped inside The Club. It was a Thursday night so it was relatively quiet. She looked around, catching the eye of one of the bartenders, Janine.

"Where is she?" Cody queried.

"Out back," the woman replied. "She's already gotten into it with one woman."

"Damnit," Cody said, grimacing.

She'd received two phone calls, one from Jazmine completely freaking out because Dakota had been drinking and then had taken off in her car. The second from the owner of The Club who'd called to tell her that her sister was drunk off her ass and causing trouble.

"Come get her, Cody," the woman had said sharply, "before I call the cops on her."

"Ya just did, Millie, I'm headed down now. Please just make sure she doesn't get back into the car, okay?" Cody had requested.

"You got it, Cody," Millie had said.

She found Dakota out on the back patio sitting in one of the chairs. A line of bottles sat on the table next to her, along with various shot glasses. She was smoking and absently watching a girl who was dancing seductively, her look directed at Dakota. Cody noted that Dakota didn't seem the least bit interested in the blond, even in her drunken state.

"So, what are we drinking to?" Cody said, pulling a nearby chair out. She sat straddling it, with her arms draped over the back.

"My fucking past coming back to fuck up my present," Dakota said snidely.

"What happened?" Cody asked, signaling to the waitress for a beer.

"The house, the Craftsman," Dakota said. "Fucking Cassandra Billings owns it."

"Fuck…" Cody said, her look a pained grimace. "Why did she do this?"

Dakota shook her head. "She says she did it to apologize, 'cause she knew I always wanted to work on a Craftsman."

"And you're not buying that?" Cody asked her look unreadable.

"Doesn't matter what I buy," Dakota said, her look wry. "Jazmine will completely flip her shit if I take the job."

Cody nodded slowly, her look considering. "Did you ask her?"

"Didn't need to," Dakota said, lifting her beer to her lips and draining the bottle.

"Why do you say that?" Cody asked, as the waitress arrived with her beer. She handed Dakota a bottle of water, winking at Cody.

"Because she freaked when I told her Cassandra owned the house, went on about how she'd tried to kill me and all…"

"Well, she did," Cody said mildly.

Dakota gave Cody a sharp look. "Why the fuck does everyone fucking think I've forgotten that! Jesus!" She slammed her hand down on the table, causing the bottles to jump and fall over, a couple of them breaking.

"Dakota!" Millie yelled from inside the bar, her voice carrying through the open windows of the patio.

"Yeah!" Dakota yelled back. She pulled out a roll of bills, threw a hundred on the table and moving to stand.

Cody put her hand out to stop Dakota's movement. "What do you think you're doing?"

"Leaving," Dakota replied mildly, her blue eyes challenging Cody.

"Yeah," Cody said, tilting her chin up, meeting Dakota's eyes. "I don't think you're leaving the way you got here."

Dakota's look changed, a nasty grin curling lips. "And you think you're gonna stop me?"

Cody narrowed her hazel eyes, her jaw muscles jumping as she clenched her teeth.

"You're telling me that you're gonna take the chance of wrapping that Berlinetta that our mother helped you rebuild around a tree because of Cassandra fucking Billings?" Cody asked, her tone grave.

She'd known exactly where to push. Dakota sat down, blowing her breath out in a rush.

"Bitch," Dakota muttered.

Cody gave her a wintery smile in return. Dakota leaned forward, putting her elbows on her knees, and her face in her hands, rubbing her face in frustration.

"I'm so fucked right now, Cody..." she said, her tone completely lost.

Cody leaned back in her chair, looking over at Dakota. "Tell me how."

Dakota looked up at Cody, seeing Cody's passive look and narrowing her eyes.

"Don't fucking shrink me, Cody," Dakota snapped.

Cody's lips curled. "Sorry, you got the wrong Falco there, Dak," she said wryly. "I don't practice."

"No, but you fucking preach," Dakota growled.

"Tell me how you think you're fucked, Dak," Cody said again, knowing that Dakota was avoiding analyzing the situation.

"I gotta tell all my subcontractors how I managed to lose this huge fucking job I promised them," Dakota said. "And I fucking iced Jazmine out earlier and I'm sure I'm screwed there now too… This just fucking sucks."

Cody nodded, licking her lower lips. "So let's go one at a time here," she said evenly. "Is the offer of the job still on the table? Or was it a complete bullshit smokescreen?"

"The offer was real," Dakota said, sighing, annoyed that Cody insisted on doing this at that moment.

"Okay, so what happens if you take the job, despite who owns the house?" Cody asked.

"What do ya mean?" Dakota asked.

"Do you trust Cassandra to pay you and see the job through?" Cody asked.

Dakota looked back at her, shaking her head, like she couldn't understand why Cody was asking all of these questions. It was a moot point.

"Yeah, I guess, I mean she'd have to sign an agreement… Considering who she is, I'd make sure my lawyers made it iron clad."

Cody nodded. "Okay, so, why can't you take the job then?"

Dakota looked at Cody openmouthed. "Did you miss the part about my girlfriend losing her mind if I do?"

"What's more important to you?" Cody asked.

"What?" Dakota asked her look puzzled.

"Is your relationship with Jazmine more important than doing this job?" Cody asked.

Dakota looked back at Cody, trying to understand exactly what she was trying to get at.

"Stop trying to figure out the end game, Dakota and answer the question," Cody said, her look pointed. "What's more important to you? Jazmine or the job?"

Dakota shook her head. "Jazmine is," she said simply.

Cody nodded, looking satisfied with that answer. "So it's my suggestion that you talk to her about the job and tell her why you want to take it."

"And then what?" Dakota asked.

"And then you let her decide," Cody said.

"Don't need to bother," Dakota said, rolling her eyes. "I told you, I already know that answer."

"Then you go back to the original question," Cody said. "Which is more important to you? Jazmine or the job."

"I fuckin' hate you, you know that?" Dakota said her tone disgusted.

Cody grinned, nodding. "I think you should talk to your girlfriend, and I think that you should listen to everything she has to say on the matter. She's earned that."

Dakota swallowed, looking back at Cody, knowing that she was absolutely right. She was letting the concern over upsetting other people override her concern for the woman she loved more than anything in the world.

She smacked herself in the forehead with the heel of her hand. "I'm so fucking stupid!"

"You do have your moments," Cody said, her lips curled in a grin. "Come on, I'll drive you home."

"I can't leave the Berlinetta here," Dakota said, shaking her head.

"I don't expect you to," Cody said, nodding to McKenna who stood waiting inside the bar. "Kenna drove me over so I could drive you home."

Dakota glanced over at McKenna, grinning, then looked back at Cody. "Always ahead of me, aren't ya?"

"It's not always easy," Cody said, moving to stand, "but I try to be."

Cody reached out to take Dakota in her arms then, hugging the woman that she truly considered family. She'd known it was imperative that she help Dakota unknot herself. It was the one thing Lyric and Savanna would have expected her to do. Cody did her best never to let her family down.

"Love ya," Cody said, kissing the side of Dakota's head.

"Love you too," Dakota said, giving Cody a slight squeeze.

Half an hour later, Dakota walked into the house she shared with Jazmine. Jazmine was standing in the kitchen and all but ran to her, throwing herself into Dakota's arms.

"I was so scared!" Jazmine said, her voice tremulous, pressing her face against Dakota's shirt.

She pulled back and looked up at Dakota. "Don't you ever leave this house in that car drunk again!" she said seriously.

Dakota lowered her head nodding, her looking downcast. "I know, babe, I'm sorry," she said, her tone repentant. "I just didn't think…"

"It only takes one time, Kota," Jazmine said softly, her eyes reflecting the fear she'd felt.

"I know," Dakota said, her look pained. "I'm sorry, what can I say here?"

"Promise me you won't ever do it again," Jazmine said, her tone vehement.

"I won't, I promise, okay?" Dakota said, returning Jazmine's direct gaze, her tone somber.

"Okay," Jazmine said, nodding, looking relieved.

"Can we talk about the job?" Dakota asked her then.

Jazmine bit her lip, but nodded. Dakota led her over to the couch in their living room. She sat down and pulled Jazmine down next to her, holding both of Jazmine's hands in hers.

"Jaz," she said her tone soft, "I want to take the job."

Jazmine winced, pressing her lips together for a moment.

"Why?" she asked, her tone plaintive.

Dakota blew her breath out. "For one thing, I've made commitments to people for work that would pay them a substantial amount of money. We're getting close to the holidays, babe, they were counting on this job. For another thing, I think that the experience I'll gain on a project like this one is invaluable and it will open up an entirely new market for me."

Jazmine nodded, her look subdued. "So you're going to take it?"

Dakota looked back at her for a long moment. "Only if you say yes."

Jazmine blinked a couple of times. "You're asking me?"

"Yes, I'm asking you."

Jazmine shook her head looking bewildered. "Why?"

Dakota looked back at her with soft eyes. "Because I love you, and I don't want to do anything that is going to endanger what we have, ever."

Jazmine bit her lower lip, tears coming to her eyes.

Dakota felt instantly sorry for her previous behavior. She touched Jazmine's cheek gently.

"Babe, I'm sorry for how I acted earlier," Dakota said. "I was pissed off and disappointed and I didn't handle it right. This whole relationship and being a responsible adult thing is still kind of new," she said with an impish grin. "But that doesn't excuse it," she said seriously. "I know that all that shit with Cassandra was awful, and could have been so much worse, and I know that it was really hard on you. So if you don't want me to do this job, I won't do it, it's as simple as that." She put her finger to Jazmine's lips then. "I love you more than anything in the entire world, and no job is worth losing you over, okay?"

Jazmine smiled, tears spilling over as she did.

Dakota pulled her into her arms and hugged her. She held her until Jazmine pulled away to look up at Dakota.

"Do you think you can trust her?" Jazmine asked, just like Cody had.

"Yeah," Dakota said, nodding.

"Not just about the money, Kota," Jazmine said. "I mean personally, emotionally."

Dakota considered that question. "That one I'm not so sure about," she said honestly. "But I will promise you that if she steps over the line, I'll quit."

Jazmine blinked a couple of times, then nodded accepting the answer. She leaned her head against Dakota's chest, closing her eyes. The thought of Dakota around the woman who'd been so very careless with her life scared her to death, but she trusted Dakota and she believed that she knew what she was getting into. She just hoped she was right.

Lifting her head, Jazmine looked up at Dakota, smiling.

"Take the job," she said simply.

"Are you sure?" Dakota asked, her eye searching Jazmine's.

"No," Jazmine said, smiling as she shook her head, "but I love you and I know that this job is what you have wanted for a long time. I want you to have what you want."

"I want you," Dakota said. "Above everything else."

"And that's the other reason," Jazmine said, smiling. "Because you say things like that."

"I mean it, Jaz," Dakota said, wanting Jazmine to understand that important fact.

"I know," Jazmine said, smiling, "but it feels really good to hear it too."

Chapter 5

"So are you going to tell me what's going on or what?" Harley asked Shiloh one afternoon when they were returning from yet another meeting downtown.

"Huh?" Shiloh queried absently as she answered another text message on her phone.

Harley looked over at Shiloh, her look pointed.

Shiloh caught her look and shook her head. "I'm just dealing with some personal stuff," she said.

"And you don't feel like we're friends enough that you can share it with me?" Harley asked her tone quizzical, the look in her eyes hurt.

Shiloh glanced sharply at Harley, seeing the look in her eyes. "It's not that," she said shaking her head again.

"Then what is it?" Harley asked, her look so openly concerned that Shiloh grimaced.

"It isn't a problem with us, okay?" Shiloh said. "I love working with you."

Harley nodded, looking somewhat relieved. "Okay, then what is it?"

Shiloh shook her head. "It's too embarrassing."

"Oh, come on…" Harley said, her tone entreating. "Tell me."

Shiloh looked down at her hands, biting her lip. "I'm getting evicted from my apartment."

"What!" Harley exclaimed, looking shocked. "Shiloh! Why didn't you say something?"

"I told you, it's embarrassing," she said shrugging and looking anywhere but at Harley.

"What can I do?" Harley asked then.

"Nothing," Shiloh said, shaking her head. "I'll be okay."

"Really?" Harley asked her tone doubtful. "What are you going to do?"

Shiloh didn't answer. In truth, she had absolutely no idea. She'd reached out to the two friends she still had, but they weren't in a position to help. They were as bad off as she was.

"Shy?" Harley queried, when she didn't answer.

"I don't know yet, Harley," Shiloh said, blowing her breath out.

"I can give you money if that will help..." Harley said.

"No!" Shiloh exclaimed, her tone sharper than she'd meant it to be. She grimaced and said, "I'm sorry, I just... It wouldn't help at this point, I'm so far behind that I'd never catch up."

Harley nodded already working on a solution.

"Well, then it's simple," she said, after a minute. "You'll move in with me."

"What? No!" Shiloh said. "I can't do that, you're my boss!"

Harley gave her a deadpan look. "Really?" she asked in a sardonic tone.

"Yes, really," Shiloh said. "I couldn't ask you to do that, Harley. I really couldn't, but thank you for the offer."

"I'm sorry, did you ask me if you could move in?" Harley asked.

"No, but—"

"No," Harley said, cutting her off. "You didn't. So you didn't ask me, I offered."

Shiloh sighed. "That's not the point, Harley. It was really sweet of you to offer, but that would really be taking advantage of you, and I can't do that."

"What if you paid me rent, would that make you feel better?" Harley asked.

"I," Shiloh stammered. "Well…" she said then, her look considering. "What would you want me to pay you?"

Harley shrugged. "Hell, I don't know. How much do you pay now?"

"Eight hundred," Shiloh answered.

"Okay…" Harley said. "So, what about like two hundred?"

"What about like six hundred," Shiloh said.

"No way," Harley said, shaking her head. "I already pay it so I'm not going to charge you crazy rent."

"What about four hundred?"

"What about two," Harley said, her smile wry.

"That's not negotiating, Harley," Shiloh said.

"I know," Harley said, "because it's not negotiable. The negotiable part was letting you pay rent at all, when I own a four-bedroom house where I use one and occasionally two bedrooms."

106

Shiloh looked shocked. "You own a four-bedroom house?" she asked, having thought that Harley was renting an apartment or maybe a house.

Harley grinned, nodding.

"Do I want to know where?" Shiloh asked.

"West Hollywood," Harley said, grinning.

"Those aren't cheap," Shiloh said, narrowing her eyes.

"What's your point?" Harley asked, raising an eyebrow at her.

"That two hundred is crazy for a room in a house in West Hollywood..." Shiloh said.

"Could be nothing, keep it up..." Harley said, her look pointed.

"Oh, I don't think so," Shiloh said, her tone sassy.

Harley gave her a narrowed look. Shiloh returned it with one of her own. Harley grinned then.

"So when do you need to move?" she asked.

Shiloh blew her breath out. "I have a three day quit or pay as of today."

Harley nodded. "Okay, well, after work today let's go over there and get started on packing."

"You don't have to do that, Harley, I can handle it..." Shiloh said her voice trailing off as she saw Harley's scowl. "Okay, okay, come help me, please," she said then, smiling ruefully.

"Much better," Harley said, grinning.

That afternoon they went to Shiloh's apartment. Harley was astounded not only by the rundown neighborhood, but by the fact that Shiloh really had very few possessions. They had her packed within two hours. The apartment was furnished so she had no furniture of her own, except for her mattress.

"Are you attached to that?" Harley asked her, pointing to the mattress.

"I got it second hand," Shiloh said, grinning. "So no."

"Okay, 'cause all of the bedrooms have furniture in them already, and the mattresses are new, so…"

"You have bedrooms full of furniture that you don't use?" Shiloh asked as they carried the two boxes of her possessions down to the car.

"Well, one of the extra rooms gets used sometimes, but the others… They haven't been used yet. I've only lived here for like eight months."

As they got in to the car, Shiloh looked over at Harley. "So who does the one room get used by?" she asked, curious.

"I sometimes have LGBT teens that stay there when they need really short term housing," she said, glancing over her shoulder as she pulled the car out on the road.

She looked over at Shiloh and saw the odd smile on her face.

"What?" she queried.

Shiloh shook her head. "You say that like it's something everyone does."

Harley blinked a couple of times, shrugging. "I have the room," she said by way of explanation.

"Sure, right," Shiloh said, her tone comically agreeable.

"What!" Harley asked laughing at the look on Shiloh's face.

Shiloh shook her head again. "You are just so…" Her voice trailed off as she tried to think of the right word. "Generous."

"Is that a bad thing?" Harley asked, worried.

"No, Harley," Shiloh said smiling softly. "It's not a bad thing; it's just a rare thing."

"Well, I like to be unique," Harley said, her lips curling in a lopsided grin.

"Well you definitely are," Shiloh said, smiling widely.

The drive to Harley's house was accomplished in short order. When Harley pulled into the residential area, Shiloh noticed many of the houses were understated with Spanish tiled roofs and were hacienda style. However, the house that Harley pulled up to had a gate that slid back out of the way, exposing a very modern looking two-story house with two balconies that Shiloh could see from the car.

"Oh my God…" Shiloh said, her tone awed.

"What?" Harley asked, glancing at Shiloh, and then saw that she was looking at the house. "Oh, it's nicer on the inside."

"It's nice on the outside," Shiloh said nodding.

Harley pulled into the very neat garage. Shiloh saw the motorcycle, a Harley Davidson V-Rod Muscle in black and red. She smiled because it looked like Harley to her.

The house that Harley led her into was astounding. Shiloh stood frozen as she looked around. She could not believe the sheer beauty of the house with its clean lines and open space. Downstairs was a huge open plan kitchen, dining, and living space. The back of the house was completely open with floor to ceiling windows that showed off a huge pool and lush green grass.

"How big is this place?" Shiloh asked her tone completely awed.

"About five thousand square feet," Harley said, grinning.

"Wow…" Shiloh said her eyes wide.

"This isn't any bigger than your parents' house," Harley said.

"Yeah, you said it," Shiloh said, glancing over at Harley. "My parents' house, not mine."

Harley pressed her lips together, her look sympathetic.

"Come on," Harley said, "I'll show you the bedrooms. You can pick which one you want to use."

"Okay," Shiloh said, nodding, still in shock.

Walking upstairs, Shiloh was no less impressed. The rooms that Harley showed her were huge and nicely decorated. They were all tasteful but simple, and airy. All of the floors were expensive-looking oak hardwood. And every bedroom had its own glass slider that led out to a balcony. Shiloh was completely blown away by Harley's home.

"This place is incredible!" Shiloh said. She she'd picked a bedroom with a built in vanity. "Two hundred a month isn't even the beginning of what I should be paying you…"

"Don't start," Harley said, narrowing her eyes. "Or I'll change my mind about you getting to pay rent at all."

Shiloh sighed, shaking her head. "You are far too generous my friend."

"No, I'm not, Shy, not in this case," Harley said, her look serious as she set the box of Shiloh's stuff on the bed. "You have been taking incredible care of me since the day you started working for me," she said sincerely, looking directly into Shiloh's eyes. "So, to me, this is just my way of returning that favor, okay?"

"They do pay me to take care of you, you know," Shiloh said, her tone informative.

Harley grinned. "Really? Do they pay you to remind me to eat? Sleep? Or to defend me against crazy lawyers, or even the AG herself? Hmm?" she asked, her look inquiring.

Shiloh looked back at Harley for a long moment, not responding.

"Yeah, that's what I thought," Harley said, her eyes softening. "You go above and beyond for me every day, Shy. So please, let me do this for you, okay?" The last was said with the sweetest, softest voice Shiloh had ever heard Harley use. It brought tears to her eyes.

She nodded, not trusting her voice to speak at that moment. Harley saw the tears in her eyes and stepped forward. She took the box Shiloh still held out of her hands and set it on the bed, then took Shiloh into her arms. After a couple of minutes, Harley released her, looking down at her.

"I'm gonna leave you alone to unpack," she said, smiling softly. "I'll be right next door if you need anything." She pointed toward her bedroom, the only room in the house Shiloh hadn't seen yet.

"Okay," Shiloh said, nodding.

A half an hour later, Shiloh knocked on the open door to Harley's bedroom. Harley had changed and was wearing black sweatpants and a black tank top. Her hair was up in a ponytail with her two rainbow braids hanging down. She was sitting on her bed, one barefoot on the floor, the other leg on the bed as she tapped away on her laptop. She looked up at the sound of Shiloh's light knock. Shiloh didn't notice because she was busy staring openmouthed around Harley's massive master bedroom.

The room itself was no less than the size of her entire studio apartment had been. One entire wall to the left of the bed was a huge sliding door that led out to a balcony that overlooked the backyard and pool. There was a very modern-looking fireplace on one wall surrounded my marble tiles. The wall behind Harley's bed had three large windows. The bed itself, although it looked like a California King, was dwarfed by the huge room. This room too was very simple in its décor, the walls were white, and the few accents in the room were shades of blue. There was a painting hanging over the fireplace. Shiloh walked over to it, and thought she recognized it, but she looked back at Harley.

"Is this Monet?" she asked, her voice reflecting surprise.

"Yeah," Harley said, nodding. "It's one of the Mornings on the Seine series," she said, grinning. "My favorite, actually."

"This isn't the one you see most often," Shiloh said, looking at the painting again.

It was beautiful, with vivid greens and blues.

"No," Harley said, shaking her head. "It's Morning on the Seine in the Rain, a reproduction, of course."

"Well, yes, I'm sure, but it's a really great one…" Shiloh said, shaking her head noting the brush strokes and texture of the oil paint used. "I imagine this cost you some money."

"Yeah," Harley said, grinning fondly, "it did."

Shiloh looked around again. "This room is really amazing too," she said, gesturing around her, then leaning to look around the corner to what had to be the master bathroom.

"Go take a look," Harley told her, grinning.

"Okay," Shiloh said, smiling as she walked toward the opening.

The bathroom was huge, and a line from the song "Rockstar" came to mind, "bathroom big enough to play baseball in." It had a steam shower with multiple heads set high and low. It also had a large bathtub with a marble surround. Everything about the bathroom screamed modern and expensive, but also seemed to fit Harley, as the tile and marble were all earth tones.

Shiloh walked back out to the bedroom and sat on the edge of Harley's bed, facing her.

"You really have done well for yourself, Harley," she said, smiling. "You should really be proud."

Harley grinned, but shrugged. "It's just a house. I bought it pretty much this way."

Shiloh canted her head. "Really? 'Cause the artwork I've seen and the décor looks very much like the Harley I know."

"Well, okay, I bought the furniture and stuff, sheesh," Harley said, grinning.

"You have really good taste," Shiloh said.

"And that surprises you," Harley said. It wasn't a question.

Shiloh looked back at Harley for a long moment. "Yeah, I guess it does. I don't know why though."

"Because you thought my dad was a biker, and he actually is," Harley said, grinning.

"Still…" Shiloh stammered. She knew that was exactly why she was surprised that Harley had such good taste.

"It's okay, Shy," Harley said, her tone sincere. "I like that I surprise people."

Shiloh looked back at the other woman, a wide smile on her face. "I can see that," she said.

Later as they sat down to dinner, the doorbell chimed. Harley pulled her iPad over to her and opened a window on it. Shiloh, who was sitting across from Harley at the dining room table, could see that she had a home security system on it.

"Oh shit…" Harley said, sighing.

"What?" Shiloh queried, leaning over to look at the iPad to see who was standing there.

She saw a girl with long dark hair. She looked very young and was dressed in raggedy jeans and a short midriff exposing top.

"It's Julie," Harley said. "Will you do me a favor?"

"Sure, what do you want me to do?" Shiloh asked as the doorbell rang again.

"Just go with whatever I say, okay?" Harley said as she hit the unlock button for the front door.

"Okay…" Shiloh said, her voice trailing off as the girl walked in.

She dropped her bag and walked over to Harley, leaning in to hug her. Harley hugged the girl quickly then sat back, pointedly putting her hands on the arms of the chair as she looked back at the girl. Heedless of Harley's inspection, Julie kissed Harley on the lips quickly. Harley pulled her head back, a look of annoyance on her face.

114

"Julie," she cautioned.

"It was just a quick kiss, Harley, geeze chillax," Julie muttered as her gaze fell on Shiloh. "Who're you?" she asked then, her tone outright rude.

"Julie!" Harley exclaimed, her voice chastising.

Julie glanced at Harley, then lowered her eyes. "Sorry," she said simply.

"This is Shiloh," Harley said, looking pointedly at Shiloh, her look warning Shiloh she was about to say something shocking. "She's my girlfriend."

Julie's head snapped up and immediately turned to look at Shiloh, her look very obviously assessing.

"Seriously?" Julie asked her tone showing that she didn't think Shiloh was acceptable.

"Are you kidding me right now?" Harley asked her look openly shocked at Julie's disrespect.

"I'm sorry," Julie said, immediately looking contrite, holding her hands up defensively.

Shiloh and Harley exchanged a look. Harley could read both hurt and offense in Shiloh's eyes and she felt bad that Julie's sharp tongue had caused it. It made her voice come out sharp when she spoke to Julie.

"What are you doing here, Julie?" Harley asked. "We talked about this…"

"I know, I know," Julie said, her look suddenly desperate. "But you gotta hear me out…"

Harley opened her mouth her look warning Julie that she didn't intend to do that.

"Harl, please!" Julie said, her voice strident.

Harley blew her breath out, her face composed in a cynical mask. "Fine, what is it this time?"

Julie gave her a surprised look. It was apparent Harley wasn't responding the way she usually did. Shiloh wondered about that, but kept silent as she watched the scene before her.

"It's José," Julie said. "He's been all over me again, and I can't seem to get him to leave me alone…" Her voice trailed off as she saw Harley's glower.

"You're supposed to stay away from that guy, Jules," Harley told her.

"I know, but that's what I'm saying, he's like all over me…" she said. Her eyes lowered then. "He wants me to work for him again."

"And you can't do that either," Harley said sharply.

"I know!" Julie practically shouted. "But what the fuck am I supposed to do?"

Harley looked back at the girl for a long minute. The only sound in the room was the drip of water from the kitchen sink. Shiloh saw Harley's head twitch slightly and knew that Harley had heard the water and was now having a hard time focusing on anything else. She stood and walked over to the sink to turn the tap off. It was part of her ADHD; the smallest sound could draw Harley's focus and drive her crazy at the same time. Shiloh was used to it now and knew her triggers.

Julie's eyes followed Shiloh's actions, and she looked at Shiloh like she was crazy. She had no idea that Harley had ADHD and that things like that would drive her crazy.

Harley too had tracked her movement, and Shiloh now had a slight grin on her face, her eyes sparkling in subdued amusement. Thinking about what Harley had asked her to do, Shiloh moved to stand on the other side of Harley, opposite from where Julie stood. She put her hand on Harley's shoulder, smoothing her hand across the back of Harley's neck affectionately, looking directly at Julie as she did.

Julie's eyes widened slightly and her lips twitched in obvious annoyance. She could see Harley's pointed look, but didn't want to deal with that at that point.

"I just need a place tonight," Julie said quietly.

Harley's lips twitched in consternation, but she finally nodded.

"Fine," she said evenly. "Go." She nodded her head toward the stairs.

"Thanks Harley," Julie said, her tone still quiet.

She picked up her bag and headed up the stairs. Harley and Shiloh watched her go. Shiloh looked down at Harley then, moving to sit in the chair next to her.

"So what's the story there?" Shiloh asked quietly.

Harley glanced at the stairs, then looked back at Shiloh.

"She was the first kid I took in," Harley said. "And at first she was really sweet, and she ended up staying here for like a week…" She shook her head. "Somewhere along the way she developed a crush on me I guess, and that's where things went bad in a hurry."

"Bad how?" Shiloh asked.

117

"Like one night she climbed into my bed, claiming she was afraid... I let her stay... It's a big bed, right?" Harley said, looking at Shiloh in askance.

"Yeah, it's huge, and if she was on the other side of it, there were miles there..." Shiloh said, nodding.

"Right," Harley said, looking slightly relieved. "But next thing I know I wake up and she's right there, and touching me."

"Oh crap," Shiloh said, her eyes wide. "How old is she?"

"Well, she's seventeen now, but she was sixteen then. Regardless..." Harley said, shaking her head.

"What did you do?"

"I stopped her, of course, explained that she was too young, underage, whatever..." Harley said. "And I basically told her she couldn't do that because I'd get my ass arrested."

"Okay..."

"Yeah, she was fine for the rest of that stay, but every time since then she's tried to make excuses to get into my bed. Sometimes she'll just be there when I wake up... It's really not a good thing. So I finally just told her she couldn't stay here anymore... But every so often she shows up and there's always a good excuse."

"Or lie," Shiloh said, her look pointed.

"Right," Harley said nodding.

"So that's why I'm your girlfriend now, huh?" Shiloh asked, grinning.

"Exactly," Harley said, widening her eyes as she grinned. "I'm hoping she won't try it if she thinks my girlfriend is here."

"Even with me in another room?" Shiloh asked.

Harley shrugged. "Hopefully she won't notice or care."

"Okay…" Shiloh said, grinning.

That night, however, true to her history, Julie climbed into Harley's bed. She saw that this "girlfriend" wasn't sleeping with her, so she figured it was that other chick's loss. She moved carefully so she didn't wake Harley up too soon, and looked down at the sleeping woman. Harley was wearing a black tank top and black underwear. Her tan made her skin glow against the white sheets. Harley lay with her head turned to one side, her left arm thrown up over her head, her right extended out to her side.

Julie wanted Harley so much and she knew that if she could just get her to see that age wasn't that big of a deal, she could be with her. She just had to get her past this stupid age shit, that's all.

She'd tried before, but she'd never been armed with this knowledge before. She smiled as she looked at Harley again, she knew she it was going to work this time, she knew it. Julie was on Harley's right side. She leaned down carefully, and kissed Harley's neck, sucking gently at Harley's skin as she moved to press her body along the length of Harley's. Harley's reaction was instant. She groaned in her sleep, her arm now under Julie's neck, pulling her closer. Julie continued to kiss Harley's neck, her hands sliding up Harley's chest, and it was obvious that Harley's body was responding. For a moment, Julie was sure that she had her.

Harley woke with a start, her body alive with sensations. For an instant, she reveled in the sensations, then it suddenly clicked in her head who was likely causing them. She wrenched her body away from Julie, shifting away from her with surprising agility.

"What the fuck?" Harley exclaimed, her anger replacing her shock as she looked down at Julie. "Are you crazy?" she practically yelled. "What the fuck is wrong with you!"

"You wanted me!" Julie yelled back, her look triumphant.

"Yeah, till I realized who you were," Harley said her tone derisive.

"What is going on?" Shiloh asked from the bedroom door.

Harley looked over at Shiloh, shaking her head. Then she looked back at Julie. "Go back to your room, now. Or leave."

Julie looked defiantly back at her, but then she nodded and got up and left the room.

"Well, that didn't really work, did it?" Shiloh said, looking chagrinned. She gave Harley a sympathetic look. "You okay?"

Harley lay back, blowing her breath out loudly. "Yeah," she said, her tone tired.

Shiloh looked down at her boss. She could see that it bothered Harley immeasurably that Julie had lied her way into her bed again. She had no idea what to say, however, so she just waited to see if Harley wanted to talk.

After a full minute, Harley sat up and got off the bed. She opened the sliding door and walked onto the balcony. She picked up her cigarettes and lighter from the table, and lit one. She stood at the railing and smoked. Shiloh joined her.

"You don't have to hang out with me," Harley said evenly. "I'm okay."

"You sure?"

"Yeah." Harley grinned. "Go back to bed."

"Okay," Shiloh said, nodding.

Shiloh turned and left. Harley stood smoking for another few minutes, then eventually went back to bed, though she wasn't able to sleep. It was a long night.

***

Dakota started the job for Cassandra a week after the fight with Jazmine. All the contracts had been signed and returned in short order. Dakota was pleased that Cassandra wasn't on the site at all the day she started. She'd received a few text messages from Cassandra telling her she was in New York, but to go ahead and get started.

It was another week before Cassandra showed up at the site. Dakota was talking to one of the sub-contractors when Cassandra's car pulled up to the curb. As she finished the discussion with the man, Dakota's eyes fell on Cassandra as she climbed out of her Mercedes. Cassandra walked over to Harley, all polish and perfect hair, to Dakota's jeans, t-shirt, and work boots.

"You do love to get dirty," Cassandra said mildly, but her dark eyes sparkled with flirtation.

Dakota narrowed her eyes at Cassandra, but didn't respond to the double-edged statement.

"Do you want to see where we are?" Dakota asked her tone businesslike.

"Of course," Cassandra said, her tone not indicating any offense to Dakota's rebuff.

Dakota walked her through the house, showing her the progress they were making refining the wood and the tilework in the bathrooms.

"We're probably not going to be able to save all of this subway tile," Dakota said, squatting down to touch the hexagonal tiles on the floor. "But we can probably save at least half, and I can find some good reproductions to fill in with."

Cassandra just waved her hand airily. "Don't worry about saving it, replace it all," she said, her tone off-handed.

Dakota made an annoyed sound in the back of her throat. "Cass, this is friggin' vintage tile…" she said in disbelief. "You don't just rip it out and replace it! I'm trying to keep this house as authentic as I can."

Cassandra looked surprised by Dakota's rejoinder.

"Well," Cassandra began, blowing her breath in an exasperated sigh, "fine, do whatever you want then."

Dakota stood up, looking annoyed at Cassandra.

"What is this, Cass?" she asked, her tone frustrated.

"What is what?" Cassandra asked impatiently.

"This," Dakota said, gesturing to the house around them. "What are you really trying to do here?"

Cassandra looked back at her for a long moment, her dark eyes searching Dakota's. Finally, she dropped her eyes, shaking her head.

"I told you," she said softly, not looking at Dakota. "I wanted to apologize to you for what happened… I knew that you wanted to work on a Craftsman, so I've had my agent looking for one." She shrugged.

Dakota looked at Cassandra, her blue eyes measuring and wary. She wasn't sure if she trusted her, but Cassandra wasn't usually one to hide her motives. She did what she did, and the people around her dealt with it.

Finally, Dakota sighed. "So you really don't care what I do with this house," she said, sounding defeated.

"That's not true, I do care," she said sadly. "I just don't know anything about all of this…" she said, waving her hand at the house.

"Would you let me teach you?" Dakota asked, surprising herself.

Cassandra raised her eyes, and Dakota could read surprise in them as well.

"You'd do that?" Cassandra said.

"If you stop wearing high heels and skirts to my job site," Dakota said with a grin.

Cassandra laughed softly, nodding. "I might be able to do that."

"Good," Dakota said, smiling.

That night Dakota told Jazmine about the encounter.

"So now you're going to teach her about Craftsman houses?" Jazmine asked, careful to keep the jealousy out of her voice.

Dakota was busy looking at something on her iPad, so she didn't see the slight flicker of jealousy in Jazmine's eyes.

"Hmm?" Dakota murmured, then looked up. "Oh, yeah, I guess. We'll see, she's not exactly much of a student," she said with a grin.

Jazmine nodded. "Well that ought to make the job harder."

"Well, I don't see the point in it, if she's not going to care about the result."

Jazmine nodded again, and changed the subject.

The next day, to Dakota's utter shock, Cassandra showed up to the work site in jeans, a blouse, and boots that were a bit fashionable, but generally resembled work boots.

"Wow," Dakota said, blinking repeatedly, "I didn't even think you owned a pair of jeans."

"I didn't," Cassandra said, winking at her. "But now I do. So teach me."

"Okay," Dakota said, leading Cassandra back to the bathroom she'd been showing her the day before.

Kneeling down, Dakota took Cassandra's hand and pulled her down as well.

"Okay, this is subway tile. It became popular at the turn of the twentieth century and was named subway tile because, well, duh, they designed it to be put in subway stations. They originally came in two sizes, three by six rectangles, and four by four squares. Eventually they came out with these patterns," she said, touching the hexagon tile.

Cassandra nodded, trying to take everything in as Dakota talked. Later Dakota told her about wainscoting and things like picture rails and chair rails. Cassandra listened attentively the entire time. By the end of the day, Dakota was tired of talking, but Cassandra was excited about the work. Even when Dakota went home, Cassandra stayed behind to walk through the house.

***

Two days after Shiloh moved in with Harley, it was her birthday. She didn't even know that Harley knew when her birthday was, so she was very surprised when she came downstairs that morning and saw an envelope with her name on it propped up on the counter. She picked it up she biting her lip. She opened it and pulled out a birthday card that was simple and cute and wished her a happy birthday.

She was fixing coffee when Harley came downstairs.

Harley walked over to her and kissed her cheek. "Happy birthday," she said smiling. "You gonna be ready soon?"

"Thanks, yeah," Shiloh said, nodding.

A few minutes later in the car, Shiloh suddenly realized that they weren't headed the usual way to the office.

"Where are you going?" Shiloh asked, looking perplexed.

Harley grinned, but didn't answer. A few minutes later, she pulled up to the curb of the Soho House of West Hollywood. She handed the valet the key to her car and a fifty-dollar bill. Then she walked over to open Shiloh's door.

"What's going on?" Shiloh asked.

"Come on," Harley said, smiling as she held her hand out to Shiloh.

She led Shiloh into the membership only restaurant and to the elevator that took them up to the rooftop garden.

"Oh my God, this is beautiful…" Shiloh breathed.

There were sweeping views of Los Angeles. There were cushioned chairs and couches, plants and trees. It was a beautiful restaurant. They were seated near the windows and had a great breakfast.

125

"This was so sweet of you," Shiloh said, sighing. "Thank you, Harley."

Harley nodded, her look expressionless.

They left the restaurant, and Shiloh expected Harley to head to the office. She didn't. Instead, she headed east on Sunset and took a right on North Doheny Drive. A couple of minutes later she pulled up to Salon Benjamin and got out, handing her key to the valet once again and leading Shiloh inside. Two hours later Shiloh was still surprised by her morning of beauty. Her hair had been colored, highlighted, cut and styled. When she emerged, her hair was a rich mahogany brown with burnished gold and copper highlights that lit her face beautifully. It was cut to frame her face and flowed down her back in waves. Harley had sat by and chatted with the staff and Shiloh the entire time.

"You are too much," Shiloh said to Harley when they were back in the car.

"Me? No…" Harley said, grinning.

Once again, Harley didn't head in the direction of work.

"Are we even going to the office today?" Shiloh asked.

"It's illegal to work on your birthday," Harley told her.

"News to me," Shiloh said, grinning.

Harley drove out to North San Vicente Boulevard and then took a right. Shiloh was once again surprised when she stopped at the Beverly Center shopping center and pulled into the parking garage. Harley got out of the car, and walked around to open Shiloh's door.

"Okay, we're just window shopping now, right?" Shiloh said, knowing full well that Harley had already spent a lot of money between breakfast and the hair salon. She'd glanced at the prices in Salon Benjamin and just about passed out.

Harley didn't respond to the question, instead she led Shiloh into the mall.

"Pick a store," Harley said, grinning.

"For…" Shiloh said, narrowing her eyes at Harley.

"It's not polite to look a gift horse in the mouth, Shy," Harley told her with a wink.

"I am not spending any more of your money," Shiloh said, folding her arms with resolve.

"Then spend yours," Harley said, handing her a credit card.

Shiloh looked at the credit card, she was damned if it didn't say her name on it.

"What did you do?" Shiloh asked Harley.

Harley smiled benevolently. "I knew you'd only let me spend so much of *my* money, so I put money on this, and you're going to have to use it, 'cause it's no longer in my name."

"You are a real brat, you know that?" Shiloh said, doing her best to look mad.

In truth, she'd never had anyone treat her like this. Her heart was touched so deeply that she had no way to express it properly. She put her arms up around Harley's shoulders, hugging her tightly.

"You are way too generous, Harley," she whispered in her ear. "I can't even begin to thank you…"

"You don't have to thank me, Shy," Harley said, looking down at her. "I just want you to have fun on your birthday, okay?"

Shiloh pressed her lips together, tears in her eyes suddenly.

"And don't do that either!" Harley exclaimed, pulling her close again so she wouldn't have to see the tears.

Shiloh leaned her head against Harley's shoulder until she could get her tears under control. When she finally had composed herself again, she stepped back and glanced up at Harley.

"So what am I supposed to do with this?" she asked, holding up the card.

"Spend it," Harley said. "Make sure you get an outfit for The Club. I'm taking you there tomorrow night."

"You are?" Shiloh asked, surprised.

"I think it's about time you meet more than just Ray, Jerich, and Devin," Harley said. "That's the best way to meet everyone."

"Okay," Shiloh said, nodding. "Where would be the best place to find something that will work for The Club?"

"Personally, I'm all about Diesel, but you could check out BCBG or Divine or Dolce... You pick."

Shiloh gave her a serious look. "Dolce? How much is on this card Harley Marie Davidson?"

Harley smiled, her blue eyes sparkling in amusement. "Trust me, I'll let you know if you're going to max it out."

"That isn't an actual answer," Shiloh said.

"But the only one you're gonna get, so get to shopping."

They spent the next few hours strolling through stores and looking at every imaginable style of clothing. Shiloh found that Harley was a lot of fun to shop with. She continually picked up crazy stuff just to make Shiloh laugh. However, in the end, it was Harley who seemed to have the eye for the kinds of things that would look good on Shiloh.

They ended up at BCBG where Harley picked up a leather mini skirt with a scalloped edge, and a lace camisole, along with a few other pieces she thought would look good on Shiloh. She also picked out couple of different pairs of booties and handed them to Shiloh.

"I'll be out there," Harley said, pointing to the chairs outside the private dressing room. "I expect to see anything that actually fits," she said with a wink.

When Shiloh put on the mini skirt, camisole, and booties she looked at herself in the mirror. She could not believe how good she looked. Harley definitely had an eye for clothes.

She walked out of the dressing room and looked around to see Harley sitting in one of the chairs chatting with a sales girl. When Harley glanced over at Shiloh however, she stopped talking. Her eyes went from Shiloh's toes, all the way up her body, a slow approving smile spreading over her face.

"You look incredible…" Harley told her. "You have to get that for The Club."

Shiloh bit her lip. "I can't wear this to work though…"

"So?" Harley said. "There's other stuff in there for work."

"Harley, this is like eight hundred dollars' worth of outfit!" Shiloh whispered loudly.

Harley grinned. "So?" she repeated. "You're getting it, or I'll use my own credit card."

"Okay, okay," Shiloh said, shaking her head and rolling her eyes.

"You need a jacket. We'll have to go somewhere else for that though... Maybe Dolce or maybe even Diesel... Hmmm..." she murmured.

She pulled out her phone to look up something. As she did, she motioned to Shiloh to go try on the other things.

The next outfit was a black sleeveless blouse with white pinstripes that draped in an asymmetrical A-line and emphasized Shiloh's small waist. It was paired with matching tailored pinstriped pants. For fun, she put on the other pair of booties Harley had picked.

"Oh yeah..." Harley said nodding. "All of it," she said decisively.

"But..." Shiloh began to protest. This was yet another seven to eight hundred dollar outfit.

Harley merely held up her own credit card pointedly.

"You are a brat," Shiloh said.

Harley just grinned and flicked her finger toward the dressing room.

At the register, Shiloh was sure she was going to faint when the total rang up to over $4,000. She looked at Harley, hoping she'd say that it had maxed the card out. She didn't.

"Harley..." Shiloh entreated.

Harley simply looked back at her with a smile on her lips.

"Now, about that jacket..." Harley said, picking up the bags and nodding toward the door.

"No," Shiloh said, shaking her head.

"Yep," Harley said. "You'll freeze otherwise."

"I have jackets," Shiloh said.

"Not that go with that outfit," Harley said, referring to the outfit Shiloh had gotten for The Club.

"No," Shiloh said again.

Harley shook her head and started walking down the walkway in the mall. Shiloh had to hurry to catch up. Harley held her arm away from her body, bidding Shiloh to take her elbow. Shiloh did, hugging Harley's arm and putting her head against Harley's upper arm.

Harley led her to Diesel. There she picked out some clothes for herself and a black jacket for Shiloh made of one hundred percent sheepskin. It was supple and soft, and had a bit of a biker look to it, with a buckle low on the waist and motocross-style quilting on the sleeves.

"Seven hundred dollars?" Shiloh exclaimed.

"I already have my card out," Harley said, taking the jacket out of Shiloh's hands and putting it up with the rest of her stuff.

Shiloh gave Harley a narrowed look, which Harley ignored.

They had lunch at the Piazza Lounge and then Harley finally took Shiloh back to the house. As they walked into the house, with Harley carrying all of the bags refusing to let Shiloh touch them, Shiloh felt a sense of unreality. She could not believe how much Harley had done for her that day, not to mention letting her live in this immensely beautiful home for $200 a month. It was crazy.

Harley took the bags upstairs and put them down in Shiloh's room. When she turned to walk out of the room, Shiloh grabbed her, hugging her.

"Thank you so much for this, you are sincerely the craziest person I've ever met," she said, smiling. "But you are also the most wonderful friend I could have ever hoped for."

Harley smiled, looking down at her. "Happy birthday, Shy."

"Thank you," Shiloh said, smiling softly.

Harley leaned down and kissed her lightly on the lips. Then she turned and left the room. Shiloh stood looking around the room and at the stack of bags sitting on the bed. She pulled the credit card out of her pocket and looked at it, wondering exactly how much was on it. She noted a phone number on the back.

She bit her lip, wondering if she should call the number to check. She debated for a while, but finally gave in to temptation. A few minutes later she wished she hadn't as the operator said that there was no limit in the card and that yes the card was billed to Harley Marie Davidson. Shiloh had to sit down after that. Harley had given her a credit card with no limit… Who did that? The level of trust that it took for Harley to do that kind of thing was beyond crazy. Shiloh doubted she knew anyone that she'd trust that far. She shook her head; the woman was just too much.

Chapter 6

Jazmine got a phone call one afternoon, two weeks after Dakota started the project for Cassandra. It was one of the workmen at the site. He told her that Dakota had been hurt and that they'd taken her to the hospital at Cedars Sinai.

"Shit!" Jazmine exclaimed. "I'm headed there now, thank you!"

She drove toward Cedar, calling Cody on the way. At the hospital she went to the emergency room and inquired about Dakota.

"Are you family?" the nurse asked.

Jazmine paused, shaking her head, thinking how annoying this was.

"Yes, she's family," came a voice from behind her. She turned to see Lyric.

"But…" Jazmine stammered.

"He called me right after he called you," Lyric told her, then nodded to the nurse. "Dakota is my daughter. We need to know how she is."

The nurse nodded. "I'll get ahold of her doctor and have him come see you."

"Okay, if she's conscious you're going to have a problem with her," Lyric said, her tone matter of fact. "So you might want to make that fast."

The nurse looked surprised, but nodded as she picked up the phone. The doctor came out a couple of minutes later, just as Cody and Savanna joined them.

"How is she?" Jazmine asked, worried.

Savanna put her arm around Jazmine, hugging her to her side.

"Ms. Falco suffered some contusions and we're fairly certain a concussion. We'll need to do a CAT Scan to be sure. She took a pretty good knock to the head, although she seems fine. I can take you back to see her."

"Thank you," Lyric said, glancing at Savanna and Jazmine seeing the relief on both women's faces.

In the emergency room, they immediately heard Dakota's voice.

"Back off, I'm not kidding you…" she was saying, her tone low and threatening.

"Oh Lord," Lyric said as she quickened her pace. "Thanks doc," she said as she passed him to get to the curtained area. "Dakota!" she exclaimed as she pulled back the curtain. The nurse who was trying to take Dakota's pulse backed up into her.

"I'm sorry, ma'am," the nurse exclaimed as she moved around Lyric and left.

Lyric looked over at Dakota who was sitting up on the bed looking highly agitated. She smiled and seemed relieved when she saw her family.

Jazmine walked over to Dakota immediately, putting her arms around her and hugging her gently.

"What happened?" she asked when they parted.

Dakota shook her head, looking embarrassed. "I was carrying some stuff, and slipped on the stairs. It was stupid."

Jazmine blew her breath out, and Dakota could tell she'd been worried it was something else. She shook her head slowly at Jazmine, as Lyric, Savanna, and Cody moved in to hug her.

"It's getting late, so we're going to need to keep you overnight," the doctor told Dakota.

"Yeah, I don't think so," Dakota said immediately.

"Ms. Falco, we need to ensure that there's nothing else going on with your head before I can release you," the doctor said, his tone authoritative.

"And I care because?" Dakota replied, in the usual acerbic manner she had when it came to doctors.

"Dak…" Cody cautioned.

Dakota looked at Cody and narrowed her eyes.

"She's right, Dakota," Savanna said, rubbing her hand over Dakota's arm. "We need to make sure you're okay before you come home, okay?" Her tone was soothing and gentle, and as usual, Dakota responded to it.

Sighing, Dakota said, "Fine."

Cody and Lyric exchanged a look, both of them grinning. No matter how tough Dakota acted, she would never argue with Savanna.

Things with Lily were fine for the first six or seven months. She took Dakota places, paid for things, insisted on buying her clothes and shoes, and anything else Dakota seemed to want or like. Dakota was always

135

suspicious, but Lily seemed to genuinely want to do things for her, so she let her.

When she heard Cody had gotten out of juvenile hall, she made a point of finding out where she'd been sent. She happened upon the house Cody was staying in on a day when Cody had been leaving with a blond in a black Ferrari. She saw the huge smile on Cody's face and wondered about it. After the car drove off, Cody made her way to the house.

She was greeted by a woman with long dark red hair, and the warmest brown eyes Dakota had ever seen before.

"Can I help you?" Savanna asked her.

"Yeah, I just wanted to ask about a friend of mine," Dakota said casually. "I was told she's here at your place."

"Who's your friend?" Savanna asked her tone kind.

"Cody Wyatt," Dakota said.

"Oh, Cody. She just left a few minutes ago, but she'll be back if you want to wait..." Savanna said, surprised that Cody had a friend. Though she realized she shouldn't be, t Cody wasn't exactly an open book.

"Where did she go?" Dakota asked, wanting to know about the woman in the black Ferrari.

"She went out with a friend of mine. She and Cody seem to have become friends."

"Friends?" Dakota asked, raising a sardonic eyebrow, her tone indicating what kind of friend she thought this woman might be.

"Oh, no," Savanna said, shaking her head. "Lyric is a great person. She's actually a peace officer, so you don't need to worry about Cody in that respect."

136

Dakota nodded, her look guarded. Cody was hanging out with a cop? But then she remembered Cody's smile at the woman and something tugged at her heart.

"Okay, cool," Dakota said to Savanna. "Well, thanks," she said, turning to leave.

"Are you sure you can't stay?" Savanna asked, sensing that this girl needed a connection and she was hopeful that Cody might be able to get her to stick around.

"Nah, it's cool," Dakota said, assuming her usual nonchalant attitude.

"Can I at least tell her who came by?" Savanna asked gently.

Dakota's eyes softened ever so slightly at the tone, but then shook her head. "Nah, I think she's better off here, and I'd rather you don't say anything about me coming by."

"But..." Savanna began, her eyes searching Dakota's.

Dakota reached out and took Savanna's hands in hers, in a very adult gesture. "Just take care of her, okay?" she said her voice both somber and serious.

She gave Savanna's hands a gentle squeeze, and then she turned and walked out the door. Savanna stared after her thinking she was missing something, but not sure what. She discussed it with Lyric later that night. Lyric agreed with her that it was likely this girl was important to Cody, but she also thought it was better that they do as the girl had asked and not mention her appearance.

"We don't want her running off to find this girl," Lyric said. "And I'm sure there's a reason the girl doesn't want Cody to know she was here. Let's just respect that, okay?"

"Okay," Savanna said, blowing her breath out, knowing that Lyric had Cody's best interest at heart.

Lyric ended up speaking with the doctor to ask about Jazmine staying with Dakota, explaining Dakota's major issue with hospitals and that the medical staff were more likely to get cooperation out of Dakota if Jazmine was there with her. The doctor finally agreed, moving Dakota to a more private room so Jazmine's presence wouldn't disturb other patients.

Lyric, Savanna, and Cody had just left the hospital when Cassandra walked into the room where Dakota was. Jazmine, who was sitting in a chair next to Dakota's bed, looked up with narrowed eyes.

"What are you doing here?" she asked Cassandra, her tone low.

Cassandra stopped her forward motion, giving Jazmine a cautious look. Then she looked over at Dakota.

"I just heard," Cassandra said. "Are you okay?"

Dakota nodded, glancing at Jazmine who did not look happy that Cassandra was there.

"Yeah, I'm okay," Dakota told Cassandra.

"But you're still here…" Cassandra said her tone leading.

"They want to do a scan to make sure I didn't scramble anything up here," Dakota said, grinning and tapping on her head with her index finger.

"Well, that should be a fruitless procedure," Cassandra murmured, her eyes twinkling with humor.

Dakota gave a short laugh, shaking her head. She caught Jazmine's sharp look and knew there was trouble brewing.

"Anyway," Dakota said, her tone more businesslike. "I'm okay."

Cassandra caught not only Jazmine's expression, but also the change in Dakota's tone. She nodded, blowing her breath out quietly.

"Please let me know if you need anything," Cassandra said, addressing Dakota and Jazmine.

"Will do," Dakota said. "Hopefully I'll be back on the job in a day or two, but I'll text you when I know for sure."

"Okay," Cassandra nodded and then left.

Dakota glanced over at Jazmine and saw that she was still looking at the door Cassandra had just left through.

"I'll be right back…" Jazmine said, moving to stand.

"Jaz…" Dakota said cautioned, but Jazmine just shook her head and walked out of the room.

Dakota made a frustrated sound, dropping her head back on the bed and wincing at the pain it caused.

"Cassandra!" Jazmine called as she strode after the other woman.

Cassandra stopped and turned around, her look unreadable.

"Yes?" she queried, her tone refined.

"Why did you come here?" Jazmine asked, her green eyes staring into Cassandra's.

"To ensure that my employee is going to be alright," Cassandra said dryly. "She was injured on my property. It could be a liability issue," she said then, her tone condescending.

"Right," Jazmine said sarcastically. "I'm sure that's the only reason."

Cassandra looked back at Jazmine totally expressionless, but Jazmine was fairly sure she could a light of triumph in her eyes.

"You stay away from Dakota, Cassandra," Jazmine said her tone direct.

"That's going to be rather difficult, Jazmine," Cassandra replied drolly. "She is working on my property."

Jazmine narrowed her eyes at the other woman, knowing that she was way out of her element when it came to Cassandra.

"We're together, Cassandra, you aren't going to change that," Jazmine said her tone assured.

"If that's true and you're quite confident of your place with her," Cassandra said her face a mask of cynicism, "then I'm not sure why you'd be attempting to warn me off."

With that, Cassandra turned and walked away. Jazmine stared after her, her mouth hanging open in surprise. She turned and walked back to the room.

"Do I still have a job?" Dakota asked mildly when Jazmine walked back into the room.

Jazmine gave her a sharp look. "What's that supposed to mean?"

Dakota shrugged slightly. "Just figured you'd gone to cuss her out, and that I'd be summarily fired for it."

"Well, your job is safe," Jazmine said, looking frustrated.

"Okay, what's going on?" Dakota asked. She was fairly sure she knew, but she wanted Jazmine to tell her so there was no doubt.

"She's after you, Dakota," Jazmine said, shaking her head. "And I don't like it."

Dakota blew her breath out, shaking her head. It was exactly what she'd thought was the problem.

"Jaz," Dakota reasoned, "even if that's true, why does it matter?"

"Because!" Jazmine exclaimed. "She's changing her tactics and she thinks we're too stupid to know it."

"Do you think I'm too stupid to know it?" Dakota asked, her tone of voice still even.

Jazmine looked back at Dakota, surprised by the question.

"I…" Jazmine began, but her voice trailed off as she shrugged.

"Trust me," Dakota said. "I'm far from stupid."

"So you know she's trying to get you back?"

"I know she's trying, yeah," Dakota said with a grin. "That doesn't mean it's going to work."

"But you took the job anyway?"

"I took the job for the reasons I told you," Dakota said. "And at the time I thought she really was just trying to make it up to me, at least I hoped that was what it was about."

"When did you decide that it wasn't just that?" Jazmine asked.

"First day she came to the site," Dakota said shrugging.

"You didn't tell me," Jazmine pointed out.

"No," Dakota said, shaking her head, "because nothing had changed on my end. I was doing the job because I needed to keep my commitments and I plan to use it to help me get other jobs. I didn't see the point in upsetting you about her intentions."

"Because you're interested?" Jazmine asked nervously.

"Exactly the opposite, babe," Dakota said. "Because I'm not."

Jazmine looked back at her for a long moment, blinking a couple of times.

"Jaz, I love you… Okay? I mean that," Dakota said, her look searching. "Do you get that I've never said that to any other woman in my life?"

Jazmine swallowed convulsively, looking sad suddenly. "I guess I'm just afraid."

"Of what, babe?" Dakota asked, her look gentle.

"Of losing you," Jazmine said.

"Not going anywhere," Dakota said shaking her head.

Jazmine took a deep breath, blowing it out as she nodded.

A couple of hours later, Dakota lay trying to get comfortable in the hospital bed. She shifted, and shifted again.

"What's wrong?" Jazmine asked as she looked up from the book she was reading.

"I friggin' hate hospitals!" Dakota exclaimed.

"What can I do?" Jazmine asked her.

"You can get over here and lay with me," Dakota said, patting the bed next to her.

"I'm not sure the hospital staff will appreciate that…"

"And I care because?" Dakota replied, grinning.

"You don't," Jazmine said, laughing softly.

Jazmine got up, setting her book down on the chair and she climbed onto the bed with Dakota, kicking her shoes off in the process. Dakota shifted to make room and lay on her side. Jazmine lay down facing her snuggling into Dakota's embrace as Dakota's arms encircled her. They both sighed grinning at each other and were asleep minutes later.

***

Harley stared openmouthed at Shiloh when she walked down the stairs in the house. She was wearing the outfit she'd bought to go to The Club that night. She'd done her makeup and her hair, and looked fantastic.

"Sweet mother of dog…" Harley breathed, her blue eyes reflecting admiration.

Shiloh laughed at Harley's expression; she was forever coming up with odd statements like that.

"I take it I look okay?" Shiloh asked, biting her lip.

"Okay?" Harley repeated incredulously. "You look freaking awesome. Maybe too good…" she said then, her look chagrinned.

"What? Why?" Shiloh asked.

"It's a gay club, Shy," Harley said. "Chock-full of lesbians who are going to find you irresistible in that outfit."

"But you'll be with me," Shiloh said.

"And?" Harley asked, her blue eyes looking back at Shiloh.

"And you'll make sure I'm safe from any would be suitors," Shiloh said simply.

"Yeah, but who's gonna protect you from me…" Harley muttered with an emergent grin.

"Oh stop!" Shiloh said, laughing as Harley held her jacket for her to put on.

They left the house a few minutes later. They had dinner at a sushi restaurant, then they made their way to The Club. The very first thing Shiloh noticed was that Harley stayed close to her; the second was the myriad of women at The Club. There were all shapes and sizes of women. There were women that were very girly with makeup and their hair and nails done, there were others that looked very masculine. Shiloh noticed she got a lot of looks, winks, and smiles from the more masculine girls, but she did notice that some of the girlie-looking girls looked her up and down too.

"You okay?" Harley asked, standing close to her.

"Yes," Shiloh said, smiling up and back at Harley.

"Just let me know if you change your mind, okay?" Harley said, having to lean down to talk into her ear to be heard over the music.

They made their way over to the group, and there was a round of introductions. Harley told her that some of the girls weren't there yet.

"Did you hear about Dakota?" Jet asked Harley.

"No, what's up?" Harley asked, signaling to the waitress as she did.

"She got hurt on the site today, so she and Jaz won't be here," Jet said.

"She okay?" Harley asked.

"Yeah," Jet said, nodding. She took the glass the waitress handed her, and handed it to her wife, then took the bottle of beer with a nod and a wink at the waitress.

"Okay, good," Harley said. Then she looked at Shiloh. "What are you drinking, Shy?"

"Um, I guess a margarita?"

Harley nodded, smiling. "So a margarita and a Blue Moon for me, thanks," she told the waitress.

"You got it Harley," the waitress said, smiling up at her.

As the waitress walked away, Shiloh noted that both Harley and Jet watched her. Shiloh looked over at Jet's wife Fadiyah, who she'd just been introduced to. Fadiyah saw what her wife was doing and merely grinned shaking her head, so apparently this wasn't a strange behavior.

"Warning," Devin said, as she and Skyler approached the table.

"What?" Harley asked, seeing the look in Devin's eyes.

"Sarah is here," Devin told her. "And she's already asked me if you are."

"Crap," Harley said, shaking her head.

"Sarah?" Shiloh queried, as she smiled at Devin and hugged her.

"Ex," Harley answered simply.

"Oh," Shiloh answered, nodding.

"Bad, bad, ex…" Devin told Shiloh. "The one I told you about…"

"Ohh…" Shiloh murmured, grimacing.

Harley narrowed her eyes at the two women. Devin looked back at Harley, a smile on her lips.

"Shiloh, you haven't met my wife," Devin said then. "This is Skyler, Sky, this is Shiloh, she's—"

"Harley's assistant," Skyler said, with kind eyes. "I know. It's nice to meet you."

"You too," Shiloh said, smiling.

A few minutes later, the drinks came and Harley handed the waitress her credit card.

"Start at tab, will ya, Jen?" Harley asked.

"Of course," Jen said, smiling. "And that's from me," she said, indicating the shot on her tray.

"Oh," Harley said, grinning and nodding.

She picked up the shot and threw it back, then kissed the waitress on the lips.

"Thanks," she said, smiling when their lips parted.

"Uh-huh…" the waitress murmured, looking back up at Harley with what Shiloh could only describe as 'bedroom eyes.'

As the waitress walked away, Jet and Skyler high fived Harley who shook her head and rolled her eyes.

"Does that happen to you a lot?" Shiloh asked, her look measured.

Harley grinned wryly. "Not all the time, no."

"I see," Shiloh said, her grin wide.

"Let's go outside, I'm suddenly feeling the need to smoke," Harley said, her tone humorous.

Harley led Shiloh outside to the patio where she grabbed two chairs near the open area for dancing, and motioned for Shiloh to sit down first. As she sat down, Harley pulled out her lighter and a cigarette, tossing the pack on the table as she did. She lit the cigarette and sat watching the women dance.

"Still okay?" Harley asked Shiloh.

"Yes," Shiloh said, her tone exasperated. "You don't have to keep checking on me Harley," she said, taking a sip of her drink. "I know I'm at a gay club, this isn't a surprise to me, okay?"

"Okay," Harley said, holding up her hands in a mock surrender.

Devin walked out onto the patio with Skyler behind her. She walked straight over to Harley.

"Incoming…" she muttered just as Sarah walked out of the door.

Harley dropped her head to her chest, shaking it.

"Is that Sarah?" Shiloh whispered, looking at the beautiful brunette who was looking in Harley's direction.

"Yeah," Harley said, as Quinn and Xandy walked out the back door behind her, followed by Jet and Fadiyah. "Hail hail the gangs all here…" Harley muttered.

"What's goin' on, Harley?" Quinn said, clapping Harley on the shoulder. She was immediately drawn to Shiloh. "And you are…?" she asked. "Quinn Kavanaugh, this is Shiloh," Harley said, watching Sarah heading in her direction out of the corner of her eye.

Quinn pulled a chair up motioning for Xandy to have a seat, as she extended her hand to Shiloh.

"Good to meet ya," she said. "You do know that Sarah's headed over, right?" she asked Harley.

"Yep," Harley said, taking a long drag off her cigarette her blue eyes narrowed slightly.

"Hey Sarah," Jet said, as Sarah passed her. It was her way of warning Harley how close the girl was.

Shiloh noted that every eye in the group was on Sarah at that moment. Devin had been right about the group keeping an eye on Harley, almost literally at that moment.

"Harley?" Sarah said tentatively. She glanced around at the members of the group who were standing around.

"Hey Sarah," Harley said. She kept her look closed off as she nodded to the other woman.

Sarah put her hands together, looking nervous. "Can we talk?"

Harley looked up at her from her seat, her lips pursed. She could feel everyone waiting for her to say no, to do just about anything but say yes.

"Please?" Sarah entreated, her green eyes sparkling with unshed tears.

Harley blew her breath out, the last thing she could handle was a woman crying. Moving to stand, she literally felt the group mentally groan. She threw Quinn a narrowed look who grinned unrepentantly.

"I'll keep Shiloh company while you're gone," Quinn told her, moving to sit in Harley's seat.

Harley walked toward the side of the building away from the group, where it would be quieter. That did not keep the group, including Shiloh, from following her movement and watching everything as she and Sarah talked. There was also a running commentary from members of the group.

"Oh, yeah, there's the apology…" Quinn muttered. "*I'm so sorry I got you knifed in my stupid bid for your attention.*" She said the last in a higher pitched voice, in a snide imitation of Sarah.

They watched as Sarah lifted the lower half of Harley's tank top and looked at the small scar where she'd been knifed.

"*Just let me kiss it and make it better...*" Quinn muttered, her lips curling in disgust.

"Yeah, but Harley's holding her own right now..." Jet said. "She's doing alright."

"For now..." Devin muttered.

"Don't assume, babe..." Skyler said.

"Right, yeah, ya see that?" Devin said, nodding toward Harley who'd just dropped her head back against the building, looking heavenward. "That's the 'I feel like shit for acting this way' movement, she's gonna cave... Fuck..." Devin said, standing up ready to intervene.

"Wait," Skyler said, putting her hand out to stop Devin. "She's got it back, she's telling her no..."

"Oh!" Quinn exclaimed, as Sarah moved close to Harley, tilting her head. "Shit, she's goin' in..."

"Not the neck..." Devin said.

"Yep, she's going for the neck," Jet said, shaking her head.

Shiloh looked around at them, trying to figure out what they meant. Did they mean going for the throat? She didn't know, and didn't feel like it was her place to ask.

"Wait, wait..." Xandy chimed in. "She pulled back just in time, I think she's gonna resist her, girls..."

"Wanna bet?" Quinn said, grinning at her girlfriend.

Xandy stuck her tongue out at Quinn.

149

"Don't stick that out unless you intend to use it," Quinn said, winking at Xandy.

"Oh, I'll use it…" Xandy replied, grinning.

"Gonna go now," Quinn said, moving to stand as the group started laughing raucously.

"Stop it!" Xandy exclaimed.

"Damnit, Sarah's going for it again… How many times…" Devin said, shaking her head.

"Yo, Harley," Rayden said, as she walked out of the bar with shots in her hand.

Harley's head snapped around and Rayden held up the shots, her dark eyes sparkling with mischief. Harley nodded, said something to Sarah, then walked toward Rayden. The group started clapping and Shiloh saw Sarah give them all a dirty look as she walked away.

"Ya saved the day again, Ray!" Jet said.

"Gotta save my girl…" Rayden said, grinning. "Hey Shiloh, ya finally made it here, huh?" she said, smiling at Shiloh, as she did the shot with Harley.

"Yeah…" Shiloh said, smiling.

Shiloh spent the rest of the evening observing and listening to the group debate about everything under the sun. At one point, she was dragged out on the dance floor with Natalia, Raine, Jovina, Cat, and Devin. Harley joined them after the first song, because there were a couple of women who were doing their best to hit on Shiloh.

Harley leaned in close to her ear. "Go with it," she told her and she winked.

Harley moved close to her and slid her hand around Shiloh's waist as she started to dance with her. Shiloh was surprised at how well Harley moved; she had a very natural rhythm. She looked up at Harley who was looking down at her, grinning. She knew then that Harley was doing exactly what Shiloh had done with Julie, pretending to be a love interest to back the other women off. It worked like a charm. It seemed that any women who were with the group tended to be left alone once claimed. Most people were afraid. There'd been a few confrontations and the group always stepped up for each other, so no one really wanted to mess with them.

As the song ended and Harley stepped back and Shiloh found that she felt disappointed. She grabbed Harley's hand and smiled up at her.

"Stay here," Shiloh said, the alcohol flowing through her veins making feel her brave.

The song that played next was Kevin Lyttle's "Turn Me On." Harley stayed a little farther away this time, but continued to dance with Shiloh.

Harley sang the bridge to her, grinning. It talked about the love interest not getting away and that she would be going home with her tonight.

"That would be because I live at your house," Shiloh said, laughing.

"True," Harley said, laughing too.

At one point, Natalia moved over to Harley.

"You need to do my class, juera!" she yelled into Harley's ear.

Harley laughed. "Not sure I could keep up."

Natalia turned around, putting her back to Harley's chest, her hands on Harley's thighs moving her body seductively to the music. Harley put her hands to Natalia's waist and moved with her, easily matching her moves. Natalia winked at Shiloh and then smiled at Raine who was watching indulgently, knowing what Natalia was doing. When the song ended, Natalia turned around to Harley.

"Your ass, in my class, tomorrow at nine!"

Harley laughed, nodding.

It was a fun evening.

As Harley drove them home at two in the morning, she looked over at a drunk-looking Shiloh in the passenger seat.

"How you doin' over there?" Harley asked, grinning.

"Oh, I'm okay..." Shiloh said, her tone singsong.

Harley chuckled. "Really feeling it, aren't you?"

"Oh yes," Shiloh said, nodding.

"Did you have fun?" Harley asked.

"I did," Shiloh said, nodding. "And I learned a couple of things..."

"What did you learn?" Harley asked, smiling widely.

"Well, I learned that butch women are sometimes called 'bois' and that you aren't really butch, but kind of butch, which apparently makes you a soft butch."

Harley laughed shaking her head. "All that, huh?"

"Oh and I saw that you are so totally hot property," she said then, sounding really drunk at that moment.

"Hot property?" Harley queried with a raised eyebrow.

"Mmmhmm," Shiloh said. "You had so many women after you…" she said, her voice trailing off as she shook her head. "I lost count."

Harley pressed her lips together, suppressing a grin. "Why were you counting?"

"Well, 'cause it was interesting," Shiloh said, sounding almost petulant.

"Interesting how?" Harley asked curiously.

"It was like they all wanted you," Shiloh said. "Do you realize how many of them kissed you?"

"That's a chick thing, babe," Harley said.

"No one kissed me," Shiloh said, sounding put out.

They pulled up to a light and Harley looked over at Shiloh, grinning.

"If you were looking to get kissed at a girl bar, babe, I think I was the one that messed that up for you."

"Yeah, how did that work anyway?" Shiloh asked. "After you danced with me, no one else even approached me."

"Well, that's the power of the group, babe, not me."

"What's that mean?" Shiloh asked.

"Well, apparently there have been a few issues in the past with people messing with women who were part of our group… Most recently, it was Rayden taking out two guys who were after Jazmine. Enough people have seen it and spread the word that people shouldn't mess with us." Harley shrugged. "So most of the time if we show girls at The Club we're interested or with someone, they back off."

"So that's why you danced with me?" Shiloh asked, looking crest-fallen.

Harley couldn't help but grin. "I liked dancing with you, Shy."

"You did?" Shiloh asked, looking shy suddenly.

Harley smiled softly, knowing that Shiloh was drunk and there-fore feeling very emotional and sentimental. She touched Shiloh's cheek gently.

"Yes, I did."

Shiloh nodded, looking happy with at that answer. When Harley started to take her hand away, however, Shiloh grabbed it, holding it with both of hers. Harley chuckled, pulling her hand and therefore both of Shiloh's to her lips. She kissed Shiloh's hands a couple of times.

"I need to shift, babe," Harley said gently, when Shiloh didn't let her hand go.

"Oh, sorry," Shiloh said, biting her lip as she let go of Harley's hand.

Shiloh watched Harley drive. She knew she'd had too much to drink, and she knew that she was talking way more than she should. Harley had been very sweet that night, very attentive, despite all the women who'd been hitting on her all night. All those women and here Harley was, driving her home to her house, where she'd invited her to live… How many women could say that? She lived with the hot property…

"They all kissed you…" Shiloh said.

Harley glanced over at her again. "We covered that, babe."

"Yeah, but I remember what a good kisser you are…"

Harley grimaced, laughing. "You were the first girl I ever kissed, Shy."

"I was?" Shiloh asked, shocked.

"Yep," Harley said, nodding.

"Wow…" Shiloh said smiling slyly. "Are you an even better kisser now?"

Harley laughed out loud. "God I fuckin' hope so!" she exclaimed.

"But you have something else too…" Shiloh said.

Harley glanced over at Shiloh, wondering where these ramblings were coming from.

"What else do I have?" Harley found herself asking.

"You have this whole sexy smart thing…" Shiloh said, gesturing with her hand at Harley as a whole.

Once again, Harley found herself shocked. It was scary the things that were coming out of her friend's mouth. Fortunately, it was a fairly short drive from The Club to the house, only twelve minutes at two a.m. Before long Harley was following Shiloh up the stairs in the house, trying to ensure she didn't trip. She followed Shiloh to her bedroom door.

"You okay from here?' Harley asked.

Shiloh nodded numbly.

"Okay," Harley said, smiling.

Unexpectedly, Shiloh reached up to hug Harley. Harley held Shiloh against her, smiling against the top of her head. Shiloh turned her head and kissed Harley's neck. Harley felt a jolt go through her, which had her stepping back and pulling her head back. She caught the confused look on Shiloh's face, but simply kissed her on the forehead and then turned to go into her room, closing the door quietly. She leaned her head back against the door, blowing her breath out. After a couple of minutes, she got changed and got into bed. Sleep was really elusive that night; in the end she got about two hours total.

Regardless, Harley got up the next morning to go to Natalia's class. She dragged a hungover Shiloh with her, but Shiloh refused to join in, she simply watched. Everyone in the group was doing their best to support Jazmine and Natalia's venture in the dance studio. Natalia and Jazmine had even brought in a kickboxing instructor to appeal to the bois.

Shiloh watched the class, specifically watching Harley, surprised once again with Harley's dancing ability. It was obvious the woman had rhythm and she seemed to pick up the steps quickly. Devin, Cat, Jovina, Xandy, Cody, McKenna, Shenin, Raine, and Zoey did the class as well. The girls all joked and poked at each other during the class, even though Natalia tended to focus on them and harass them to work harder. Shiloh stood with the 'bois' and listened to their conversations, finding much of it amusing.

"No, she's cute," Quinn was saying at one point.

"She's not family though," Skyler said, shaking her head.

"Ya sure about that?" Jet asked, raising a black eyebrow.

"What do you know?" Tyler asked, grinning at Jet.

"I shouldn't kiss and tell," Jet said, grinning slyly.

Quinn, Skyler, and Jericho all looked back at Jet with varying degrees of shock.

"Before Fadiyah!" Jet said, holding up her hands. "Before, seriously!"

"Better have been," Skyler said, eyeing Jet pointedly. Then she looked over at Quinn and Jericho. "She was a bit of a slut before, though…"

"Slut?" Jet repeated, her look offended.

"Tramp?" Skyler asked, grinning.

"Whore?" Quinn supplied.

"Player, please!" Jet said, laughing.

"Same difference," Rayden put in.

"Not to me," Jet said. She glanced at Shiloh. "Shiloh, what do you think?"

Shiloh looked back at Jet, who was one amazing-looking woman with her black hair and light green eyes.

"I think I like player better too," Shiloh said, grinning.

"See?" Jet said giving the others a wry look.

"So when's the rematch?" Shiloh asked Quinn then.

"Wot?" Quinn queried, sounding very Irish.

"With Harley," Shiloh said, nodding toward the dance floor.

"Oh…" Quinn said, grinning. "Yeah, I dunno, Harley needs to make the call."

"I need to get in on that…" Jet said, shaking her head.

"She already beat the Mas," Quinn said. "Ya thinkin' the Fastback?'

"Yeah…" Jet said, grinning.

"Come on then," Quinn said, her look challenging.

"Oh Lord," Kashena said, as she and Sierra walked up.

"What?" Jet queried.

"You planning to race the Fastback?" Kashena asked, having come in during the last part of the conversation.

"Yeah, maybe, why?" Jet asked.

"You're her best asset," Jericho told Jet, reminding her that her boss frequently referred to her that way.

"And if you're dead…" Kashena said, grinning as her dark blue eyes sparkled.

"That's all you care about, boss? Harsh," Jet said, shaking her head. "Just harsh, Kash…"

Kashena laughed, as did the rest of the group.

"Where's Baz?" Jet asked.

"Ashley's not feeling well. Neither is the baby, so…" Kashena said, shrugging.

"That sucks," Jet said, pressing her lips together. "Fadi is talking about a baby," she said, widening her eyes and grimacing.

"Not quite ready for that level of domesticity?" Quinn teased.

"Hey, at least I made a commitment and married my girl," Jet countered.

"I don't hear Xandy complaining," Quinn said, grinning.

"Alright bois…" Jericho said, shaking her head.

In the car on the way to the restaurant where the group was having lunch, Shiloh told Harley she thought she did well in the class. Harley simply grinned, rolling her eyes. They'd just pulled into the lot of the restaurant when Harleys' phone rang. She answered it on the hands free.

"'Lo?" she answered.

"Harley?" a woman's voice queried uncertainly.

"Yeah…" Harley replied, looking like she didn't recognize the voice.

"It's Roslynn… from San Francisco," the woman said, adding her location when Harley didn't respond.

"Oh… Hey, how are you?" Harley said, grinning now.

"I'm good…" Roslynn said. She was silent for a few moments. "So you had said that when I was in L.A. I should look you up… And I'm coming to LA…"

"Okay…" Harley said, her tone leading. "When will you be here?"

"On Thursday," Rosylnn said. "I'd really like to see you, if that's possible."

"That would be great," Harley said, smiling now. "Where are you staying?"

"Umm," Roslynn stammered. "Well… You had said… umm…"

Harley smacked her forehead with her hand. "I said you could stay with me, didn't I? Of course, no problem at all."

"Are you sure?" Roslynn queried.

"Yes, I'm sure," Harley said, smiling. "Are you flying in?"

"Yes, to LAX," Roslynn said.

159

"Text me the info, I'll pick you up."

"Okay," Roslynn replied. "That would be great. I'm really looking forward to seeing you again."

"Yeah, me too," Harley said warmly.

"I'll text you, and I'll see you Thursday," Roslynn said.

They hung up a minute later. Harley and Shiloh got out of the car and walked into the restaurant.

"We were beginning to think you weren't going to make it," Rayden said, grinning.

"Got a call just as we got here," Harley explained, holding a chair out for Shiloh.

"We're getting a houseguest," Shiloh said, grinning.

"Huh?" Devin queried.

"Roslynn is coming down," Harley explained.

"The hot brunette from Pride?" Quinn asked, her eyes bright.

Harley grinned and nodded.

"Well, alright then!" Quinn said, holding her hand up to high five Harley.

Harley shook her head, even as she did the high five.

"You two were loud," Devin said. She glanced over at Shiloh. "Get headphones," she told her winking.

"Seriously?" Harley said to Devin.

"You don't realize how loud you were," Skyler said, grinning. "Trust me, she needs headphones."

Harley looked at Shiloh. "Don't listen to those two," she told her.

"I heard you too," Cat said, grinning. "And I always thought Jovi was loud," she said, winking at her girlfriend.

"I am," Jovina said, "but Ros was louder."

"Okay, we need to stop talking about this now," Harley said, looking embarrassed.

"It's a good thing when they're loud, Harley," Jet said, grinning. "It means you're doing it right."

"Is that what it means?" McKenna asked, winking at Cody.

"It means someone's doing something right," Cody agreed, laughing.

"It's definitely a good thing, though," Zoey said, her hand in Jericho's.

"Never heard a complaint yet," Jericho replied, smiling widely.

"And you never will," Zoey told her.

"Can we please stop talking about this now?" Harley asked, sighing.

"When's the hottie comin' in?" Quinn asked, ignoring Harley's request. She was always interested in stirring up trouble.

"Thursday," Harley said, shaking her head.

"So you'll bring her to The Club Friday?" Xandy asked.

"I guess," Harley said.

"You will," Rayden said, grinning.

"Is that an order?"

"Yep," Rayden said without hesitation.

"Fine, now can we change the subject?" Harley asked.

The group laughed and continued with their lunch.

Chapter 7

Wednesday night Harley was getting ready for bed when Shiloh knocked on her open bedroom door.

"Harley?" Shiloh queried.

"Yeah?" Harley replied from the bathroom.

"Guess who's back?" Shiloh said, her look pointed.

"Fuck, seriously?" Harley asked, turning around to lean against the vanity sink.

"Yep," Shiloh said, nodding.

"Son of a…" Harley muttered.

"What do you want to do?" Shiloh asked.

Harley blew her breath out, shaking her head. "I don't know… how far are you willing to help me on the 'girlfriend' angle?"

"I will do whatever you need, Harley," Shiloh said sincerely.

"Would you sleep in here tonight?" Harley asked hesitantly.

"I said I'd do whatever you need, Harley, I meant it."

Harley blew her breath out, nodding. "Okay, cool, thanks."

"You need to go talk to her," Shiloh said.

"I don't wanna," Harley said, grinning then.

"Do you wanna talk about credit card limits?" Shiloh asked, her look pointed.

"I think I'll talk to Julie," Harley said, as if it had been her idea all along.

Shiloh chuckled as Harley walked past her toward the door. She returned a few minutes later.

"How'd that go?" Shiloh asked.

"I got the same excuse as last time, but she swears she'll stay in her own room tonight."

"You believe her?"

"Not as far as I can throw her," Harley said, shaking her head.

"I didn't think so," Shiloh said, grinning.

"Okay, so we sleep in here together," Harley said, looking hesitant again.

"Will you relax? Sheesh!" Shiloh said, rolling her eyes. "I don't think I snore or anything," she added with a grin.

Harley looked back at her for a long moment, then grinned, shaking her head. "I just don't want to ask too much here."

"I see it this way," Shiloh said, as she climbed into the bed. She grabbed Harley's hand and dragged her down on the bed with her. "If she manages to compromise you, you get arrested and I'm out of a job, so…"

Harley laughed when Shiloh pulled her down on the bed. She lay down on the left side of the bed, then looking over her.

"So it's all about you?" Harley asked, grinning.

"You got it," Shiloh said, winking at Harley.

Shiloh looked over at Harley, seeing that Harley had laid down about three feet from her.

"You think Julie's gonna believe that I'm your girlfriend if you're sleeping way over there?" she asked, raising an eyebrow at Harley.

Harley pursed her lips. "I guess not," she said, moving closer. She lay on her side, her right arm extended out to the side, her left arm resting on her hip.

Shiloh moved closer, putting her head in the crook of Harley's extended arm, her moss-green eyes looking into Harley's. They both grinned. It was an odd situation they had found themselves in.

"You know, if you touch me, I probably won't burst into flames or anything," Shiloh said. It seemed that Harley was pointedly not doing so.

"So pushy…" Harley muttered, putting her hand on Shiloh's waist gingerly. "Is that better?"

Shiloh moved a little closer, putting only about four inches between their bodies as they faced each other.

"More convincing, yes," Shiloh said, nodding.

They were both silent for a few minutes, then Shiloh looked at Harley again.

"Why did you do it?" she asked.

"Do…what?" Harley asked, looking perplexed.

"The credit card," Shiloh said, her eyes searching Harley's. Harley looked hesitant to answer. "And, yes, I called about the balance, before you try to bullshit me."

"Oh," Harley said, her eyes widening slightly. Then she shrugged. "I wanted you to be able to have whatever you want, when you want it."

"Do you know how risky that is for you?" Shiloh asked, her tone worried.

"Why?" Harley asked her look open and sincere.

Shiloh sighed. "I wouldn't do anything crazy, but you don't know who else might... Please tell me you don't do that for everyone..." Shiloh said, her voice reflecting the troubled look in her eyes.

Harley smiled softly. "I know you wouldn't do anything crazy, Shy, that's why I trust you with that card. And no, I've never done that for anyone else."

Shiloh drew in a deep breath, nodding, feeling both relieved and her heart swell emotionally at the same time.

"You are such an amazingly generous, kind person, Harley," Shiloh said.

"And I hear a 'but' in that statement," Harley said, grinning.

"The 'but' is that you worry me."

"What are you worried about?"

"That you'll let the wrong person in and they'll take advantage of you and you'll get hurt," Shiloh said honestly.

Harley looked back at her, her blue eyes softening at Shiloh's statement.

"Well, now I have you here to keep me from getting into too much trouble, right?" she said, grinning.

"If you'll actually listen to me," Shiloh said.

"Well, there is that," Harley said, grinning.

Eventually they fell asleep. At one point during the night, Shiloh heard a click at the door, and knew without a doubt that Julie was looking into the room. She saw the shaft of light from the hallway and moved closer to Harley, sliding her hand up Harley's arm. Harley was asleep, but responded to Shiloh's closeness and brought her right arm up to hold her closer, sliding her left hand further around her waist. Shiloh shuddered at the feel of Harley holding her, but did her best to appear asleep to Julie. The door clicked closed a couple of minutes later. Shiloh glanced over her shoulder to insure that Julie had indeed left, she had.

Laying her head back against the hollow of Harley's shoulder, Shiloh knew she should move away from Harley at that point. But she really didn't want to. Harley was still sound asleep, so she really didn't see any harm in staying where she was. Taking a slow deep breath through her nose, she could smell the cologne Harley wore, and once again Shiloh felt an almost electrical current go through her. She sighed softly and did her best to go back to sleep.

At one point during the night Shiloh got up to go to the bathroom and when she came back, settled on her side, this time with her back to Harley, but still with Harley's arm under her neck. She was chastising herself, even as she scooted back closer to Harley. Once again, Harley responded to her proximity and her right arm came up to encircle her shoulders, her left hand slid over her waist. Shiloh fell asleep, doing her best to ignore the thoughts that were swirling around her head, memories of years ago, and of the recent night at The Club.

Apparently, falling asleep thinking those kinds of thoughts caused dreams she definitely couldn't squelch. There were thoughts of Harley's hands and lips on her, touching her, kissing her, and then there were vivid visions of what could have happened in her bedroom all those years ago. In her sleep, Shiloh writhed, her body pressing back against Harley's. She woke to the sensations of Harley's hands on her body and it took her a few seconds to realize she was no longer dreaming.

Harley was still asleep, but her left hand at Shiloh's waist was pressing her back against Harley's body sensually. Harley's right hand was splayed between her breasts, her thumb brushing upward across an extremely hard nipple. Once again, Shiloh knew she should move away, but her body refused to listen to anything her brain had to say. Instead, she lay in Harley's arms, writhing against the other woman as her body turned into molten liquid, quickly going up in flames. Suddenly she was coming and doing her best not to scream knowing that would wake Harley. Still she was surprised that her gasping and writhing didn't do that. Apparently, Harley was a heavy sleeper, even when aroused.

Shiloh lay breathing heavily, astounded by the ease with which a mostly unconscious Harley had brought her to orgasm, when men she'd dated had almost never succeeded after as much as an hour of effort. She was fairly sure she knew why women were hounding Harley now, if this was any indication; the woman was a rock star in bed. Even her kiss years before in her bedroom had set all kinds of sensations off in her body. Apparently, her skills had done nothing but improve with practice.

Shiloh turned over, looking at Harley as she slept. Her eyes moved over the smooth, tanned skin. She had a very attractive face, especially with her very blue eyes framed by long eyelashes. Her white blond hair fell a couple of inches past her shoulders, cut into layers, with the rainbow colored section extending four inches past the blond.

Her ears had multiple piercings, five in each ear, in four of which she usually wore graduated silver hoops, the largest of which was only the size of a nickel. In the fifth piercing, the one highest up on her ear, Harley had a small silver chain with a rainbow feather extended from it at the end.

Harley Marie Davidson was very much her own person, and very different from anyone Shiloh had ever known. Staring up at her in the dark, Shiloh realized that she had always known that Harley was destined to be part of her life. She still had no idea how, but she also knew now that she was attracted to her, and had always been. It was a rather sobering thought.

The next morning, Harley woke to the realization that she was holding Shiloh extremely close. She grimaced and tried to extricate herself carefully before Shiloh woke up. The last thing she wanted to do was to freak Shiloh out by appearing to come on to her. She was too late, however, because Shiloh looked up at her, her moss-green eyes bright in the morning sunlight coming through the windows above the bed.

"Good morning," Harley said, grinning.

Shiloh smiled softly. "Good morning."

Harley gave her a chagrinned look, lifting her hands to indicate their location on Shiloh's waist and at her back.

"Sorry about this," she said. "I guess I'm too much of a creature of habit when there's a body in bed next to me..." she said, her voice trailing off as she grimaced.

"It's okay," Shiloh said, smiling.

Harley blew her breath out in relief. "Whew, good," she said, grinning.

"Julie did come in during the night," Shiloh told her.

"Seriously?" Harley asked.

"Yeah," Shiloh said, nodding. "She opened the door, and must have watched us for a few minutes, then I heard the door close again."

"Well, hopefully this worked then," Harley said. "So much for her promise though, huh?"

"Yeah, you really need to stand firm on her not staying here, Harley."

"I know," Harley said, sounding resolved as she nodded. "Guess we should get ready for work though, huh?"

"Yep," Shiloh said, grinning.

They both got up and started getting ready for work, each of them going to their own bathroom. An hour later when Shiloh got downstairs where Harley stood fixing her coffee, she was stunned.

Harley was wearing dark jeans that were fashionably tattered in a couple of places, a black tank top with a colorful design on it, and her two-inch heeled Harley Davidson boots. What was surprising was the long black lapelled jacket that fell to her mid-thigh. The sleeves were pushed up her forearms exposing a thick linked silver bracelet on one arm and her thick-banded leather and stud watch on the other. She also wore her usual six silver rings. At her throat, she wore a double-looped black leather tong-style necklace with angel wings dangling from the cord. The most surprising thing was that she also wore makeup, not a lot, but eyeliner and a little bit of mascara that made her blue eyes stand out even more, and a slightly tinted lip gloss that drew Shiloh's eyes right to her lips. Her hair was down and smooth, and the rainbow section wasn't in braids for once. It blended with the rest of her hair, the rainbow colors standing out. She looked... *hot* was the only word Shiloh could think of.

"What?" Harley grinned, seeing Shiloh's astounded look.

"You look..." Shiloh stammered. "Wow..."

Harley smiled, looking pleased by the sparsely worded compliment. "Thanks."

"Is this for that meeting with the AG later? 'Cause she's straight, you know?" Shiloh said, winking at Harley.

"And married to a man she's majorly hot for," Harley said. "It's legendary, and I do have a TV you know. No, remember, Roslynn comes in today..."

"Oh, right," Shiloh said, not believing she'd actually managed to forget that. She wondered remotely if she'd blocked out the thought. "Well, now I'm feeling jealous," she said, her grin wry, even as her mind said, *touch of truth to everything.* A thought she quickly tamped down on.

"Why?" Harley asked her look amused.

"'Cause you don't dress up like that for me," Shiloh said, winking at Harley.

"Stop being straight, we'll talk," Harley responded jokingly.

"One never does know," Shiloh replied, her tone teasing.

"Ohhh..." Harley said, grinning.

"Holy fucking shit!" Julie said as she walked into the kitchen her eyes on Harley instantly. "Harl, you look hot!"

Harley laughed, shaking her head. "Well, at least it's unanimous, but you two are starting to make me feel nervous, Jesus…" she said blowing her breath out slowly.

***

Dakota had gone back to work three days after her accident. She'd recovered quickly. She still had a couple of nasty bruises, one of which was on her shoulder where she'd collided with the railing on the stairs, but she felt better. Cassandra didn't show up to the site for a few days, and Dakota took it as a sign that she was done making a play for her attention.

A week later, Dakota was sitting in bed on her iPad with Jazmine next to her reading a book. Dakota's phone rang. She put her Bluetooth in as she continued to scroll through the pictures she was perusing for ideas.

"Yo?" Dakota answered her phone.

Jazmine could only hear Dakota's end of the conversation, but she knew who it was immediately.

"Hey," Dakota said, grinning. "Yeah, I'm looking right now… What were you thinking? You what? No… Cass, you can't… Are you kidding me right now? No, that… no…" She chuckled. "Why would you do that?" she asked, her tone exasperated. "I know, but… No, just because they call them that… They're not… Cass, they're not… I'm not bullshitting you. I'll show you… No… I refuse, you can't make me." She said the last teasingly. She laughed then, and Jazmine felt her ire rise instantly, but she did her best to hide it.

The conversation continued and Jazmine had to finally get up and leave the room to keep from making a nasty comment. Dakota found her sitting in the living room twenty minutes later.

"What's up, babe?" Dakota asked, sitting next to her on the couch.

"She's calling you on your off time now?" Jazmine asked.

"I get calls from the home owners all the time, babe," Dakota said, her look pointed.

"Yeah, well, she knows how I feel about her... So..." Jazmine said.

"Babe..." Dakota said her tone entreating.

"I know, I know," Jazmine said, grimacing. "But it just bugs me when I hear you laugh at something she said... You should hate her guts like I do..."

Dakota wet her lips, scraping her teeth over her lower lip.

"I don't have time for that," she said evenly. "I'm doing a job, it's not personal, Jaz."

"Her coming on to you is personal, Dakota."

"She wasn't coming on to me, babe, she was talking about putting blinds up over the stained glass we just installed. It was ridiculous and I told her that."

"She's always coming on to you, Dakota. She's just trying to romance you now."

"Oh God, seriously babe?" Dakota asked.

"Yes, damnit!" Jazmine exclaimed angrily.

Dakota dropped her head back against the couch, shaking it. "I don't know what else I can do here, Jaz... I'm seriously in on this project... If I quit it now we're gonna lose a lot and my business'll take a major hit..."

Jazmine pressed her lips together, swallowing convulsively as she nodded.

"Jazmine," Dakota said, sitting up and taking Jazmine's hands in hers. "Babe, I'll quit if you really want me to, but I'm telling you, we won't be doing any expanding of the studio if I do... We'll lose a serious chunk of change at this point."

"How much?" Jazmine asked almost instantly.

Dakota blew her breath out, doing some quick calculations in her head. "About a hundred and fifty kay."

"That much?" Jazmine asked, stunned.

"Yeah, I had to front the equipment rentals and the materials babe, the same as any other job, but the materials for this job were insane..."

"That's it, that's what she's doing..." Jazmine said, her tone strident.

"What babe?" Dakota said her tone annoyed.

"She's trying to ruin you, so she has a hold over you again..."

"Oh Holy hell, seriously, Jaz?" Dakota said, her tone telling Jazmine she thought she was crazy.

"You don't think she'd do that?" Jazmine asked.

"I think everyone will do something at some point, but what you're not hearing is that it wouldn't ruin me, it would fuck me business-wise for a while, but that's it."

"She's up to something, Dakota, damnit!" Jazmine exclaimed.

Dakota looked back at the woman she loved and really wasn't sure what else she could do or say at that point. She reached out, putting her hand behind Jazmine's neck and pulled her to her, to kiss her deeply. Minutes later, she was making love to Jazmine, reminding her with her body exactly who she wanted. Afterwards they lay on the couch, both of them trying to catch their breath. Dakota lay next to her, her hand still on Jazmine's skin.

"I love you…" Dakota whispered next to Jazmine's ear. "Only you, only ever you."

***

Harley was driving to work that morning and the stereo was on as usual. As one song ended and another started, Harley started nodding, glancing over at Shiloh.

"A while back you asked which song I think is most me," she said. "Well there are a few of them, but I'd have to say this is the best one right now."

"Okay," Shiloh said, nodding. She turned up the volume so she could hear the words. The song was "I Am an Illusion" by Rob Thomas.

As the song ended, Shiloh turned the stereo down and looked over at Harley.

"You think that song fits you?" she asked.

"I think a lot of it does, yeah," Harley said, grimacing.

Shiloh blinked a couple of times, then pursed her lips.

"Okay, let's look at it," she said. She pulled out her phone and looked up the lyrics. " 'The confusion running around your head'... Is that the ADHD?"

Harley nodded, grinning at Shiloh's thoroughness.

" 'Take back my unkind words'... Harley you almost never speak unkindly," Shiloh said, but then she nodded, "so, if you did, you'd feel bad... I see... Okay, now this next set... talks about you being the place where things go bad? What do you mean by that? In relationships?"

Harley drew in a breath and blew it out, nodding.

"What makes you think it's your fault the relationships fail?" Shiloh asked, her look sharper than she meant it, but she didn't like Harley taking on all the responsibility for that.

"Well, I am the common denominator, Shy..." Harley said.

"Relationships fail for lots of reasons, Harley. It doesn't mean that because yours fail there's something wrong with you."

Harley didn't answer, but Shiloh could see that Harley didn't believe her.

"How are you an illusion?" Shiloh asked then.

Harley's lips twisted in a sardonic grin. "I apparently look quite different to you today, right?"

Shiloh gave her a searching look. "You look really great today, Harley, but it's still you... You're not pretending to be something you're not."

Harley looked contemplative, then shrugged. "I dunno..." she said finally.

It was obvious she was done being expansive, so Shiloh left her alone for the time being. It was definitely an insight into the way Harley saw things though, and it bothered her to no end that Harley didn't think she was as amazing as she was.

Later that morning, Shiloh had to remind Harley that Roslynn's plane was due in at one o'clock. Harley had been working industriously on the program for the Criminal Division. They had a meeting with Midnight and Sierra that afternoon about it that had just been scheduled.

"You better get going," Shiloh told Harley at eleven.

"How long is it to LAX?" Harley asked, loathe to stop what she was doing.

"About an hour and forty-five minutes. As it is, you're screwed if you hit traffic. Go!" Shiloh told her.

"Okay," Harley said. She saved her work and then stood up. "You're gonna meet me at the AG's office, right?"

"Yes, I'll meet you there, I'll get a ride over with Rayden," Shiloh said, nodding.

"Okay, I'll see you there," Harley said, smiling.

Two and a half hours later, a harassed Harley drove up to the sidewalk at LAX, looking for Roslynn. It was impossible to miss the stunning brunette with a body that wouldn't quit. *Holy Mother of Dog...* Harley thought as she saw her. Roslynn was wearing skintight jeans, three-inch black heels and an emerald-green top that hugged her body in all the right places.

Harley pulled up next to where Roslynn was standing and opened the passenger window of the Z.

"I'm sorry I'm late, traffic was crazy!" she said, throwing the car in park and climbing out.

"It's okay," Roslynn said, smiling brilliantly.

Harley strode around the front of the car to Roslynn, who was only an inch shorter than Harley in her high heels. She reached up to hug Harley who obliged happily. She took the other woman in her arms, letting the scent of Roslynn's perfume envelop her.

When they parted, Harley turned and opened the passenger door for Roslynn and waited for her to get into the car. She put Roslynn's suitcase in the trunk and got in the driver's side.

She put the car in gear and headed out of the airport arrivals area. Disturbed's "Intoxication" was playing. Roslynn listened to the words and liked them, especially the first verse. They were very possessive and aggressive, but sexy at the same time. Harley sang the words as she got onto the freeway, weaving around cars expertly.

Roslynn thought Harley was definitely as hot as she'd remembered. There was just something about the woman that had attracted her from the moment she'd met her during the Pride Parade in San Francisco.

The Pride parade had just begun and as usual, Roslynn's friends had made her late getting there!

"Damnit I'm going to miss them!" Roslynn had exclaimed, moving toward the street. The crowd was huge and she had a really hard time getting through it. She squeezed past a couple of people, but ran into a

woman who pushed her back. Roslynn stumbled into someone, and she felt a pair of hands grab her by the shoulders to keep her from ending up on the pavement.

"Oh my God, thank you!" she exclaimed as she looked up into the bluest eyes she'd ever seen.

"No problem," Harley said, smiling. "You might not want to go that way," she said, nodding toward the mean-looking femme woman who'd pushed her.

"I guess not," Roslynn said, rolling her eyes. "I guess chivalry is dead."

Harley grinned. She leaned down so she could be heard over the passing motorcycles. "Chivalry's not dead, babe, she's just a bitch," she said with a wink.

"Oh… I like that," Roslynn said, smiling up at Harley. "I'm Ros," she said, extending her hand to Harley.

"Harley."

"Will you be out later?" Roslynn asked as her friends yelled to her from the sidewalk.

"Not sure," Harley said, laughing.

"We're going to Q Bar tonight, come there!" Roslynn said, as she started moving back toward the sidewalk. "I'll buy you drink and thank you properly!"

After the hot brunette disappeared into the crowd, Quinn and Jet had insisted that they hit Q Bar, just to see what a proper thank you looked like.

"So, I'm really sorry," Harley said, her hand on the stick shift as she shifted to speed around another car, only to have to slow because of traffic again. "But I have a meeting this afternoon that I cannot miss... Once it's done, I'm all yours, but..."

"It's okay," Roslynn said, nodding. "I'll hold on to the 'all yours' part," she said with a wink.

Harley laughed, nodding. "Okay."

"Is this meeting in like five minutes?" Roslynn asked pointedly.

"No, like forty-five minutes, why?" Harley asked.

"Well, you're driving kind of fast..." Roslynn said.

"Oh, sorry, no, this is how I drive on a regular basis," Harley said, looking chagrinned.

"Oh," Roslynn said, nodding. "Oh wait, I remember, this is the car that beat all your friends on the drive up to Pride, right?"

Harley smiled widely. "Yeah," she said.

"I never did hear what you did for a living though..." Roslynn said, her voice trailing off as Harley scratched her back exposing a flash of gold and *was that a gun?* "Are you a cop?"

Harley looked over at her confused, but then she saw that Roslynn was staring at her waist. She glanced down and realized her jacket was open, exposing the gun at her hip.

"Oh," she said, grinning. "Yeah, well... kind of... I'm actually a programmer, but I'm also a sworn peace officer, so... I work for the State Department of Justice," she said, gesturing to the badge and gun.

"I see," Roslynn said, nodding.

"Does that bother you?" Harley asked, knowing that some people were freaked out by guns.

"No…" Roslynn said flirtatiously. "It's actually pretty sexy."

"Oh, well…" Harley said, pressing her lips together in mute appreciation. "Alright then."

They drove in silence for a couple of minutes, as they hit another area of traffic. Roslynn watching Harley drive, seeing the way she moved with the music and sang to her music, now Bon Jovi's "It's My Life." Roslynn remembered the sex had been amazing, and she'd really hated to let Harley go two days later when Harley had planned to drive back to LA with her friends.

"I have to say," Roslynn said at one point, her dark green eyes sparkling, "that you look absolutely amazing."

Harley grinned almost shyly, inclining her head. "Well thank you. You look pretty damned good yourself," she said, putting her hand out to slide from Roslynn's knee to her mid-thigh.

Roslynn shuddered at the feel of Harley's hand. She'd had so many visions of what this meeting with Harley again would be like. She'd wanted to jump Harley the second she'd seen her get out of the sleek black sports car. God she was one seriously hot woman! She had a wild child vibe, but also just had a completely sexy look about her.

"I was really nervous coming here," Roslynn said.

"You were?" Harley asked, surprised. Someone like Roslynn seemed so confident, she couldn't even feature the woman being nervous about anything.

"Oh my God, yes!" Roslynn said.

"Why?" Harley asked, giving her a sidelong glance.

"I didn't know if you really remembered me… You were kind of drunk that night…" Roslynn said.

"Not that drunk," Harley said. "And only as drunk as I was because the group was buying me shot after shot. It was my first run with them, I guess we were celebrating."

Roslynn nodded. "Well, I just… We had so much fun… I was nervous about things being weird this time, you know?" Then she tilted her head. "Are you sure it's okay for me to stay with you? I feel like I kind of backed you into a corner on that one, and I didn't mean to."

Harley smiled, as she moved around yet another car and shifted into a lower gear to speed up. She glanced at the clock as she did, conscience that she was getting close to being late for her meeting.

"No, it's totally fine," Harley told her. "Hell, if nothing else, I have a total of four bedrooms, so…" she said, letting her voice trail off to indicate that if things didn't work out, she could stay in one of the other bedrooms.

"Well, I was really hoping to stay in your bedroom…" Roslynn said, her voice full of sexual innuendo.

Harley smiled widely, her tongue against her teeth as she did. "Well, okay then," she said, looking pleased at the thought.

Harley's phone rang then. "Excuse me," she said to Roslynn as she hit the button for hands free. "'Lo?" she queried.

"Harley?" Shiloh said.

"Yeah, Shy, what's up?"

"You are going to make the meeting, right?" Shiloh asked.

Harley grimaced. "I'm trying, but traffic is complete shit. I'm coming, I promise."

"Good, 'cause I really don't want to have to explain to Midnight why you're not here…"

"I know, I know," Harley said, wrinkling her nose up in consternation. "I'll make it, I promise," she said as she downshifted again to zip around a car.

"Try not to wrap yourself around a tree in the process please," Shiloh said, hearing the car's engine rev up.

"It's LA, we don't have trees, lampposts maybe…"

"Not funny, Harley…" Shiloh said seriously.

"Sorry," Harley said, grinning impishly, "I'll be there, promise."

"Okay, drive safe, see you in a few."

They hung up then.

"Did she say Midnight?" Roslynn asked.

"Yeah," Harley said, nodding.

"And you work for the Department of Justice…" Roslynn said. "Are you seriously meeting with Midnight Chevalier?"

Harley chuckled, nodding.

"Oh my God…" Roslynn said, shaking her head. "I had no idea that you were *that* connected, wow…"

Harley shrugged. "It's just work."

"Impressive work," Roslynn qualified.

Harley shook her head. She didn't think it was a big deal. Her phone rang again then, and Harley rolled her eyes.

"Sorry," she said, as she answered the second call. "'Lo?"

"Agent Davidson…" came a different female voice.

Harley rolled her eyes heavenward, shaking her head, as she said, "Hello, ma'am."

"It's Midnight, Harley…" Midnight said, sighing.

"Yes, ma'am," Harley said, grinning.

"We are going to see you today I hope," Midnight said casually.

"Yes, ma'am, I'm on my way there right now," Harley said, banging her head against the headrest of her seat.

"Okay, good," Midnight said, smiling at her end. "Drive carefully please," she said then. "I want you alive, even if you're a little late."

"Yes, ma'am."

"Midnight," was the response. "Say it Harley," she said, in a feisty tone.

"Yes, ma'am, Midnight," Harley replied, grinning again.

"Hopeless," Midnight said, chuckling. "See you soon."

They hung up a moment later.

Harley glanced over at Roslynn and saw that she was avidly watching her.

"Midnight Chevalier just told you to be careful," Roslynn said as if she couldn't fathom such familiarity with such a local celebrity.

"Yeah," Harley said, with a wry grin. "It sucks that she's heard about my driving."

"That's how you see it?" Roslynn asked, looking shocked.

"Well, that and the fact that she doesn't trust me to show up for our meeting... Of course that's probably because I missed our last conference call... so..." She shrugged.

Roslynn shook her head. "You certainly aren't a name dropper are you?"

Again, Harley shrugged, grinning.

Twenty minutes later they walked up to the Attorney General's Office building. Shiloh was pacing outside the building and smiled with relief when she saw Harley striding toward her.

"Oh thank God!' she said, rolling her eyes. Then her eyes went to Harley's laptop case. "Oh good, you remembered, I was worried..."

"I never forget this," Harley said, grinning.

"No, I guess you don't," Shiloh said, smiling.

"Oh, Shy, this is Roslynn. Roslynn this is Shiloh. She's my assistant and resident best friend," she said, winking at Shiloh.

"It's nice to meet you," Shiloh said to Roslynn, already completely jealous of the woman's appearance. She looked very glamorous.

"You too," Roslynn said, smiling.

"You have your ID with you, right?" Harley asked Roslynn as they headed in the building.

"Yes, why? Roslynn asked.

"Security," Harley said, gesturing at the CHP officers standing in the entry. "And if you want to meet Midnight, you're going to need it," she said, winking.

"Are you serious?" Roslynn asked looking stunned.

"I'm sure she won't mind," Harley said. "Midnight's pretty cool."

"Harley, you head up," Shiloh said. "We're already late. I'll get Roslynn checked in and up there as soon as I can, okay?"

Harley nodded. "Okay, thanks, Shy," she said, smiling. "See you up there."

With that, she lifted her jacket aside to show the CHP officers her badge and they waved her through.

An hour later Roslynn was extremely impressed with Harley Marie Davidson. Midnight Chevalier was incredibly gracious meeting her. She had nothing but extremely good things to say about Harley, and proclaimed her as one of her most valuable assets in the department.

"With a doctorate from MIT," Midnight had said, "she's definitely one of the most educated agents I have." The last was said with a wink at Harley.

On the way to Harley's house, Roslynn looked over at Harley.

"You have a doctorate from MIT?" she asked.

Harley nodded, not looking too impressed with herself.

Roslynn shook her head. "I barely have a bachelor's from a local college," she said, "and you don't even mention a doctorate from an Ivy League school…"

Harley glanced over at her. "I guess that's not what you're used to?"

"No, not hardly," Roslynn said, smiling.

A few minutes Roslynn was further rendered mute with shock when she saw Harley's house.

"You have got to be kidding me..." Roslynn muttered as she walked inside. She looked back at Harley her mouth hanging open. "You have all this..." She shook her head in amazement.

In the couple of days she'd spent with Harley in San Francisco, there'd been no bragging by Harley about any of this kind of thing. She'd said that she lived in West Hollywood when she'd invited her to stay with her if she was ever in town. But that had been the extent of information she'd provided. Even earlier in the day when she'd mentioned that she had four bedrooms, Roslynn had no idea it would be four bedrooms in a house like the one she was standing in at the moment.

"Come on, I'll show you the upstairs," Harley said, grinning.

"Okay," Roslynn said, nodding, still looking completely shocked.

Harley carried her suitcase up the stairs, and showed her the other bedrooms, then finally her own room. Roslynn couldn't begin to form a cognitive sentence for a good minute.

Harley noted the shock on Roslynn's face, and she knew that she'd surprised the woman. She'd meant it when she'd told Shiloh that she liked to surprise people, never being what people expected.

"So the bathroom is this way," Harley said, when the silence stretched.

Roslynn nodded numbly.

"You mentioned wanting to take a shower," Harley said, grinning.

"Right, yes," Roslynn said, suddenly coming back to earth.

"Okay, well, everything you should need is in there," Harley said, smiling.

"Okay, um," Roslynn stammered.

Harley put her small suitcase on the massive bed and Roslynn nodded gratefully.

A half an hour later, Roslynn walked back into the bedroom wearing only a towel, her hair swept up in a bun. Harley was working on her laptop. She'd shed her jacket and was sitting with one leg up on the bed and the other on the floor.

"Do you ever stop working?" Roslynn asked.

Harley shook her head, her eyes still on her computer screen.

Roslynn walked over to the side of the bed. "Maybe you just need a reason to," she said and dropping the towel.

Harley's eyes caught the flutter of the falling towel, which had her looking up. Her lips parted in shock, her eyes sweeping from Roslynn's head to her feet then back up to her eyes. She quickly saved her work and set the laptop aside, turning to put both feet on the floor facing Roslynn. Roslynn moved to stand between Harley's parted legs, putt her hands to Harley's face, and leaned down to kiss her. Harley's hands immediately slid around her body, pulling her close as their lips met hungrily.

Roslynn moaned loudly moving to straddle Harley's waist. She held Harley's head in her hands grasping at her hair, as Harley's lips moved to her breasts. In minutes, she was crying out in her orgasm, her body pressing against Harley's desperately. Then she kissed Harley deeply, her hands grasping at Harley's shoulders. Harley broke the kiss as she heard keys in the front door and looked at the open bedroom door. She slid her hands under Roslynn's thighs and lifted her up. Roslynn wrapped her legs around Harley's waist. Harley grinned as she carried her over to the door, kicked it closed, and then returned to the bed.

Roslynn pulled off Harley's tank top, sliding her hands over her skin, her nails grazing it and causing Harley to shudder slightly. Roslynn looked down at Harley, her eyes so heated that Harley was almost certain she could feel flames lick out from them.

"I want you to fuck me," Roslynn told her, her voice husky.

Harley felt her breath catch in her throat. She slid her hands up Roslynn's back, clasped her shoulders, and moved her onto her back in one swift movement. Roslynn groaned loudly, and felt her whole body come alive as Harley looked down at her. She scooted back on the bed quickly, never taking her eyes off Harley.

"I want to feel you against me," she told Harley.

Harley shifted, putting her still jean clad legs between Roslynn's and did exactly what Roslynn wanted, moving her body over Roslynn's, causing friction in all the right places. Roslynn's nails bit into Harley's skin as she grasped at her, pulling her closer as she orgasmed over and over again.

At one point, Harley positioned herself next to Roslynn who then took the initiative and unbuttoned Harley's jeans. She pushed them down as Harley kicked off her boots. Within minutes, Harley was naked and Roslynn was sliding her body over Harley's, kissing her neck and feeling Harley groan lowly in her throat. Harley's hands buried themselves in Roslynn's hair that was now hanging loose, holding her where she was. Roslynn took that cue and moved her lips over Harley's neck, kissing, licking, and sucking at her skin. Harley came with a gasping groan, her body taut and pressing against Roslynn's.

Shiloh heard their lovemaking and did everything she could to block it out. The worst part was hearing Harley's voice raised in her excitement. Shiloh actually felt her body respond to the sound. Suddenly she realized that it wasn't just men that needed to take cold showers sometimes. She did exactly that, and then went to sit in the part of the house that was farthest from Harley's room. It was going to be a long visit, apparently.

Chapter 7

The next night, everyone was meeting up at The Club. Devin and Skyler came to Harley's house, planning to take Shiloh with them to The Club, since Harley would have Roslynn with her and her Z only held two people.

Roslynn wore tight bootcut jeans and a black body-hugging shirt that was off the shoulders and with silver and rhinestone accents. She also wore three inch heeled boots with a rhinestone boot jewel. Her makeup was darker, but artfully done to make her dark green eyes glow.

Next to her Shiloh felt absolutely dowdy once again. She'd opted for a casual outfit that night, figuring that Harley wouldn't have time to rescue her like she had the week before. Shiloh wore jeans, a pair of the booties that she'd gotten for her birthday, and an army-green silk tank top that Harley had insisted she get since it almost matched her eyes. She did her makeup softly, not over the top. Even so, Harley smiled at her when she came downstairs to join the group.

"You look great," Harley told her, smiling.

Shiloh simply chuckled and shook her head.

They all left the house a few minutes later and were at The Club ten minutes after that. After the reintroductions, most of the group had already met Roslynn in San Francisco, Harley made her way out to the patio to smoke and have a beer. Roslynn went with her. Not too long after that, Shiloh spotted Sarah heading for the patio. She immediately texted Harley to warn her.

Harley got the message, and looked up just as Sarah walked out.

"Harley," Sarah said, as if she hadn't known that Harley was outside. "We never finished our talk."

Harley looked back at Sarah, as Devin, Skyler, Quinn, and Xandy stepped out onto the patio. She glanced back at her friends, then shook her head, looking back at Sarah.

"Sarah, this is Roslynn," Harley said, gesturing to Roslynn sitting across from her. "Ros, this is Sarah, my ex."

Sarah and Roslynn exchanged a look and nodded at each other. Sarah walked away then, but only strolled as far as the bar. She sat down on a bar stool, looking over at Harley and the group.

"Great, so she's gonna stare at ya for the next four hours…" Quinn muttered, rolling her eyes.

"Where's Shy?" Harley asked, glancing around.

"She went to the bathroom," Devin told her. "She knows we're out here."

Harley looked worried for a moment, but then she nodded. It didn't escape Roslynn's notice and she narrowed her eyes. Though no one except for Devin saw. Rayden, Grayson, Jericho, and Zoey joined the group a few minutes later. Harley looked around, then stood up. She leaned down and kissed Roslynn on the lips.

"I'll be right back," she said and walked inside the bar.

As she'd half expected, Shiloh had been cornered by one of the butches and she was being chatted up rather extensively.

"Hey, Shy, there you are," she said, putting her hands on Shiloh's shoulders possessively. "We're out here," she said, nodding toward the patio.

"Okay, great," Shiloh said, sounding relieved. "I'm gonna go join my friends now," she said, smiling at the butch.

"Well, now wait…" the woman said, putting her hand out to stop Shiloh from leaving.

"Honey," Harley said, looking at the butch, "she's straight."

The butch looked shocked by, but then grinned. "Well, I can fix that."

"If anyone is gonna fix that, it's gonna be me, so…" Harley said, her tone very matter of fact. So much so that Shiloh glanced up sharply at Harley, who winked at her.

Finally, the butch nodded, looking disappointed, and Harley steered Shiloh towards the patio.

"Gonna be you, huh?" she queried as they walked out the door, a smile on her lips.

"Uh-huh," Harley said, grinning with her tongue between her teeth, her blue eyes sparkling mischievously.

Harley sat back down at their table, looping her foot around a chair leg from the next table to drag it closer to her so Shiloh could sit down.

"What happened?" Quinn asked, having noted Harley's departure and return with Shiloh.

"She had to rescue me again," Shiloh said, grinning.

"Gonna keep happening," Devin said, shaking her head. "Or you're gonna have to get ugly or something," she said with a wink.

"Right, okay, sure…" Shiloh said, rolling her eyes.

"Or ya could just switch sides," Quinn said, winking at Shiloh outrageously.

"Or that," Harley said, grinning.

"I keep hearing that suggestion…" Shiloh said, laughing as she shook her head.

"What do you expect?" Rayden asked. "You are hanging out with a bunch of lesbians."

"Well, that's true," Shiloh said, grinning.

Roslynn stood up causing everyone to stop and look at her. She was a very hot looking woman and it didn't go unnoticed.

She leaned down, kissed Harley's lips, and said, "I'll be right back."

The group watched as Roslynn sauntered over to the bar, and started talking to Sarah.

"What the…" Quinn muttered.

"What is she doing?" Devin asked, as they all watched Roslynn lean in closer to Sarah.

Shiloh glanced at Harley and noted that she was looking on, her face expressionless.

"Holy crap…" Rayden said as Sarah stood, looking at Roslynn with definite interest.

"Alright then," Jet said glancing at Harley. "Who else needs a shot?"

Harley put up a finger, as did a couple of the others. Jet signaled the waitress, circling her finger, and then holding her fingers an inch apart to indicate a shot. The waitress nodded and walked over to the bar.

After the shots, Harley lit a cigarette and leaned back in her chair. Shiloh slid her hand into the crook of Harley's arm, squeezing it gently.

"You okay?" Shiloh asked softly in Harley's ear.

"Yep," Harley said, glancing at Shiloh.

"She's just trying to make you jealous, you know," Shiloh said.

"I know," Harley said, sounding blasé.

Everyone watched as Sarah and Roslynn walked over to the dance floor and began dancing. There were rounds of "What the fuck?" and "Are you friggin' kidding me?" from pretty much the entire group. Cat, Jovina, Natalia, and Raine joined them, glancing in the direction the group was looking in to see what was going on.

"Isn't that Roslynn?" Cat asked, as she sat down.

"She's dancing with Sarah?" Jovina asked.

"Yep," Rayden said.

"Uh-huh," Jet murmured.

"What the fuck?" Cat asked.

"Well said," Quinn said, grinning.

"And not something someone else hasn't already said over and over," Harley said, grinning.

"What the hell?" Jericho asked as she and Zoey joined the group.

"Yes, we know," Raine said, grinning.

As the group continued to discuss the varying degrees of shock they felt, Shiloh kept her hand on Harley's arm.

"You know, you could just fight fire with fire," Shiloh told Harley softly.

"It's fine, don't worry about it," Harley said, shaking her head.

"I don't think so," Shiloh said, her tone low.

Harley turned her head to look at Shiloh, and suddenly felt Shiloh's lips on her neck. She couldn't even breathe for a moment.

When she found her voice, she breathed, "Shy…"

Harley's tone was so quiet that no one else heard it, but Shiloh did, and she was bound and determined to make Roslynn pay attention. She felt Harley's left hand touch her face, her fingers flexing as Shiloh nuzzled her neck deeper.

"Shy… Ya gotta stop…" Harley said, her voice still low. It was just between the two of them.

Devin, however saw what was going on, since she was standing closest to the two. She touched Skyler on the shoulder and canted her head ever so slightly. Skyler's lips curled in a grin, knowing exactly what Shiloh was doing. It was clear how much it was affecting Harley.

Roslynn had also apparently noticed, because she stopped dancing. Right about that time, Shiloh moved away from Harley's neck, her moss-green eyes issuing a challenge to Roslynn. By this time everyone in the group had noticed what Shiloh had done and could see that Harley was no longer paying any attention to Roslynn. They all started to grin, and little by little, the group made a unanimous decision without even discussing it. They absolutely loved Shiloh. They also decided Roslynn needed to be taught a lesson.

Roslynn walked over to Harley, who had her head turned toward Shiloh and was talking to her in low tones. Roslynn stood, waiting for

Harley to notice her. She could see the varied looks from the group, none of which looked very pleased with her. Finally, Harley turned her head to look up at Roslynn, mostly because Shiloh had just told her that Roslynn was standing there.

"Hi," Harley said, grinning, her blue eyes completely guileless.

"Hi," Roslynn said, smiling tightly. "Come dance with me," she said then, wanting to get away from the group to talk to Harley.

Harley's eyes looked behind Roslynn toward the bar, and saw Sarah once again sitting on the barstool.

"Nah, I'm good," Harley said, picking up her beer and lifting to her lips.

"Come on…" Roslynn said, her tone cajoling. "I want to dance with you…"

Harley looked back at her, her blue eyes turning slightly icy. "I don't dance. You were fine though," she said, gesturing towards Sarah.

"I," Roslynn stammered, "but…" She tried to begin again, but she couldn't stand the look in Harley's eyes. She was being dismissed and she was damned if she was just going to take it.

She turned around and walked back over to the bar and ordered a drink.

Quinn ordered another round of shots from the waitress, whispering something in her ear as she did. The waitress looked over at Harley and nodded emphatically. When she brought back the shots, she held Harley's aloft while the group looked on. Then slowly she put the shot between her ample breasts, and straddling Harley's lap. She took Harley's head in her hands and bent it toward the shot. Harley, knowing exactly what her friends were doing, grinned and did exactly as they wanted her to. She slid her tongue over the waitress's skin, and then picked up the shot with her teeth, drinking it without touching the glass. Then she dropped it into her hand and kissed the waitress deeply while the group cheered.

For the rest of the night, the hotter femme members of the group payed extra attention to Harley. At one point, Jazmine and Dakota arrived, and they'd already been told via text what was going on. Jazmine walked out onto the patio, glancing around to make sure Roslynn had a good vantage point. She took a handful of Harley's hair from behind, pulled her head back, and kissed her deeply.

"And hello to you too," Harley said, chuckling, her eyes widened in reaction.

Eventually, Roslynn made her way back over to Harley, this time bringing with her a shot.

"Will you do this one for me?" she asked, refusing to look at anyone but Harley.

Harley gave her a measured look. Roslynn looked back at her silently pleading. Finally, Harley nodded.

Roslynn kneeled between Harley's legs, pressing her body seductively against her. Harley's eyes watched her closely. Roslynn pulled the top of her shirt down to just above the nipple and tapped the spot with her finger. Harley grinned and leaned forward, licking the spot slowly. Roslynn took the saltshaker from the table, sprinkled some on her skin, and then looked back at Harley. Harley obliged by leaning forward again, this time sucking at the skin with salt on it. Roslynn held up the shot and Harley and drank it, her eyes never leaving Roslynn's. Roslynn slid the lime over her lips and Harley leaned in to kiss her deeply. Roslynn wrapped her arms around Harley's neck, kissing her back with fervor. When their lips parted, Roslynn hugged Harley, but had her eyes on Shiloh.

"I'm sorry," Roslynn whispered in Harley's ear.

Shiloh simply narrowed her eyes, but didn't say anything. The rest of the group looked on, but didn't say anything either. It wasn't quite the night they had expected.

The next morning Shiloh sat in the kitchen, looking at the clock repeatedly, knowing that Harley had likely forgotten that she'd promised Natalia to come to her class that morning. When it got to eight o'clock and she'd still heard no movement from upstairs, Shiloh sighed and got up.

She knocked lightly on Harley's bedroom door but got no answer. Shaking her head she took a deep breath, feeling like she was entering the lion's den, or in this case the lionesses den. She walked in and saw that Harley was lying on her stomach in bed, her arms around the pillow under her head, and her back bare. Shiloh was temporarily taken aback by the long tattoo down the middle of her back. It looked like Asian letters that started out red at the top and then with each symbol went through all the colors of the rainbow. Shiloh hadn't even known that Harley had tattoos.

Roslynn was lying on her side facing Harley, but not nearly as close to Harley as Shiloh would have expected. Shiloh wondered remotely and hopefully that perhaps Roslynn's little show the night before had put Harley off a bit. She immediately tamped down on that thought; Harley wasn't really one to hold grudges. The fact was, Harley deserved whatever happiness she could get, and Shiloh wanted that for her. Even if she'd already put Roslynn in the category of the women Harley'd already been with who were attention whores.

She stepped over to the side of the bed, and reached out to touch Harley's shoulder.

"Harley?" she queried softly, not wanting to wake Roslynn up.

"Mmm?" Harley murmured, turning her head toward Shiloh and opening one blue eye slightly.

"It's eight and you told Nat you'd be there this morning," Shiloh said, grinning.

Harley made a groaning noise in the back of her throat, and rubbed her face on her pillow tiredly.

"Okay," Harley said into her pillow. "I'm up."

Shiloh grinned, resisting the urge to remind Harley that until she was technically upright, she wasn't. She saw that Roslynn's eyes were now open and narrowed at her. Shiloh just gave her a pointed look, indicating that she didn't care. Then she turned and walked out of the room.

"Seriously?" Roslynn muttered.

Harley levered herself up on her forearms looking over at Roslynn. "What?"

"She comes into your bedroom whenever she wants?" Roslynn asked, her tone ridiculing.

Harley regarded her for a long moment. "She came to remind me of a promise I made to a friend. That's what friends do for each other."

With that, Harley climbed out of bed and walked towards the bathroom. Roslynn stared after her, thinking that she'd just screwed up again. She knew that what she'd done at The Club the night before was stupid. She'd just been so irritated by how much attention Harley had paid to Shiloh, "rescuing" her, she'd felt the need to react. Harley, however, hadn't reacted the way she'd expected, and her friends all seemed to now resent her as well. Knowing she needed to get back into Harley's good graces, she climbed out of bed and got dressed.

Shiloh was sitting in the kitchen when Harley walked downstairs. Harley wore black Capri leggings, a black tank top with a rainbow pulse beat on it, and a heart shape in the same rainbow line, and black tennis shoes. Shiloh handed her a cup of coffee with a grin.

"I need to smoke," Harley said, taking the coffee and heading out to the backyard.

Shiloh followed her, cup in hand.

"So how are you this morning?" Shiloh asked.

Harley lit a cigarette and looked back at her through the smoke.

"Alright, I guess," Harley said, shrugging.

Shiloh's phone chimed and she checked the message. Harley saw Shiloh smile and start to answer the text.

"Who's that from?" Harley asked, her blue eyes sparkling with interest.

"No one," Shiloh replied with an embarrassed grin.

"Uh-huh… Tell." Harley said, smiling.

"It's that Agent Salinas," Shiloh said.

"From CPU?" Harley asked looking surprised.

"Yeah, you know he's been stopping by my desk a lot…" Shiloh said, biting her lip.

"Oh ho!" Harley replied her eyes wide. "So what did he say?"

"He wants to take me out…" Shiloh said, her look chagrinned.

"What's that look about?" Harley asked.

Shiloh shrugged. "I don't know, I guess I'm just nervous about dating again."

"They're not all going to be like that last asshole," Harley said, having heard the story finally of why Shiloh's parents had disowned her.

"I know," Shiloh said, picking at the plant that sat on the table they were sitting at.

Harley narrowed her eyes slightly, seeing Shiloh's agitation and not sure what it was about. Roslynn walked out of the house then, so Harley didn't have a chance to pursue the matter. A little while later Roslynn and Harley left to go to the class. Shiloh had decided not to go.

At the studio, Roslynn noticed that once again all the femmes in the group seemed to pay an inordinate amount of attention to Harley. Roslynn stayed apart from the group sensing they didn't want to associate with her. During the class, it became very evident to Roslynn that Harley could indeed dance, contrary to what she'd said at The Club the night before. Roslynn commented on it on the way back to Harley's house.

"So you can dance…" Roslynn said, looking over at Harley.

"Never said I couldn't," Harley said.

"You said you don't," Roslynn replied.

"True," Harley said, noncommittally. "You seemed like you'd found a willing dance partner," she said then, her tone impassive.

"You didn't seem to mind," Roslynn shot back, instantly on the defensive.

"I didn't," Harley said simply.

"Did it make you jealous?"

"Did I seem jealous?" Harley asked, her tone still frustratingly impassive.

"No, you seemed really cozy with your assistant!" Roslynn snapped.

Harley looked over at Roslynn, her blue eyes widening slightly at Roslynn's outburst.

"Did it make you jealous?" Harley asked evenly.

"Yes!" Roslynn exclaimed.

Harley licked her upper lip, looking at Roslynn pointedly as if to say *that was the point*. Roslynn realized she'd been beaten at her own game. She'd allowed her jealously of Shiloh's obviously close association with Harley to cloud her judgment and make her do something stupid.

Sighing loudly, Roslynn shook her head.

"I'm sorry," she said, putting her hand on Harley's hand. "I was really stupid and I shouldn't have done that to you, especially not in front of all your friends."

Harley's look flickered, as she looked over at Roslynn. "Ros, what my friends think or don't doesn't really matter. When I'm with someone, I'm with them and no one else and I think they should have that same level of commitment if they want to be with me." She looked over at Roslynn then. "And if that's not what you want here, Ros, that's fine, but I need to know that and you need to move into one of the other bedrooms during your stay here."

Roslynn pressed her lips together, nodding. "You're right. You're totally right," she said, looking contrite. "And I do want to be with you, I really do… Last night I was just…"

"Just what?" Harley asked when Roslynn didn't continue.

Roslynn blew her breath out. "I was jealous and I let that make me do something stupid."

Harley nodded. "Okay."

"Can we try again?" Roslyn asked looking hopeful.

"In terms of…" Harley asked, wanting to make sure they understood each other now.

"In terms of making it up to you," Roslynn said, sliding her hand up Harley's arm. "We could go out tonight again, and I promise I won't even think about anyone else but you."

Harley narrowed her eyes slightly, wondering if this was even a good idea.

Finally, she blew her breath out, nodding. "Okay."

Roslynn sensed that Harley wasn't exactly sure about them at that point. She was going to prove to Harley that she had nothing to worry about.

That night they went to The Club. A few members of the group were there, but not in the numbers they were the night before. Roslynn did as she'd said and paid attention only to Harley, refusing to allow any jealous feelings she had about any other woman in The Club to show. It was a much better night.

Harley and Roslynn spent a lot of time together and many late, late nights. Shiloh worried about Harley, but knew that she needed to stay out of their business. The fact was Harley was an adult, and if she wanted to stay up all hours of the night with the woman she was dating, then that was her business. It was, however, harder and harder to get Harley out of bed in the mornings to go to work.

One morning, a week and a half after Roslynn had arrived in Los Angeles, Shiloh walked into Harley's bedroom after Harley had hit the snooze button so many times the alarm had stopped going off. It was the second day in a row that Harley had done that.

"Harley," Shiloh said, touching her shoulder. She deliberately didn't whisper, not caring if she woke Roslynn up.

Harley didn't move. Shiloh put her hand on Harley's shoulder fully and was surprised to find that it was quite warm. She shook Harley's shoulder lightly, repeating her name, louder this time. Roslynn stirred, giving Shiloh a dirty look, a standard for her lately whenever Harley wasn't looking. Shiloh didn't pay any attention to her, she was more worried about Harley's lack of response.

"Harley!" Shiloh said again, louder this time shaking her friend harder.

Harley gave a slight groan, then looked up at Shiloh. She could immediately see that Harley was sick. Her normally bright blue eyes were very dull.

"Are you getting sick?" Shiloh asked, putting her hand to Harley's forehead. "You definitely feel like you have a fever."

"I don't feel good," Harley said, sounding like a little kid suddenly.

205

"I'm gettin' that," Shiloh said, grinning. "You want to take the day? Rest?"

Harley nodded, sniffling as she did.

"Okay, I'll email Rayden," Shiloh said. "Can I get you anything?"

Harley just shook her head and closed her eyes again.

Shiloh left the room then, doing her best to tamp down on the irritation she was feeling. She knew that Harley was getting sick because she hadn't been getting enough rest. Harley hadn't been getting enough rest because Roslynn was apparently insatiable when it came to going out and partying, and then coming home and having sex for hours on end. Even Shiloh was tired from all the late night noises. Even so, both she and Harley had gone to work every day and Harley hadn't slowed down in the slightest. But now Harley was sick. Shiloh was curious to see how Roslynn would handle this development.

She found out an hour later when Roslynn came downstairs with her suitcase.

Shiloh was sitting at the dining room table with her laptop answering work emails. She saw the suitcase and made a rude sound, shaking her head.

"What?" Roslynn snapped immediately.

"Now you're leaving?" Shiloh asked.

Roslynn shrugged. "I was supposed to go back four days ago," she said, her tone not the least bit contrite.

"So, you stick around long enough to wear Harley completely down, and now you're just going to leave when she's sick?" Shiloh asked acerbically.

Roslynn gave a short offended snort. "I have a life too, you know!"

"Yeah?" Shiloh queried her look and tone openly hostile. "Where's your life been for the last week and a half?"

"I don't answer to you," Roslynn snapped. "If you want Harley so bad, why don't you go climb into bed with her now."

"Now that you're out of it, I just might," Shiloh shot back. "You can go ahead and leave now."

"I'm waiting for a cab," Roslynn replied primly.

"Wait outside," Shiloh said, her tone brooking no argument.

"Bitch!" Roslynn snapped.

"You say that like it's a bad thing," Shiloh replied, staring Roslynn down.

Roslynn finally picked up her suitcase and slammed out of the house. Shiloh pulled up the house security system and locked the door behind her, then opened the front gate, indicating that she expected Roslynn to wait out on the street. She smiled as Roslynn made her way out to the street, tripping on the rail the security gate slid on. She then closed the gate.

"Bye bye…"

She texted Devin to let her know what was going on with Harley and that Roslynn had just left. They'd been in communication all week about the goings-on at the house. It had been Devin who'd warned Shiloh to stay out from between Harley and Roslynn.

"She left? What!? What a using little bitch!" came Devin's texted reply.

207

"I made her stand out on the street to wait for her cab," Shiloh replied with a little devil emoticon.

"You go girl!" Devin replied. "Let me know how Harley's doing, I'll come by and check on her and you tonight. You need anything?"

"No, I just want Harley to get better and to get that wench out of her system," Shiloh replied.

"Fortunately, our girl has a short attention span when it comes to women," Devin texted.

"Why did she have to be so awful? Harley was so excited about her coming here."

"I know, I hate it too," Devin replied.

Later Devin told Skyler what was going on.

"She really just picked up and left?" Skyler asked, surprised.

"Yeah," Devin said, nodding. "Now that she ran Harley into the ground, she left Shiloh to deal with the aftermath."

Skyler looked back at Devin, her light green eyes narrowed. "You want her with Shiloh, don't you?"

Devin looked back at her wife and grinned. "Would that be so bad?"

Skyler shook her head. "But Shiloh is straight."

"Did she look straight that night at The Club when she was kissing Harley's neck to make Roslynn jealous?" Devin asked.

"Well, no, no she didn't," Skyler said, grinning.

"And Shiloh actually cares about Harley. She's not after her money or her car or her connections, she just cares about her."

"Okay, babe, but does Harley feel the same way?" Skyler asked.

Devin hesitated. The time Harley had just spent with Roslynn would indicate to anyone else that she didn't. But then again, a lot of people didn't know Harley the way she did.

"I think you'd be surprised," Devin said, smiling.

Skyler narrowed her eyes at her wife, knowing that Devin was forever scheming when it came to her friends. She wanted everyone of her friends as happy and in love as she was with Skyler. She'd done her best to push Quinn and Xandy together originally too. She'd also found a girl for Skyler's best friend and co-pilot Jams and for Skyler's little brother, so she did have a good track record.

Skyler sighed. "Well, I just hope it doesn't go south on you," she said, shaking her head.

"It won't," Devin said confidently.

Shiloh let Harley sleep for four hours, checking on her frequently. At one in the afternoon, she went into the bedroom and kneeled next to the bed. Harley was pale, her skin almost ashen. Shiloh blew her breath out. She touched Harley's forehead and was sure it was warmer now that it had been that morning. She went into Harley's bathroom, looking in the medicine cabinet for a thermometer and for something to help break the fever. That's when she noticed there wasn't a bottle of medicine to be found. There were little brown bottles lined up with various colored labels on them with words like, Lavender, Chamomile, Eucalyptus, and Sage, but no medicine. She thought it was strange, but closed the medicine cabinet and went back into the bedroom. She kneeled back down and carefully put the digital thermometer in Harley's ear. She grimaced as the thermometer displayed 103 degrees.

"Harley," Shiloh said, touching Harley's shoulder. "Harley," she repeated louder this time.

"Mmm?" Harley murmured, opening her eyes blearily.

"Hon, your temperature is high, we need to get it down. Can you tell me where you have like Tylenol or Motrin, or something?"

Harley shook her head. "I don't have any," she said, her voice the barest whisper.

"Okay, I can go get some," Shiloh said, moving to stand.

"I don't take medicine, Shy," Harley said simply.

"What?" Shiloh queried, not sure she'd heard Harley right.

"I don't take medicine."

"Ever?" Shiloh asked her tone shocked.

Harley simply shrugged.

"Okay, hold on for a minute," Shiloh said. She got up again and went to get a cold washcloth from the bathroom.

She walked back in and laid it on Harley's forehead, then sat on the bed next to where Harley lay. She picked up her phone to text Devin.

"She doesn't take medicine?!" she texted.

"Oh, she's still not taking stuff huh?" Devin replied. "She told me that at MIT, I figured it was some kind of hippy thing."

"Well it's not and she's got a 103 temp!"

"Keep an eye on that, if it goes over 103 or doesn't come down we're going to need to take her to a hospital."

"How's that going to go over with her no meds policy?"

"I don't think we'll care at that point."

Shiloh put her phone down and touched the cloth on Harley's forehead. It was already hot. She went to the bathroom and cooled it again, then put it back on Harley's forehead. She went downstairs and got a bowl of water to keep by the bedside. She picked up a couple of dishtowels as well. Back in Harley's room, she put the towels in the cool water, and lay them on Harley's back and over the back of her neck. Harley sighed, reaching her arm out and touching Shiloh's hand.

"What is it, Harley?" she asked gently.

Harley mumbled something, but Shiloh couldn't understand. She lay down putting her face next to Harley's.

"I didn't catch that…" she whispered.

"Stay," Harley repeated.

"I'm not going anywhere," Shiloh told her. She brushed her hair back off her face. "I'm staying right here with you, okay?"

Harley nodded, closing her eyes slowly again.

They spent the day with Shiloh consistently changing the cloths, doing her best to cool Harley's fever. She'd managed to get it down to 101 degrees but it wouldn't drop any lower. She'd searched online for a few natural remedies. When Harley was deeply asleep she'd done a search of the bathroom cabinets and found that Harley did have some herbs, but not the ones Shiloh had read about. Shiloh texted Devin to ask her to get some elderflower, yarrow, and some natural ginger, plus a steeper to make the tea with. Devin had responded immediately and said she'd be there with the stuff as fast as she could.

True to her word, Devin arrived an hour later with a bag of items.

Devin took over watching over Harley as Shiloh made the first of three different teas that had been suggested. While she was gone, Harley stirred to find Devin sitting next to her. She looked perplexed.

"Hi," Devin said, brightly. "Shiloh's making you some kind of tea with some kind of yicky herby stuff in it to try and break your fever."

A grin tugged at Harley's lips at Devin's description of the tea.

"You got a good one there," Devin told Harley. "Don't be stupid and ignore it."

Harley looked perplexed again. "Shy?" she asked with a scratchy voice.

"Yeah, Shy, Harley," Devin said, sighing. "She's been taking care of you since the day she walked back into your life. So be smart and do something about that when you feel better, okay?"

"She's... straight..." Harley said.

"Yeah, yeah, whatever," Devin said airily. "She's in love with you, Harley, don't be a dumb ass for once."

"Gee... thanks..." Harley muttered.

"Anytime," Devin said brightly.

Shiloh came back a few minutes later with a cup of tea.

"Harley, you need to take this," Shiloh said, seeing that Harley's eyes were open now.

Harley nodded, looking extremely tired. Shiloh moved to the other side of the bed and set the tea down so they could help Harley sit up.

"Okay, I put some sugar in it to make it a little more palatable," Shiloh said, handing it to Harley who reached up with shaking fingers.

"Never mind, I have it," she told Harley, holding the cup to her lips. "Just drink, babe… Carefully…"

Devin heard the endearment and suppressed her smile. She knew she was right about how Shiloh felt about Harley. She still wasn't completely sure about Harley, but she had a feeling she was right there too.

Harley took a few sips of the tea, grimacing at the bitterness.

"Well you're the one who doesn't want to take nice tasteless Tylenol…" Shiloh said, winking at Harley with a smile.

Harley took a few more sips then moved her head away.

"Okay, I'll add more sugar to the next batch," Shiloh said, grinning at Devin.

The two of them laid Harley back down on the bed. Shiloh pulled the covers up over her and then walked Devin downstairs.

At the front door, Devin turned to Shiloh. "How do you feel about Harley?"

Shiloh looked surprised by the question but took a moment to think about how to respond.

She shrugged. "She's the best friend I've ever had."

Devin nodded slowly. "But what about romantically?"

Shiloh's eyes widened, then she bit her lip.

"Oh boy," Devin said. "I can see we need to talk."

"I need to get back up to Harley."

Devin smiled thinking that alone answered her question. But Shiloh needed to come to that realization herself. She nodded.

"Okay, well, let's talk as soon as she starts getting better," Devin said, winking at Shiloh.

"Thanks for getting the stuff for me," Shiloh said, sighing. "I guess I'm going to learn about this homeopathic stuff, huh?"

"Looks like," Devin said, noting that Shiloh avoided the topic of them talking.

Another sign as far as Devin was concerned.

Devin left, and Shiloh went back up to check on Harley. She was sleeping again. Shiloh looked down at Harley, thinking about the questions Devin had asked. She wasn't ready to fully examine her feelings for Harley. She knew that desire wasn't always love, and she didn't even know if the desire was mutual. That made her think of something, so she texted Devin.

"Hey, I have a question for you when you get a chance. What is the deal with Harley and her neck?"

She'd wondered it after the first night at The Club, when the group had been talking about Sarah going for Harley's neck. She'd also noticed that the night they'd come home from The Club, Harley had practically jumped when Shiloh had nuzzled her neck. Then that night at The Club with Roslynn, Harley had seemed deeply affected when she'd kissed her neck to try and make Roslynn jealous.

Devin finally texted an hour later when she'd gotten back to her house. "Harley's biggest turn on."

Shiloh read that and sighed, she'd figured it was a turn on, not her biggest though. To Shiloh, it meant that Harley wasn't necessarily attracted to her, just affected by anyone kissing her neck. She felt a sense of disappointment and did her best to ignore it. She fell asleep that night, sitting up leaning against the headboard of Harley's bed with her hand on Harley's shoulder.

The next day, Harley didn't seem to be feeling much better, so Shiloh emailed Rayden again. She checked Harley's temperature and it was down to 100, so she made a point of brewing more tea. By mid-afternoon, she was feeling well enough to sit up and watch TV. She insisted on watching a series on DVD: *The L Word.*

"Don't know if you'll like it though," Harley said, grinning.

"Why?" Shiloh asked.

"It's about gay women in LA," Harley said.

"'Cause I don't know any of those?" Shiloh asked wryly.

Harley chuckled, causing herself to cough. "I see your point," she said when she was able to talk again.

Shiloh went down to the kitchen and heated up some soup from a can, thinking she needed to make Harley some homemade soup. When she got back upstairs, there was an episode of *The L Word* on and two women were making love. One of the women had short dark hair and was very slim hipped with a very androgynous look about her, reminding Shiloh of Dakota.

"She looks kind of like Dakota," she said to Harley as she handed her soup. "Easy, it might still be a little hot," she cautioned, catching Harley's grin.

"Yes, Mom," Harley said.

"Don't make me smack you when you're sick," Shiloh said, raising an eyebrow at her.

Harley grinned unrepentantly. "And you're right, she does look like Dakota a bit. That's Shane."

"Okay…" Shiloh said, settling next to Harley on the bed and watching the show. "Who's that? Wait, isn't that the woman that played in *Flashdance*?"

Harley chuckled. "Yeah… She was hot in that too. The character's name is Bette."

"I see is she the one you like the best there?" Shiloh asked.

"Mmm…" Harley stammered. "Yeah, her or Carmen. Carmen is way hot."

"Which one is that?" Shiloh asked.

"Wait…" Harley said. A few minutes passed, then a Latina came on the screen, and Harley pointed. "That is Carmen," she said, sighing.

Shiloh screwed up her face in assessment. "I dunno… I think Shane's hot."

Harley looked back at Shiloh. "Really now?"

"Well, yeah, if I had to pick," Shiloh said. "Oh, or that one!" she said when another woman came on the screen.

"She's totally butch," Harley said.

"So?" Shiloh asked.

Harley shook her head grinning. There was a ring of the doorbell then, and Shiloh picked up Harley's iPad to check the front door. It was Devin. She hit the button to open the door for her.

"We're up here!" Shiloh called.

Devin walked in, her eyes immediately drawn to the screen as two women were kissing and making all kinds of noise again.

"Oh, *The L Word*, good choice..." Devin said, grinning as she walked over to kiss Harley who was sitting against the headboard.

"Okay, who do you think is hottest?" Harley asked her.

"Definitely Shane," Devin said nodding. "The carpenter was pretty hot too," she said, referring to the other woman that Shiloh had found hot.

"So you're both into butches. Way to solidify the stereotype, girls," Harley said, grinning as she winked at them both.

"Excuse me?" Devin asked, as she kicked off her shoes and lay across the bed. "Have you seen my wife?"

"Yeah," Harley said, grinning.

"Is Skyler considered butch?" Shiloh asked.

"Soft butch," Harley said.

"Yeah, and you got nothing to say, Harley, so are you," Devin told her.

Shiloh looked over at Harley, her look surprised. "You'd be considered butch?"

Harley chuckled, nodding. "Yeah, by most people. You don't remember that conversation in the car on the way home from the bar that first night?"

"Hmmm, I don't remember much about that night, no," Shiloh said, looking at Harley as if she was trying to see the 'butch.' "So Shane is butch too?"

"She's actually got that whole androgynous thing going on, so she's a bit harder to peg," Devin explained.

Shiloh nodded, trying to understand all the subtleties of lesbians and their ways.

"So what makes butches different from other lesbians?" Shiloh asked curiously.

Devin and Harley exchanged a look; they'd both heard these kinds of questions before.

"Well, butches tend to be the more masculine of the women," Harley said.

"And they're also usually the best gentlemen you'll ever find," Devin said, smiling over at Harley. "They open doors for you, some of them still stand when you enter a room, they pick up the check…"

"Or give you a credit card with an unlimited credit limit," Shiloh said, raising an eyebrow at Harley.

"You did what?" Devin asked, her eyes wide.

"It was for her birthday," Harley said, shrugging, as she pointedly looked back at the TV.

"Uh-huh," Devin said, her look knowing. "Did ya cancel it after her birthday?"

Harley didn't answer, she was focused on whatever was happening on the show. Devin picked up a pillow and tossed it at her.

"Hmm?" Harley murmured. "What?"

Devin shook her head, grinning. "Did you cancel the credit card after Shiloh's birthday?"

"What?" Harley asked, looking confused for a moment. "No, wait, why?"

"'Cause it's only 'for my birthday' if it was only on my birthday, Harley," Shiloh said.

Harley looked at Shiloh, then over at Devin, who nodded with a grin on her lips.

"Whatever," Harley said, waving her hand dismissively.

"Whatever she says," Devin said, looking at Shiloh and rolling her eyes. "Shy, how many people would you trust like that?"

"Not one person on this Earth," Shiloh responded.

"Me either," Devin said pointedly looking at Harley.

Once again, Harley's focus had shifted back to the TV, but she sensed she was being watched.

"What?" she asked looking between the two women, sounding exasperated.

Devin shook her head, sighing and turning onto her side to watch the show. Shiloh smiled, seeing that Harley was looking vexed. As she watched, Harley set her foot at Devin's butt and shoved her over, making Devin laugh.

"Brat!" Devin exclaimed.

"You're one to talk, troublemaker," Harley said.

They spent the afternoon watching TV. Eventually Harley started to get tired again, so Shiloh turned it off and got her settled in bed again, making sure she was comfortable. She walked with Devin downstairs and started checking the refrigerator to see if they had the items she needed to make soup. Devin sat at the bar counter across from her.

"So, how much do you love her?" Devin asked out of the blue.

"What!" Shiloh exclaimed, shocked by the question.

"You heard me," Devin said, smiling.

"What makes you think I do?" Shiloh asked her look blasé.

"You do," Devin said, her tone sure. "I just want to know how much."

"You can love friends, you know."

"Yeah, you're right, you can," Devin said, nodding. "But you're in love with her too."

Shiloh's mouth dropped open, then she busied herself getting out vegetables and looking in the freezer for chicken.

"At least you aren't denying it," Devin said, smiling from her perch.

"I'm not saying anything," Shiloh said, shaking her head.

"Right, which means you're not denying it."

"So I have to deny it to make it not true?"

"Pretty much, yeah."

Shiloh looked back at Devin, and could see that part of her really wanted to deny it, just so she could keep denying it to herself. Finally, Shiloh blew her breath out, shaking her head.

"I wish I could lie and say I'm not," Shiloh said simply.

"Why?" Devin asked. "Why would you want to lie about that?"

"Because," Shiloh said, shrugging, "she's my boss, she's my friend… Because I'm frigging terrified."

"What are you afraid of?" Devin asked, looking surprised.

"What am I afraid of?" Shiloh repeated, her look asking Devin if she was crazy. "Do you know she hasn't even asked about Roslynn?"

Devin looked back at Shiloh, her look considering. "You're thinking that if she can dismiss someone like Roslynn from her mind so easily, she could do the same to you?"

"Exactly!" Shiloh said.

Devin looked pensive, then finally shook her head. "Shy, Harley doesn't dismiss people from her life."

"What do you mean?" Shiloh asked, looking confused. "You just said…"

"I know what I said," Devin said, "And I was saying that it's what you think, but the thing is Harley doesn't have the ability in her to be cruel enough to dismiss people from her life. She lets things go that don't hold her attention. Unfortunately, sometimes that includes women."

"Unfortunately for who?" Shiloh asked.

"For Harley and for the women I suppose," Devin said. "But you have to ask yourself a question here. What are you willing to risk to find out if you can hold her attention?"

"I don't know," Shiloh said, shaking her head. "I mean, Jesus you saw Roslynn. She was one of the hottest women I've ever seen. Plus, if the noise level was any indication, she obviously knew what she was doing in bed, so… Where am I going to measure up in either of those areas?"

"And you think Harley's only about looks and sex?" Devin asked.

That question brought Shiloh up short and she furrowed her brows. She hadn't really thought about it that way.

Devin nodded, seeing that Shiloh was suddenly unsure of her own logic.

"You're telling yourself all kinds of stuff, Shiloh," Devin said, "because it would be easier if you didn't want her. But that's not going to make it go away, trust me."

"You know about this kind of thing?" Shiloh asked.

"God, yes!" Devin said, rolling her eyes. "Do you know how hard I had to work to catch and keep Skyler?"

"What? No way," Shiloh said. "I've seen you two together, she thinks you're the most awesome thing she's ever seen…"

"Now, she thinks that now," Devin said. "But believe me, she pushed me away every way to Sunday and back to Friday… she wanted nothing to do with me. But I kept at her until I could prove to her that I loved her and that I wanted to be in her life, no matter what her demons were," she said wistfully. "You don't have any old demons to worry about with Harley, she is who she is, no games, no bullshit. That, my friend, is priceless."

"But I might not hold her attention," Shiloh said, her biggest fear coming back to bear.

"Not gonna know till you try," Devin said. "But I can tell you that having someone like Harley decide to make you their own, is the most incredible thing in the entire world. Why wouldn't you want to fight for something like that?"

Shiloh looked back at Devin, her face drawn in an unhappy line. She didn't know how to answer. She was afraid to answer.

Chapter 8

Dakota was sitting by the pool, her sunglasses over her closed eyes. She was wearing shorts and a tank top and was baking in the Mediterranean sun, but in some crazy way it felt good. She knew she was getting way too much sun, but she didn't care. Part of her wondered if she'd end up with skin cancer, but the other part of her didn't care. She thought about how her life had been before, and how it was now… same shit, nicer wrapper.

Then there was a cold hand on her thigh. She jumped.

"Jesus your fucking hands are like ice!" she exclaimed.

"Sorry," Cassandra said smiling. "I was inside where the cool air is."

Dakota rubbed her leg. "I'm thinking you need to get your circulation checked," she said, her tone annoyed.

Cassandra straddled Dakota's waist. "I think you just need to get my blood pumping like you're so good at doing," she said, sliding her hand up Dakota's chest.

Dakota looked at Cassandra through her sunglasses. She wasn't a bad-looking woman. At forty, she still had honey-blond hair with no signs of gray, thanks to her hairdresser. Her skin was taut and wrinkleless, thanks to God knew how many plastic surgeons and vats of Botox. Her body… now that was her own. She was very agile in bed, not that it ever served Dakota's needs, but she definitely moved well.

Cassandra also had a lot of money, and was desperate to use as much of it as necessary to keep Dakota with her. They'd been together for a month, and Cassandra had been willing to take her anywhere she wanted, buy her anything she wanted. Dakota was smart; she played hard to get, and Cassandra wanted her more. Recently, she'd seen a Bugatti that she wanted, but instead of telling Cassandra, she played it cool. She made a point of finding a magazine that had the exact model in it that she wanted and left it open to that page. Cassandra had thus far ignored the hints, so Dakota knew it was time to step it up.

She stopped Cassandra's hand in its exploration of her nipple.

"Not in the mood," Dakota said.

"I can change that," Cassandra said smiling.

Dakota lowered her sunglasses slightly, looking back at Cassandra cynically.

"You think so?" Dakota asked doubtfully.

"I know what gets you hot…" Cassandra said confidently.

"Do you?" Dakota asked, reaching out a hand to flick her finger upward against a taut nipple.

Cassandra gasped loudly and her breathing quickened. She pressed closer to Dakota, but Dakota sat back, crossing her arms in front of her chest.

"What do you want?" Cassandra asked, her eyes glowing with desire.

"Nothing," Dakota said, her tone bored.

"You have to want something," Cassandra said, pressing against Dakota's body again, longing for her hands to touch her.

Dakota sighed, shaking her head.

"I know you want something," Cassandra said. "I've seen that car you've been looking at."

"It's a three point four million car, Cass!" Dakota said, knowing damned good and well Cassandra could afford it.

"If it's what you want..." Cassandra said.

She turned around to lay her back against Dakota's chest, her body between Dakota's legs. She slid her hands down Dakota's thighs, laying her head back against her shoulder.

"Touch me..." she insisted.

Dakota grinned behind her. She slid her hands up Cassandra's torso stopping just below her breasts. Her thumbs brushing upward, but not quite reaching very hard nipples. Cassandra groaned, pressing back against Dakota, her hands grasping at Dakota's legs.

"Dakota please..." Cassandra begged.

"What do you want?" Dakota asked, her lips right next to Cassandra's ear.

"You... God... You..." Cassandra said, her breathing coming in sharp rasping breaths.

"That's right..." Dakota said, her fingers tightening on Cassandra's torso, pressing Cassandra back against her body. "You want me..."

"Yes, yes... please..."

"I want the Bugatti," Dakota told her. "And I want it in my name."

"Okay, okay, Dakota please..." Cassandra said, her body trembling.

"Promise me," Dakota growled seductively against Cassandra's ear.

"I promise, I promise…" Cassandra said, willing to promise anything at that moment.

"Good girl…" Dakota said, brushing her thumbs upward over Cassandra's nipples making her come immediately.

Two days later, Dakota got the Bugatti she wanted, to the tune of $3.4 million.

"Holy hell… Where did you find it?" Dakota asked as she looked reverently at the fireplace mantel that had just been brought in by two of the workers.

"I have been searching high and low for something that actually came out of a Craftsman back east," Cassandra said, smiling. "You like it?" she asked, seeming almost giddy.

"It's incredible, Cass…" Dakota said running her hands over the cherry wood. "It's authentic Craftsman. Do you know how you can tell?"

"No," Cassandra said, shaking her head and smiling indulgently. "How?"

"You see here," Dakota said, touching the two lengths of wood on the sides of the mantle. "This tapered column style is classic Craftsman; it even has these mini rafter tails." She indicated to the small pieces of wood against the upper part of the mantle.

Cassandra nodded. "The tapered columns are one of the main features of a true Craftsman," she said. "I remembered what you told me. That's why I thought this mantle was perfect."

"It is, you did really good on this one," Dakota said, grinning. "Now about that tile…" she said, her eyes falling on the tile that had been sent over to the site.

"Not as good?" Cassandra asked grimacing with one eye closed.

Dakota laughed out loud and shook her head.

"I'm still looking, I promise!" Cassandra said, holding up her hand like she was being sworn in. "There was one Art Nouveau tile that I saw that I really want to get my hands on. It's a really great dark sage green with a four-leafed flower pattern in darker greens. Art Nouveau is the right time frame, right? The twenties?"

Dakota nodded and smiled at the excitement in Cassandra's voice. She could see that the rich socialite was finally excited about something. Dakota was beginning to wonder if Cassandra had indeed done some changing. Everyone at the site broke for lunch then, which left Cassandra and Dakota alone in the house together.

"Jazmine isn't happy that you're working with me, is she?" Cassandra asked.

"No, she's not," Dakota said honestly.

Cassandra nodded. "She still hates me,"

"Well, you did almost let me die, Cass…"

"I know," Cassandra said, grimacing. "I'm the one that caused the wounds that could have killed you. I know… I've actually wanted to talk to you about that a few times…"

"Okay," Dakota said, sitting down on the stairs, her look open. "Talk."

Cassandra was so surprised by the sudden opportunity that she was unable to formulate a thought. She'd honestly expected Dakota to

227

completely shut her down the minute she'd brought up the idea of talking about what had happened. She moved to sit on the stair just below Dakota, leaning against the rail, her leg extended out to the side, so her foot was against the other railing. Dakota noted the cute little designer work boots she wore.

"How much did you pay for those?" Dakota couldn't help but ask.

"What?" Cassandra said, lifting her foot and turning it this way and that. "They're really cute, they're Frye boots, and they were very cheap only three hundred."

Dakota coughed, shaking her head. "Only you would by three hundred dollar work boots that were designer."

"Well how much were yours?" Cassandra asked.

Dakota looked back at her and grinned. "Well, they're Under Armour and I wear them every day so I need good quality ones, and still they were less than half of what you paid."

"I see," Cassandra said. "My boots aren't poor enough," she said, with a grin.

"They're very you," Dakota said, grinning.

They were both silent for a couple of minutes.

"So," Cassandra began, still not sure what she wanted to say. "About what happened… What I did… to you… I know that nothing will ever make up for that and you don't know how much I've regretted my actions every day since then…" She looked up at Dakota. "I don't want to make excuses," she said, "but you should know that I did check myself into a facility when I left here after that incident."

Dakota looked surprised and nodded slowly. "Okay…"

"The doctors thought that I must have had some kind of psychotic break… You know I was on so many different medications at one point…" She reached up putting her hand on Dakota's leg. "Still, I'm not trying to make excuses. You are right, I could have killed you, and no matter what I say now, or what my reasons are, you'd have still been dead and I would never have been able to forgive myself."

Dakota looked back at her, wanting to believe that Cassandra hadn't meant to kill her. She hoped that she could trust what Cassandra was saying this time. Cassandra knew that Dakota was looking for signs that she was lying or pretending to be sorry about something she wasn't. Cassandra withstood Dakota's inspection, her look completely open and honest. Dakota decided that either Cassandra was telling the truth, or she'd become a damned good actress in the last so many months.

"Okay," Dakota said again. "So the opportunity to work on this house really is exactly what you said, your apology."

"My crazy way of apologizing, yes," Cassandra said, smiling sadly.

Dakota blinked a couple of times, nodding as she tried to assimilate what Cassandra was saying. Cassandra could see that she was having a hard time believing her sincerity, and she couldn't blame her. Things with Dakota had gone so badly, and had been so violent and angry and dangerous that it was a wonder that neither of them had ended up dead. What Cassandra hadn't told Dakota was that she'd nearly killed herself by driving drunk and high at breakneck speeds in the Alps. She'd been trying to outrun the demons that had possessed her to do such a horrendous thing to Dakota.

"Is there any chance you'll ever be able to forgive me?" Cassandra asked, knowing she was really pushing her luck at this point.

229

Dakota smiled softly. "I'm working on this house, aren't I?"

The smile that lit Cassandra's face suddenly was almost painful for Dakota to see.

"And you're doing an amazing job," Cassandra said, nodding and smiling still.

Then she looked at Dakota. "Jazmine really does hate me, doesn't she?"

"She doesn't trust you."

Cassandra pressed her lips together in consternation. "I wouldn't trust me either," she said honestly.

"You wouldn't?" Dakota asked, looking surprised.

"No," Cassandra said, shaking her head, "because I think I'm in love with you, Dakota."

"Holy hell…" Dakota breathed.

"What the fuck!" Jazmine raged as she paced back and forth in front of their bed.

Dakota sat on their bed with her legs pulled up to her chest, watching Jazmine pace.

"This is exactly what I thought, this is it! Goddamn her!" Jazmine yelled, throwing her hands up in frustration. "I knew it! I knew it!"

Still Dakota made no comment, knowing that nothing she could say to Jazmine at that moment was going to be heard. She needed to wait for her to calm down.

"No, that's it, no… You're done, you're not going back there," Jazmine said then, standing with her hands on her hips and her feet wide apart.

"Why?" Dakota asked mildly.

"Are you fucking kidding me?" Jazmine asked looking stunned.

"No, I'm honestly asking you what you think has changed here," Dakota said, her tone slightly lower this time, indicating that she was doing her best to keep her cool.

"Didn't you just tell me that she admitted that she's in love with you?" Jazmine asked sarcastically.

Dakota's eyes narrowed slightly at Jazmine's tone, her lips twitching with the effort to not react solely to that.

"Jaz, I know you're upset," Dakota said evenly, "but watch your tone with me right now."

Jazmine stared back at Dakota, her mouth hanging slightly open at the rebuke. Dakota could see the play of emotions across Jazmine's face: shock, anger, assumption, rejection, and right back to anger.

"Whoa!" Dakota said. She held up a hand as she saw the fire in Jazmine's eyes suddenly, and her hands ball into fists. "Just stop and think for a minute, Jazmine… Think!" Dakota all but yelled.

When she could see that she wasn't getting through, Dakota got off the bed and walked over to where Jazmine stood. Reaching out she touched Jazmine's face and Jazmine stared up at her, her mouth still tight in anger.

"You want to be with her, right? That's why you want to stay with the job," Jazmine said, finally letting fly all of her concerns and fears. "You want her, you want that…"

231

"No!" Dakota said, raising her voice so she could be heard over Jazmine's ranting. "How many fucking ways do I have to say it?"

"Your actions speak for themselves," Jazmine practically spat.

"Yeah?" Dakota asked, sharply. "What do the actions of a raving lunatic say?"

"You think I'm a raving lunatic?" Jazmine asked hotly.

"I think you're acting like one right now."

"Because I don't want you to keep working for someone that wants to fuck you?" Jazmine countered.

Dakota gave a short derisive laugh. "Lots of women want to fuck me, Jazmine, that doesn't mean I'm going to do it."

"Well, this one has a big pocket book, so…" Jazmine said, her tone trailing off nastily.

Dakota looked like Jazmine had just slapped her. In truth she felt like she had. Jazmine could literally see the mask drop over Dakota's face, closing her completely off. Without another word, Dakota stepped back, walked around Jazmine to heading for their closet, and went inside and quietly closed the door.

Jazmine hadn't moved when Dakota walked out of the closet three minutes later. She now wore boots and a jacket. She picked up her keys off the dresser and pocketed her wallet, then walked out of the room.

For the next four hours, Jazmine told herself that she was completely justified in what she'd said. Multiple texts and calls to Dakota went unanswered. In hour five, Jazmine started to worry. Dakota wasn't drunk this time, but she was obviously upset. Jazmine started wondering if she should let the Falcos know what was happening. It took another half hour for her to draw up the courage to make that call. No matter how vindicated she felt about what she'd said, she knew that if something happened to Dakota as a result of her sharp tongue, the guilt would be on her head.

She reached out to Cody, too afraid to call Lyric or Savanna.

"Cody, it's Jazmine," she said when Cody answered her phone.

"What's up, Jaz?" Cody asked, glancing over at McKenna who was holding Ana.

"I'm a little worried about Dakota, have you seen her?" Jazmine asked.

On her end, Cody's brows furrowed. "No, why, what happened?"

"We kind of had a fight," Jazmine said.

"Okay…" Cody said her tone leading.

"Cassandra admitted to Dakota that she's in love with her today," Jazmine said, her voice tinged with anger.

"Well, we kinda figured there was an angle there," Cody said reasonably.

"Yeah, but for her to admit it and Dakota to still want to work for her…" Jazmine said her tone querulous. "It just sounded wrong to me, and I got mad…"

Cody closed her eyes on her end, she could tell by Jazmine's hedging and justifications that something had gone very wrong.

"What did you say to her?" She asked, her tone accusing now.

Lyric and Savanna both looked over at Cody sharply, hearing the tone in her voice.

"Jesus, Cody!" Jazmine exclaimed, as she started to feel the guilt starting to creep in to her heart.

"What did you fuckin' say, Jazmine?" Cody said sharply.

"I was really pissed off..." Jazmine said her tone tremulous now.

"And?" Cody bit out.

"And I said that Dakota wanted Cassandra because she had a big pocket book," Jazmine blurted out, trying to rush through it like it would lessen the impact.

Cody's mouth dropped open in shock, then she shook her head, her mouth contorting in a grimace of disgust.

"We'll take it from here," she said simply then hung up the phone.

"What happened?" Savanna asked the second Cody hung up the phone.

"Cassandra admitted to Dakota today that she's in love with her, and fucking Jazmine accused Dak of wanting Cassandra because of her money."

"Oh, Jesus..." Savanna said, looking worried instantly.

"Okay, start calling around see if we can locate her," Lyric said. "Cody, text her."

Dakota was driving at breakneck speeds, music pouring from the speakers in an attempt to drown out her thoughts. She was done, she was just done, was what kept running around in her head. She'd given the whole domesticity thing a try and this is what she got for it. *Fuck it!* she thought viciously as she slammed her foot down on the gas pedal. The Ferrari Berlinetta leapt forward. She'd dumped a lot of money into restoring the car, and had paid particular attention to the engine, giving it as much speed and power as it could handle.

Visions of time spent with Lyric in her garage working on the car flashed through her head. She shook her head, pushing the vision out. It was just replaced with pictures of baby Ana, or Cody, or... Savanna. Dakota closed her eyes for a moment, feeling a vicious stab of pain go through her heart. If she managed to kill herself this time, what would Savanna think? That she failed her? That Dakota had never really cared? That Dakota hadn't really appreciated the gesture of adopting her... Tears coated her eyes suddenly. *Damnit!* This was what fucking loving people got you, you couldn't even take the easy way out. *Son of a bitch!*

As if Savanna sensed Dakota thinking about her, Dakota's phone rang. She looked over to see on the display that it was Savanna. She'd ignored numerous phone calls from Lyric, Cody, McKenna, Jazmine... even Jet had tried calling. She didn't answer, but this was Savanna...

Sighing she touched the hands free on the phone.

"Yeah?" she answered, her voice completely toneless.

At her end, Savanna grimaced at hearing Dakota so far down.

"Dakota, honey?" Savanna said gently. "Honey, come home..." Lyric, who sat beside her, squeezed her hand. "Dakota, I know you can hear me... Please come home, babe, we just want to see you're okay."

"I'm okay," Dakota said automatically.

"I said we want to see you, Dakota," Savanna said, her voice still soft. "Please come home, honey."

Dakota didn't answer, she just grit her teeth in an effort to resist Savanna's soft entreaty.

"Dakota... Please honey..." Savanna said, her voice growing more worried. "You have to know that we love you and that we are here for you. We will take care of you, please honey, just come home."

It almost worked, she almost managed to shut her heart down and would hang up in a second. Then Savanna sniffled, and Dakota knew she was lost. Tears came instantly to her eyes. The woman that had become the mother she'd never really had was crying, and it was her fault.

"Okay," Dakota said, her voice affected by the tears in her throat. "I'm coming home."

"Okay," Savanna said, sounding relieved. "Now can you please slow down for me too?"

Dakota gave a short astonished laugh. "How did you..." she began to ask.

"I know Ferrari engines, Dakota, all my girls drive them," Savanna said, smiling through her tears.

Dakota smiled fondly, knowing Savanna included her as one of her "girls." It broke her heart a little more.

"I'm coming home, and I'll take it slow," Dakota told Savanna, willing to promise anything to get her mother to stop crying.

"Thank you, honey, we'll see you soon."

"Okay," Dakota said, nodding.

"Love you," Savanna said then.

"Love you too, Dakota replied, feeling her heart ache.

A half an hour later, the dark silver-gray Ferrari pulled up to the front of the Falco home. As she climbed out of the car, Dakota felt exhausted suddenly. As she rounded the front of the Ferrari the front door opened, and Savanna ran out to grab her up in a hug. Dakota held Savanna, burying her face in Savanna's long mahogany hair.

"Okay, honey... Okay..." Savanna said soothingly, her hands rubbing Dakota's back.

Lyric, Cody, and McKenna watched from behind them, all of the smiling. It still amazed them that tough little Dakota would crumple so easily for Savanna and no one else. Savanna was always the Falco ringer when it came to Dakota.

When Savanna finally let Dakota go, she took her hand and walked her into the house. The other three parted to let them pass. Savanna proceeded to sit Dakota down at the dinner table and holding both of her hands, she looked into Dakota's eyes.

"Before we worry about anything else," Savanna said. "When did you eat last?"

Dakota shook her head tiredly. "I'm not hungry," she said her voice reflecting her exhaustion.

Savanna's lips tightened in dismay. She glanced back at Lyric who stood behind where Dakota sat. Lyric nodded, gesturing with her head toward the spare bedroom. Savanna got the message and smiled, moving to stand.

"Okay, honey, let's get you to bed then, come on," Savanna said tugging Dakota back to her feet.

An hour later, Dakota was asleep in the guest bedroom. Cody and McKenna had gone back to their house, and Lyric and Savanna lay in their bed.

"What the hell was Jazmine thinking saying that to her?" Lyric asked, her tone indicating how crazy she thought that it was.

"Jazmine isn't near as confident as everyone thinks," Savanna said. "And I think that her stupid comment came from that place in her."

Lyric looked back at Savanna for a long minute. "You do realize that I'm not Cody, right?"

Savanna gave her a narrowed look. "I think I know you're not Cody, but I also know how smart you are, so I figure you'd get it."

"Sorry, babe, no psych degree here," Lyric said.

"Okay," Savanna said, settling closer to Lyric. "First of all, Jazmine is majorly indebted to Dakota, for the million she invested in the studio. Further, she's living in the house that Dakota bought and now Dakota is talking about paying for an expansion to the studio…"

"Okay…" Lyric said, nodding slowly. But she still didn't understand.

"What people say to you is never personal," Savanna said. "It's a reflection of their own experience of life."

"You're getting all psych-y on me again…" Lyric said with a grin.

"What Jazmine said to Dakota wasn't a reflection of what she thought of Dakota, it was a reflection of what she thought about herself."

Lyric looked back at her for a long moment, "So Jazmine saying that Dakota is only interested in Savanna because of her money, is really Jazmine saying that she feels like shit because she's living off of Dakota?"

"Exactly!" Savanna said, nodding.

"Hmmm," Lyric murmured, "well, that really kind of backfired on her, didn't it?"

"When someone isn't recognizing their own issues, it really does tend to do that."

"So are we going to hate her or not...?" Lyric asked.

"Dakota loves her," Savanna said. "So no, we're not going to hate her. We're going to help, that's what we're going to do."

"Yes, ma'am," Lyric said, grinning.

***

After three days, Harley finally started feeling somewhat better. Shiloh was there every step of the way. After multiple steam showers when the congestion kicked in, Shiloh quickly learned why Harley had all the brown bottles in the medicine cabinet, they were essential oils. She used eucalyptus with the steam to help clear her head. Shiloh learned to brew tea from a few different herbs and roots, one of which was ginger. She even learned to make cough syrup out of various roots, cinnamon, honey, and fresh ginger. It was definitely a different experience.

The fourth morning, she woke with Shiloh lying next to her as she had for the last three days. Breathing in the smell of the eucalyptus and lavender vaporizer next to the bed, Harley smiled. Shiloh had been a champion when it came to learning how to take care of her without medications. Looking at Shiloh as she slept, Harley couldn't help but feel completely moved by everything Shiloh had done for her. What's more, she hadn't treated her like she was crazy for not just popping a few pills. She'd been beyond attentive, spending hours on end changing cloths on her forehead and back to keep her cool. She'd been sitting up and talking whenever Harley was feeling up to it or watching L Word with her. She'd made chicken soup from scratch and any number of batches of tea for her. She'd been absolutely amazing.

She touched Shiloh's cheek, her look so tender that when Shiloh opened her eyes, she felt her breath catch in her throat. Their eyes met and neither could tear themselves away. Harley gently brushed back her hair, her eyes searching Shiloh's.

"Thank you for taking care of me, Shy…" Harley said softly.

"You don't have to thank me, Harley. I did it because I care about you."

"Then thank you for caring about me enough to take care of me," Harley said, her eyes sparkling with emotion.

Shiloh smiled softly. "How are you feeling this morning?"

"Better," Harley said. "Still kind of congested though."

"Do you want to do a shower to help?" Shiloh asked.

"Yeah I think I will," Harley said, nodding.

A half an hour later Harley climbed out of the shower, wrapped herself in a towel, and walked into the bedroom. Dropping the towel, she climbed back into bed, having exhausted herself with a coughing fit in the shower.

Shiloh came into the bedroom a few minutes later, having heard the shower turn off. She saw Harley lying on her stomach. Her back was bare, and her arms were around the pillow under her head. Once again, Shiloh was struck by the sheer sexiness of that picture. She was also reminded of the tattoo that extended two feet down her back.

Shiloh sat down on the bed next to where Harley lay. Harley immediately sensed her there, and moved to put her head in Shiloh's lap, her arms encircling Shiloh's hips like they had been around the pillow previously. Shiloh smiled fondly and slid her fingers through her hair, her nails grazing Harley's scalp.

Harley moaned in pleasure. "That feels so good..."

"Good," Shiloh said, smiling, continuing her ministrations.

Eventually she moved her hands to Harley's back, smoothing over her skin, and once again grazing her nails over Harley's bare skin.

"Don't ever cut your nails... ever..." Harley murmured.

Shiloh laughed softly. "Okay, got it."

Harley sighed happily, turning her head to nuzzle Shiloh's abdomen affectionately. Shiloh bit her lip, enjoying Harley's closeness thoroughly.

"Can I ask you a question?" Shiloh said at one point.

"Mmmhmm," Harley murmured, her head still against Shiloh's stomach.

"What do these mean?" she asked, touching the tattoos on Harley's back.

"They're Chinese," Harley said. "The red one represents love, the orange hope, the yellow joy, the green is for nature, the blue is strength, and the purple is courage."

Shiloh smiled, smoothing her hand over the symbols. "They all sound like you."

"That's supposed to be the idea," Harley said, grinning.

"I didn't even know you had tattoos."

"Those aren't the only ones I have," Harley said, grinning.

"Where are the others?"

"Got one on each ankle, one on my right hip, and one over my left breast."

"Wow," Shiloh said, "what do they look like?"

"You can see the ankle ones, but the other two... Well..."

"Well what?" Shiloh asked when Harley's voice trailed off.

"Those are a bit more intimate."

"Oh," Shiloh said, biting her lip and grinning.

"So when you decide to stop being straight, we can talk about those two," Harley said, lifting her head to wink at Shiloh.

"I see," Shiloh said, her look narrowed. "Okay, let's see the ankles."

Harley shifted her feet under the covers and stuck one foot out. Shiloh had to crane her neck to see it. It was two rainbow-colored lightning bolts with the word "Pride" in black script between them.

"That's cool," she said, smiling. "And the other one?"

Harley did the same with the other foot. That tattoo was the classic Harley Davidson logo in black, orange, and white.

"Guess that gives 'identifying tattoos' a whole new meaning, huh?" Shiloh asked, grinning.

Harley chuckled. "Yep."

"Don't they hurt to get?" Shiloh asked.

"Some spots hurt more than others, but it's not super painful, more jarring than anything else."

"Still, I'd be too chicken to get *one*," Shiloh said. "Let alone, what? Like ten."

Harley grinned. "Yeah, like ten."

"Are you going to get more?" Shiloh asked.

Harley shrugged. "Don't know till I decide I want one, so… Hard to say."

"But for the most part no one can see them," Shiloh said.

"I'm stealth like that, yeah," Harley said smiling mischievously.

"Why?" Shiloh asked.

Harley shrugged. "I guess cause of my dad."

"He doesn't like tattoos?" Shiloh asked.

"He has tons of them," Harley told her. "I don't want people judging me because of my ink, like they do him."

"Oh," Shiloh said, nodding, "I see."

She shook her head then, there were so many things about Harley that weren't what they seemed. She was a brilliant and extremely dedicated programmer, but seemed so easy and free in her life. She had a wild look about her, but was the sweetest human being Shiloh had ever encountered.

"You really do like to surprise people, don't you?" Shiloh asked.

Harley gave an impish grin, her blue eye sparkling.

"I'll take that as a yes," Shiloh said, nodding. "Okay, what can I get you to eat?"

"I'm okay, not really hungry."

"Tough," Shiloh said. "You're going to eat something, even if it's toast."

Harley gave her a baleful look, but her grin seconds later spoiled it. "Fine," she said, sighing.

"I need to go shopping today, we're running out of stuff," Shiloh said offhandedly as she got up.

"Cool, we can do that," Harley said, nodding.

"You're still sick," Shiloh said.

"I could do with a little bit of time out of this house."

Shiloh gave her a narrowed assessing look. "We'll see."

In the end, Shiloh allowed Harley to drive them to the local market. Shiloh could tell that Harley was still feeling sick, because she was driving the speed limit and the volume of the music in the car was really low.

"You really still don't feel great, do you?" Shiloh commented.

"Uh-uh," Harley murmured. "But I needed to get up and move around a bit. I can't stand lying in bed all that time."

Shiloh nodded. "I know, that's why I allowed this little trip," she said with a wink.

"Ah," Harley said her grin wry.

"So do you get sick often?" Shiloh asked.

"No, almost never, actually," Harley said. "I was a bit run down, that's probably why it hit me."

Shiloh nodded, pressing her lips together to keep from saying something about the person who'd run her down. Harley caught the look, a narrowed her eyes slightly, knowing Shiloh wanted to say something but didn't.

"So can I ask why you don't take medicine?" Shiloh asked after a couple of minutes.

"It's mostly because of my dad, I mean, that's how it started anyway," Harley said, her thumbnail rubbing at the seam of her jeans.

"Why?" Shiloh asked, wanting to know more about how Harley's mind worked.

"Well, remember the night of the infamous kiss?" Harley said, grinning.

"Who could forget that?" Shiloh said, smiling widely.

"Well, I don't know if you remember that I was really tired that night…"

"I remember, you actually fell asleep at one point," Shiloh said.

"Yeah…" Harley said, grinning. "Well, it was because the day before that my dad had been shot on the job, and I'd spent the whole day and night in the hospital with him and my mom. My mom completely falls apart when my dad is hurt, she's really dependent on him…"

Her voice trailed off for a moment, Shiloh could tell there was more to that story, but she didn't want to get Harley off track by asking, so she mentally filed it away for a later time.

"Anyway, he was okay, but he was in a lot of pain and he started taking painkillers and became addicted to them. That summer really sucked. We found out that he has an addictive personality, which work-wise is great, but not so much with things like narcotic painkillers. He almost lost his job and things were a real mess during that time. So I decided then that I wasn't going to get attached to any kind of medication."

"In case you have an addictive personality too?" Shiloh asked.

"Oh, I do, I already know that."

Shiloh nodded, her look contemplative.

"What?" Harley said, grinning.

Shiloh shook her head. "I guess that makes sense. It still surprises me… But it does explain a couple of things."

"Like?" Harley asked, her tone amused.

"Like a week and a half of needing headphones," Shiloh said, her look pointed.

Harley grimaced. "I'm sorry about that."

"Which part?" Shiloh asked.

Harley was obviously taken back by the question, and narrowed her eyes slightly.

"What did I miss?" she asked.

Shiloh looked contrite immediately. The last thing she'd wanted to do was to complain about Harley's girlfriend.

"Nothing, it's not important," Shiloh said, shaking her head.

"Shy, if it's bugging you, it's important," Harley said, reaching over touch Shiloh's hand.

"You're addicted to her, aren't you?" Shiloh said evenly.

Harley was surprised by the question, but looked considering. Finally, she nodded.

"I guess I was in a way," she said, "but probably not in the way you think."

"What way do you think I'm assuming?" Shiloh asked.

"I think you mean that I'm addicted to her as a person."

Shiloh looked back at her and shook her head. "No, I know you're not, because you didn't bat an eyelash when she wasn't there anymore."

Harley nodded. "Okay, so maybe you did know what I meant," she said, grinning.

"You meant the sex," Shiloh said.

Harley looked contrite, but nodded.

"It doesn't bother you that she just left like that? When you were sick?" Shiloh asked.

Harley shook her head dismissively.

"It doesn't make you mad?" Shiloh asked persistently.

"Why should it?" Harley asked, pulling into the parking lot at the store.

"Because it was kind of a fucked up thing to do…" Shiloh said, her tone upset.

Harley pulled into a parking space, turned off the car and turned to Shiloh, taking both of her hands in hers.

"The person who mattered was the person who didn't leave, Shy."

Shiloh had no idea how to take what she'd just said. She wanted to ask questions, but didn't know what to ask and if she'd like the answers anyway. She nodded, blowing her breath out.

They got out of the car and did the shopping they needed to do. A half an hour they were on their way back home.

"Can I ask you a question?" Shiloh said.

"Of course," Harley said.

"Why did you kiss me that night?"

Harley smiled. "Because you wanted me to," she answered simply.

Shiloh's eyes widened. "How did you know that?"

Harley grinned. "I saw it in your eyes."

Shiloh looked back at her shocked, but then nodded.

"So you aren't in love with Roslynn," she said then. "Right?"

"Right," Harley said, surprised in the change of topic.

"Have you ever been in love?"

"Once," Harley said, smiling fondly.

"Really?" Shiloh asked. "Who? Wait, not Devin…"

"No," Harley said, chuckling.

"It was a woman right?" Shiloh asked. "I mean, you've never dated men, have you? Or have you?"

"No… no men," Harley said, shaking her head vehemently. "Lots of women, but no men."

"So did you know you were gay in high school?" Shiloh asked.

"Not really, no," Harley said. "I just knew I was never interested in guys."

"But then you kissed me."

"And that was the end of my high school career," Harley said, grinning.

Shiloh bit her lip, wincing at the reminder. "I've apologized for that, right?"

Harley chuckled. "Yes, you've apologized for that, Shy, more than."

Shiloh nodded, looking relieved.

They arrived home and carried the bags inside. Even though Harley was still sick, she insisted on carrying in the bags herself. Shiloh made herself busy putting things away. Then she told Harley to get herself back upstairs and back into bed to rest for the remainder of the day. Harley grinned at being ordered to bed like a child, but did as she was told.

Shiloh walked into the bedroom a little while later, finding Harley lying in bed on her side. She'd taken the time to take off her jeans and her boots, but that was it. Shiloh moved to sit down next to Harley on the bed, resting her back against the headboard, as she had for days now. And as she had for as long, Harley moved close to her, putting her arm over Shiloh's legs. Shiloh moved her hands through Harley's hair and Harley sighed.

Shiloh's mind was alive with questions and thoughts. Harley could sense it, and after a few minutes, she looked up at Shiloh.

"What's up?" Harley asked.

Shiloh looked down at her, surprise evident on her face.

"How did you…" Shiloh started to ask.

"You're practically vibrating, Shy," Harley said, grinning as she sat up. "I can tell your mind is going. I just wondered if it was anything you wanted to talk about."

"You're supposed to be resting," Shiloh said.

Harley looked back at her knowing she was being evasive. "I'm resting. I'm sitting here, not running a marathon."

Shiloh blew her breath out, shaking her head. "I'm not sure I even know what's going on in my head right now."

"So just talk and hopefully things will get clearer," Harley said.

Shiloh grimaced. "Or a really big mess, really fast."

"Okay, what's that mean?" Harley asked, turning to look at Shiloh, her eyes searching.

"It just means that some things are sometimes better not discussed," Shiloh said.

"That's never been my experience," Harley said. "Things not discussed tend to make things fester and get blown completely out of proportion in your own head."

Shiloh looked back at Harley for a long moment, just shaking her head.

Harley watched Shiloh, knowing that she was wrestling with something. She thought she knew what it was.

"Devin said that she thinks you're in love with me," Harley said unexpectedly, causing Shiloh's eyes to widen. "Is she wrong?"

Shiloh blinked a couple of times, swallowing convulsively. She looked almost terrified by the question, and Harley felt like she'd managed to back her into a corner. She hadn't meant to.

"Would it help," Harley said, her look direct, "if I told you that the one woman I've ever loved was you?"

Shiloh looked stunned, her mouth opened in shock, her eyes widened. Then she grimaced sadly. "That really makes me feel worse," she said. "Harley... I had no idea..."

250

"There's no way you could have," Harley said. "I never said anything and I would never have even now, but…"

"But what?" Shiloh asked.

"I need you to answer my question, Shy," Harley said seriously.

Shiloh finally nodded. "Yes, Devin is right. I am in love with you."

"And why is that hard for you to say?"

"Because I'm afraid," Shiloh said simply. "Because I've never felt like this for anyone and I'm not sure what to do, or say… But mostly, I'm afraid that I have no idea how you feel about me now."

"You have no idea how I feel about you?" Harley asked in disbelief.

Shiloh heard Harley's tone but didn't fully understand. She suddenly felt like she'd missed something important.

"Shy, who do you work for?" Harley asked.

"The Department of Justice," Shiloh said. Then at Harley's narrowed look, she added, "For you."

"And who got you that job?"

"You."

And where are you living?"

"With you," Shiloh said.

"And who remembered your birthday?"

"You," Shiloh said, sighing.

"Do you need a billboard?" Harley asked, grinning.

"Shut up!" Shiloh said, laughing.

Harley moved closer to her. "I was in love with you in high school, and you broke my heart, but I never stopped loving you."

The hope that bloomed on Shiloh's face was like bright warm sunshine.

"Are you saying...?" Shiloh began, not daring to hope.

"I'm saying that I love you, Shy," Harley said seriously. "And I always have."

"And you just thought you'd tell me now?" Shiloh said, her tone slightly chiding.

Harley stared openmouthed at her for a moment. "Until Devin told me that you were in love with me and that I shouldn't be stupid, I had no idea if you were just a good friend, of if you wanted more."

"You had a woman in your bed for the last week and a half before you got sick!" Shiloh exclaimed in her defense.

"Yeah, just not the woman I really wanted in my bed," Harley said. "Until I got sick."

Shiloh looked back at her then, her eyes sparkling mischievously.

"And you still are sick," she said. "And you should be resting..."

"Well, there's a matter that needs to be settled first," Harley said, her tone serious.

"What matter is that?" Shiloh asked, worried about Harley's change in tone.

Without a word, Harley moved closer, her lips hovering just above Shiloh's. Shiloh felt her breath catch in her throat. Her breathing became shallow as she anticipated the kiss, but Harley didn't kiss her, she kept her lips right where they were. Shiloh could feel Harley's breath on her cheek, then Harley's hands slid around her waist, grasping at her gently. Shiloh felt her pulse quicken and, moving another inch closer to Harley, she felt her lips brush her cheek, and her hands press her body closer.

Shiloh's hands were trembling as she put her hands against Harley's chest, her right hand grasping at Harley's tank top. Harley's lips grazed her lips and Shiloh moaned softly when they didn't stay. Her fingers flexed against Harley's exposed skin. She felt Harley smile slightly and tighten her hands against her waist. Then one hand moved up her back to hold the back of her neck as Harley pulled back looking down into her eyes.

"Do you want me, Shy?" Harley whispered breathlessly.

"Yes," Shiloh breathed instantly.

Harley's lips touched her softly. It wasn't a full kiss, it felt more like a promise of a kiss. Then Harley moved back, wetting her lips as she looked down at Shiloh.

"I think we should go out," she said.

"What?" Shiloh asked, her voice breathless with desire. Her utter confusion was written all over her face.

Harley grinned. "On a date," she said. "I think we should go out on a date."

Shiloh opened her mouth to tell Harley she was insane, but she could see the sincerity in Harley's eyes. It made her stop for a second.

"Why?" Shiloh asked.

"Because I want to do this right with you," Harley said. "I want to romance you, show you what this will be like and then if you still want me... Well, then we'll go there."

"Can't just go there now and go out later, huh?" Shiloh asked her voice tinged with humor.

Harley bit her lower lip, her blue eyes shining with the most incredible look of love Shiloh had ever seen. Shiloh was willing to do anything to keep that look on her and no one else.

"Okay, a date, sure, let's go on a date… Can we do it tomorrow?"

Harley laughed at her rushed speech.

"Yes, we can do it tomorrow night," Harley said, smiling.

"Good," Shiloh said. "'Cause I'm not sure how many more cold showers I can take!"

Harley laughed out loud at that one.

Chapter 9

Dakota spent two days sleeping, texting her foreman to tell him she wouldn't be on the site for a few days. When she emerged from the extra bedroom, she spent hours playing with Ana, and when Ana was asleep she'd sit in the backyard smoking. Savanna watched Dakota from the window, wanting to talk to her, but knowing that she shouldn't push too hard. She knew that Dakota would say something when she was ready to. She'd at least make an end road.

That end road came late in the afternoon on the third day at the Falco home. Savanna had just gotten back from the home she ran for LGBT kids. She'd stopped at the grocery store and was carrying the bags into the house. Dakota saw and jumped up to help, stubbing out her cigarette. When all of the bags had been brought in, Savanna expected Dakota to disappear, but she didn't. She stayed in the kitchen, helping Savanna put things away. Savanna knew it was a sign.

"So how are you, honey?" Savanna asked as Dakota came out of the pantry.

Dakota stopped in the pantry doorway, leaning against the door-jamb looking like she was trying to decide how she was. Finally, she blew her breath out.

"I dunno," she said, shaking her head. "I just feel like… Like I'm done, ya know?"

"Done?" Savanna repeated.

"Yeah," Dakota said. "I just can't keep doing this…"

"What part of this, Dakota?" Savanna asked warily.

Dakota's face clouded with tumult. "I'm not sure, maybe all of it. I don't know."

"Does that include us?" Savanna asked her look expectant.

Dakota took longer to answer, her eyes dropping from Savanna's. "I don't know, maybe."

Savanna looked back at Dakota shocked by her statement. Shocked and hurt.

"That's not how this works, Dakota," Savanna said, her tone slightly sharp. Dakota heard it and looked surprised. "You don't just get to toss us aside when you're done with us," Savanna said, feeling anger and burning tears sting her eyes.

Shaking her head knowing she was about to burst into tears, Savanna left the room. She went upstairs to her bedroom lay down on the bed to cry. She heard the front door open and close and then heard Dakota's car start. She cried harder, knowing that she might have done irreparable damage to her relationship with Dakota, but her anger at Dakota's casual mention of being 'done' with them had hurt her to the core. They'd opened their hearts to Dakota and she'd seemed so very happy with them. But at the first sign of trouble, she ran? That wasn't right! Savanna's heart ached painfully. She knew that Dakota was reacting like so many street kids would, but she'd put so much of her heart into the girl, and for her to just turn like that… It hurt so much.

Lyric found her still lying on the bed two hours later. She immediately strode over to the bed and kneeled in front of where Savanna lay.

"What's wrong? What happened?" Lyric asked, her tone alarmed and worried at the same time.

Fresh tears started then as Savanna thought about having to tell Lyric what Dakota had said. Lyric had spent so much time with Dakota, rebuilding the car, talking to her about different things, trying to give Dakota the role model she'd needed for years. In Savanna's mind, Dakota was throwing that back in their faces and it made her heart hurt all over again.

On the job site the following day, Dakota sat smoking on the outside stairs. She remotely heard the sound of skill saws, hammering, and power tools all around her. Music played on her phone as loud as the phone would go. She sat with her elbows on her knees, her head down, and no one bothered her. No one except Cassandra. She recognized Dakota's dark, forbidding visage. She'd seen it a number of times over the two years they'd been together.

"What's wrong?" Cassandra asked, sitting on the stair below Dakota's feet.

"Nothing I want to talk about," Dakota said flatly, taking another long drag off her cigarette.

"Is there anything I can do?" Cassandra asked.

Dakota's eyes narrowed. "I think you've done quite enough."

Cassandra's head came up slightly, realizing this was apparently about Jazmine.

"You had a fight with Jazmine?" Cassandra asked.

"Cass... don't, I mean it."

"Yes, yes, I know," Cassandra said, rolling her eyes. "I'm not allowed to talk to you about her. I understand that, but maybe I can help."

"How?" Dakota asked looking cynical.

"I don't know, by being a sounding board for you, or something…" Cassandra said shrugging helplessly.

Dakota didn't answer. She simply sat and smoked until the cigarette was down to a nub, and then she lit another one.

"Chain smoking, always healthy," Cassandra commented. Seeing that Dakota didn't even crack a smile, she sighed heavily. "So Jazmine was angry about what I told you…"

"Angry I expected," Dakota said.

"What didn't you expect?"

Dakota didn't answer, she started to bounce her knee in agitation.

"Did she kick you out?" Cassandra asked.

"Is that hope I hear in your voice?" Dakota countered darkly.

Cassandra pressed her lips together, blowing her breath out through her nose. "I'm sorry, it probably was, but the question remains…"

"I left," Dakota said, her tone low. "She can't kick me out, it's my house."

"Oh yes, I'd heard you sold the Bugatti," Cassandra said, grinning. "And made the investment I didn't."

Dakota nodded.

"But you apparently also invested in some real estate, which was wise too."

"Does that surprise you?" Dakota asked.

"No, it doesn't," Cassandra said. "I should have let you do more with all of this," she said, gesturing to the house and meaning real estate in general.

Dakota was silent.

"Is there anything I can do?" Cassandra asked tentatively.

Dakota narrowed her eyes. "Like what?"

Cassandra blinked a couple of times, having not expected that question.

"To help…" Cassandra finally said.

Dakota blew her breath out through her nose, her lips twisting in a sardonic grin.

"I get that you think you love me, Cass, but it's never going to happen, okay?" Dakota said her voice more gentle than Cassandra would have expected it to be.

Cassandra drew in a deep breath, nodding as she expelled it. "You really love her."

"Like a complete dumbfuck, yeah," Dakota said.

Cassandra grinned at Dakota's term. Leave it to Dakota to be so cynical, even when in love. She nodded then, blowing her breath out again.

"You know," Dakota said, "the simple fact that you were willing to tell me you were in love with me, says something."

"What does it say?" Cassandra asked, looking somewhat defeated.

"It says that you're open to love," Dakota said. "And that's not something I think you ever were before."

"Neither were you," Cassandra replied her look pointed.

Dakota blew her breath out, nodding. "I know."

"I heard that you're part of a family now, is that true?" Cassandra asked.

Dakota grimaced, emotional pain lancing across her features as she nodded.

"What is it?" Cassandra asked. She'd never seen pain like that in Dakota before.

"Nothing…" Dakota said, shaking her head, as she did her best to fight back the tears that wanted to come out.

She knew that she'd hurt Savanna the day before at the house, and she was terrified that she'd never be able to mend that hurt. She'd slept in her car the night before, and even doing that felt like a betrayal of everything Lyric and Savanna had done for her. It made her feel sick.

As if thinking about them had conjured her, Dakota looked up and saw Lyric standing at the end of the walkway, on the sidewalk, looking at her. Cassandra saw Dakota's look and followed her line of sight to Lyric. She stood up and walked up the stairs into the house, touching Dakota on the shoulder as she walked past her. Dakota stood up. She wasn't sure what Lyric was doing there, but felt like she should be standing for whatever was about to happen.

Lyric looked back at her for a long moment, and then started to walk toward her. Dakota stepped down the two steps to put her on level ground. Her body was tense. She wouldn't blame Lyric for hitting her, she deserved whatever was coming. She knew that. She was stunned when Lyric took her into her arms immediately, hugging her fiercely.

"You're not leaving our family, Dakota," Lyric told her, her voice gruff. "So you can get that stupid fucking thought out of your head right now."

Dakota felt tears stinging her eyes, as she nodded against Lyric's shoulder.

"I'm sorry," Dakota said when Lyric stepped back.

Dakota looked up and saw that Savanna was now standing at the end of the walk, her arms crossed in front of her. Dakota strode over to her. She stood in front of her with her head lowered.

"I'm sorry, Savanna… I didn't mean what I said, I just…" Dakota said tearfully.

"You just don't know how to be in a family," Savanna said, "and we need to teach you that."

With that, Savanna put her arms around her. Dakota responded by throwing her arms around Savanna and bursting into fresh tears. Lyric watched her wife and her daughter, smiling with tears in her eyes.

Cassandra watched the scene from the house and felt a sense of loss; she knew she had only had the slimmest chance of getting Dakota back. With people like this to support her, the girl was truly lost to her. Part of her was happy for Dakota, however, and it was that part of her that she decided to concentrate on.

Dakota was smoking in the backyard when Jazmine arrived at the Falco home. Savanna answered the door, and opened her arms to the other woman seeing how unhappy she looked. They had talked on the phone a few times, and Savanna had told her what her thoughts were on the matter. Jazmine had taken it all in and had thought about little else for the last three days.

Without a word, Jazmine walked over to the sliding glass door, looking out to where Dakota sat. Her heart beat hard in her chest. She knew that this conversation could go well, or terribly wrong. She was terrified.

"Just stay calm," Savanna told Jazmine. "No matter what she says to you, remember she had a right to be angry about what you said. So don't try to justify it, it will only piss her off again, okay?"

Jazmine took a deep breath, nodding, knowing that Savanna was right. She'd regretted her statement moments after it was out of her mouth. She'd now had days to see how very wrong she'd been. She just had to manage to stay calm enough to tell Dakota everything that had been in her head.

She opened the sliding glass door and stepped out. Dakota glanced back, blinking once when she realized who it was, her face expressionless. Then she turned her head forward again.

"Can we talk?" Jazmine asked softly.

Dakota didn't answer for a long moment. Finally, she gestured to the chair next to where she sat. Jazmine sat down looking at Dakota's face and seeing that she was still hurting from what had happened between them. It broke her heart a little bit more.

"Dakota," Jazmine began softly. "I'm so sorry for what I said to you. It was incredibly stupid and thoughtless and it really wasn't directed at you."

Dakota raised an eyebrow. Her blue eyes flicked to Jazmine as she took a long drag on her cigarette.

"Let me explain, okay?" Jazmine said her voice beseeching.

Dakota nodded slowly, her look closed.

"When I said that you were more interested in Cassandra's money, I really wasn't talking about you… I mean, God, I know how not about money you really are… You've been so incredibly generous with me and I think that what I said was more a reflection about how I felt about taking so much from you without giving back… You know? I just had all these feelings of inadequacy; I was never able to give you as much as you gave and I just… I guess I let it get all screwed up in my head and I threw it out at you… And you didn't deserve that… And I understand if I've ruined everything, but I love you so much and I just… I needed to tell you this, and tell you how sorry I am…" She looked down at her hands, tears from her eyes dropping on them.

She was afraid to look at Dakota, afraid that she'd see the ice cold mask she'd seen the night Dakota had left. Her heart was breaking all over again for what she may have lost. She knew without a doubt that if she truly lost Dakota, it was all her own fault.

She heard Dakota blow her breath out slowly.

"You said you know I'm not about money," Dakota said, her tone even.

Jazmine looked up at her, nodding her head.

"But you think that you need to give me money to keep me," Dakota said then.

Jazmine winced at the inference. She hadn't thought about it that way before. She thought about it now.

"I guess money is just the easiest way to define things," Jazmine said. "Whether I'm doing my share in the relationship."

Dakota nodded slowly thinking about what Jazmine had just said.

"Do you have any idea how valuable love is?" Dakota asked her.

Jazmine shook her head slowly.

"And do you have any idea how little of it I've had in my life up until I had you?" Dakota asked then.

Jazmine's tears started again as she shook her head.

"That's what you gave me, Jaz," Dakota told her. "And that was worth so much more to me than fucking money ever could be."

Jazmine closed her eyes, blowing her breath out as she felt the stab of pain in her heart. Dakota was talking in past tenses and she knew she'd lost her. She wrapped her arms around herself and bent forward, taking short gasping breaths.

Suddenly Dakota was there, kneeling in front of her, looking up at her.

"Do you love me, Jaz?" she asked softly.

"Yes," Jazmine said breathlessly.

"And do you believe that I love you?" Dakota asked then, her voice serious.

"Yes," Jazmine said, nodding, tears still sliding down her cheeks.

Dakota stood, taking Jazmine in her arms as she did, and Jazmine wrapped her arms around Dakota's waist crying in earnest.

"Can I come home now?" Dakota asked, grinning against Jazmine's hair.

"Please?" Jazmine asked.

Dakota chuckled.

Savanna watched from the kitchen window, her heart swelling seeing her girl happy again.

***

It was Shiloh and Harley's date night and Shiloh dressed with care. She wore a teal blouse with an empire waist and a lace up neckline, exposing a decent amount of cleavage. She also wore a black hi-low skirt; the front was short, and back was sheer black that fell to her knees. She added black heels. She took her time with her makeup, making sure it accentuated her eyes and made her skin absolutely glow, although she was sure excitement was doing that too. She took her time to curl and style her hair so it fell in silky waves. As she looked in the mirror at the finished product, she was pleased.

She walked downstairs and saw Harley was in the kitchen. Once again, she was completely taken aback by Harley's attire. She wore black pants that fit her snugly but perfectly, black dress boots and a sapphire-blue dress shirt left open at the throat. Around her neck, she wore a silver flat linked chain and her usual riot of earrings and rings on her fingers. Instead of her usual thick black leather-banded watch, she wore a sleek silver Movado watch with a sapphire-blue face. Over the shirt she wore a black tailored jacket that was a combination of formal and casual, with leather accents on the lapels and pockets. She wore eyeliner and a touch of mascara and just a little color on her cheeks and lips. She looked absolutely amazing.

"Oh, I think I got the hotter look…" Shiloh breathed, her eyes reflecting her awe at Harley's appearance.

Harley smiled, her eyes twinkling as she turned and picked up a bouquet of flowers. She walked over to hand them to Shiloh. She leaned down as she did whispering in Shiloh's ear.

"And I think you look much hotter," she said. Her eyes swept over Shiloh again. "You look amazing, Shy," she said her tone impressed.

Shiloh bit her lip, smiling as she smelled the flowers.

"These are beautiful," Shiloh said. "When did you have time to do this?"

Harley grinned. "I have my ways…"

"I see," Shiloh said, smiling.

"Shall we?" Harley asked, gesturing toward the garage.

Once in the car, Harley drove them to Santa Monica, toward the pier. She led Shiloh to a restaurant near the pier called The Lobster. It had beautiful views of the ocean and Santa Monica Pier. Shiloh was very impressed with Harley's excellent taste.

They had appetizers, dinner, wine, dessert, all the while talking about whatever occurred to them at the time. Shiloh had known that Harley was an engaging conversationalist but she was still pleasantly surprised by Harley's wit and intelligence during their dinner.

"So how did you get into computers?" Shiloh asked at one point.

By this time they'd taken their drinks out to the terrace where Harley could smoke. They were sitting at a small table across from each other. Shiloh couldn't help but notice how Harley's eyes sparkled in the setting sun.

"I got into them in high school, really," Harley said. "Remember Mr. Saran? He was the most incredible teacher…"

"The computer lab guy," Shiloh said, nodding, remembering the man with the glasses and the pocket protector, the classic geek.

"Yeah, he was really smart, and he knew so much about computers… I would sit and talk to him for hours and he's the one who talked to me about programming. He showed me how to work in C Sharp when it was getting more popular and I loved it…" Harley said, smiling widely and Shiloh could see the joy in her eyes.

"I can see that," Shiloh said, smiling brightly.

"I got really into it in my junior year, and then in my senior year I just got better and better. I knew what I wanted to do then. I had applied for the scholarship to MIT, before…you know… All that stuff happened."

Shiloh grimaced, nodding.

"Fortunately I'd gotten the award of the scholarship before I got kicked out, and as long as I was able to pass the GED they didn't care about what had happened."

"And I'm sure you passed the GED with both eyes closed," Shiloh said grinning.

"Oh yeah," Harley said, rolling her eyes. "So friggin' easy."

Shiloh shook her head, knowing it would have been for Harley, since what most kids didn't pass was the algebra portion of the test. Harley could do algebra in her sleep!

"So what about you?" Harley asked then. "What happened for you after high school?"

"I went to business school," Shiloh said. "My dad wanted me to work for his church."

"And how'd that go?" Harley asked.

"It was okay, at first, I just did whatever they wanted in those days."

Harley nodded, remembering that well.

"You do know that it wasn't me that told my dad about the kiss, don't you?" Shiloh said then, addressing her biggest concern.

"Didn't matter to me if it was you or not," Harley said, her look completely honest.

"It matters to me, Harley," Shiloh said, reaching out to touch Harley's hand. "I need you to know that it wasn't me that tried to get you kicked out. It was my best friend, Kim."

"Oh, I remember that one for sure," Harley said, her look pointed.

Shiloh tilted her head slightly, giving Harley a narrowed look. "What does that mean?" she asked.

"'Cause she tried to come at me."

"At you?" Shiloh asked.

"On to me," Harley replied, with a shrug.

"When?" Shiloh asked her tone shocked.

"Right about the time I was tutoring you," Harley said.

"Are you serious?" Shiloh asked, stunned.

"Yeah…" Harley said, grinning. "I guess she didn't tell your dad that part, huh?"

"No, no she didn't," Shiloh said, her look irritated. "That little bitch!"

Harley laughed out loud at her exclamation. "Guess she didn't tell you either?"

"No! She acted like you were white untouchable trash…" She thought back to the things that Kim used to say about Harley. "Oh my God, she wanted you and that's why she talked like that…"

Harley pressed her lips together, her blue eyes sparkling.

"What?" Shiloh asked.

"She came over to try and console me when I got kicked out," Harley said. "Like really console me…"

"Wow…" Shiloh said, her voice sharp. "She tried to ruin your life and then actually tried to screw you literally… never spoken to her again after I found out she was who told my dad about you and me, so…"

"Really?" Harley said, surprised by that statement.

"Really! I wouldn't forgive her for that. I told her that I was confused about the kiss and she made me out to be crazy. Little did I know she was making a play for you instead. What a little…"

"Doesn't matter now, does it?" Harley asked.

"No, it doesn't," Shiloh said, biting her lip and looking over at Harley. "What matters is that I'm here with you now."

Harley grinned, nodding. "And I'm really glad you are," she said, her blue eyes looking directly into Shiloh's eyes.

They talked for a while longer, and then decided that they'd go to The Club to round out their evening.

Walking into The Club with Harley as her date was a very different experience. Harley held her hand and led her over to the group's table. Everyone knew they were on an official date and were very happy.

"Now this is the right of it!" Quinn said, hugging Shiloh and kissing her on the cheek.

Shiloh smiled shyly, the red-haired Irishwoman was always kind to her, and she found it very sweet.

"Happy for you two," Devin said, hugging Shiloh. "Hold on to her with both hands," she whispered in Shiloh's ear, making her smile widely.

"I'll try," Shiloh said.

The rest of the group was also full of congratulations and smiles. Harley was extremely attentive the entire evening, getting Shiloh drinks, holding her hand, or having her arm around her. At one point, Shiloh glanced up to see Harley looking to her left with narrowed eyes. Shiloh followed her line of sight and saw the butch that had been chatting Shiloh up the night of Roslynn's misadventure.

"What's that about?" Shiloh asked Harley.

"Just warning her off," Harley said, leaning down to kiss her ear.

"I see," Shiloh said, shivering at the feel of Harley's lips on her ear. "Maybe if you dance with me, it'll really tell everyone," she said, smiling up at Harley.

"By your command," Harley said, gesturing to the dance floor.

Shiloh led the way with Harley right behind her. They danced to a couple of fast songs and then the DJ slowed it down. Shiloh looked up at Harley to see if she wanted to leave the floor, but instead she felt Harley's hand slide around her waist and pull her close. Harley's lips grazed her temple. Shiloh slid her hands up around Harley's neck, pressing closer and feeling Harley's hands slide further around her back to gather her closer. Shiloh had her face right at Harley's neck.

She inhaled the intoxicating scent of this woman she'd been craving so much. Closing her eyes, she let herself completely experience every moment of their dance. She felt the rise and fall of Harley's chest as she breathed. She leaned her head against Harley's chest and could feel her heartbeat. She could not believe how wonderful it felt to in this woman's arms.

Shiloh slid her hands down Harley's arms, feeling the strength in them, and feeling so happy she couldn't even think of a way to express it adequately. She felt Harley glance down at her, evident by the way Harley's neck muscles shifted. Shiloh looked up, her eyes connecting with Harley's. Her breath caught in her throat as Harley lowered her head and kissed her lips. Harley's lips were soft and warm. Shiloh felt the gentle sucking and the wetness between their lips, but her body felt it all the way to her core. As if there was a direct connection between her lips and her groin, she felt a pulse start, and she jumped significantly as Harley's hand came up to cup her face. She deepened the kiss, her lips taking on a more demanding quality.

Shiloh moaned softly against Harley's lips and her hands grasped at the front of Harley's shirt. She felt a corresponding expelling of breath from Harley, and Harley's hands grasping at her back, pulling closer, caressing Shiloh's back. When their lips parted, Harley leaned down to put her lips next to Shiloh's ear.

"God, Shy, I want you so much…" she said, her voice husky with desire.

Shiloh felt a thrill go through her unlike anything she'd ever felt before in her life.

Turning her head she said, "I want you too, now, right now…" She was practically pleading.

Without a word, Harley stepped back, taking Shiloh's hand in hers, and led her off the dance floor. She walked over to the table, picked up her jacket, and handed Shiloh her purse.

"We're out," Harley said, her tone telling the group everything they needed to know.

There were a series of looks and knowing grins exchanged, as many of them nodded politely.

In minutes, Harley and Shiloh were in the car and Harley was driving as quickly as it was safe. Soon they were getting out of the car in the garage. Harley opened the passenger door for Shiloh, taking her hand to help her out. She closed the car door behind Shiloh and then pressed her back against the car as she kissed her again, making them both extremely hot. Harley turned and led Shiloh into the house turning off the alarm as she walked past it.

Shiloh stopped suddenly, causing Harley to turn around to look at her. The look in Shiloh's eyes held so much desire Harley could only gasp as she took her face into her hands to kiss her again. Their bodies pressed as close together as they could possibly get. Shiloh was grasping at Harley's shirt, unbuttoning it so she could slide her hands inside. Harley tore her lips away from Shiloh's, groaning loudly at the feel of Shiloh's hands on her torso.

"Shy, Shy…" she murmured, as she lowered her lips to Shiloh's again, pulling at her, wanting her so desperately.

They made it as far as the stairs. Harley kicked off her boots, as she pulled Shiloh's shirt up over her head. She laid Shiloh against the stairs, kissing and licking her skin while Shiloh's hands buried themselves in her hair.

Harley reached around Shiloh, unclasping her bra with the expertise born of a lot of experience with women and their undergarments. She kissed the more sensitive skin, as she pushed Shiloh's skirt up on her hips, putting her body between Shiloh's legs, still fully clothed. Harley pressed her body against Shiloh's and felt Shiloh's body shudder. She moved her lips to Shiloh's nipples, feeling Shiloh go ridged and heard her gasping and groaning moments later as she came. Harley kept up the pressure of her hips against Shiloh's groin, causing her to come again.

Shiloh felt like she was turning to liquid as Harley expertly guided her to orgasm after orgasm. Her hands grasped at Harley's shoulders, and then moved to her torso as she tried to pull Harley closer to her. After at least three orgasms, Shiloh felt Harley move away, and she groaned, trying to pull Harley back to her. She heard Harley chuckle and then she felt her body being lifted.

Just like the old movies, Harley carried Shiloh upstairs and into her bedroom, laying her down at the end of the bed. She took her time to remove all of Shiloh's clothes, her lips and hands never losing contact with Shiloh's skin. Harley brought her to her climax twice more.

Shiloh pulled Harley up so their eyes met again. Slowly she got up off the bed, standing to face Harley as she pushed the shirt off Harley's shoulders and unbuttoned her slacks. Harley obliged by assisting her in removing her clothes. Shiloh's hand went to the tattoo above Harley's left breast, it was a yin and yang symbol, but rather than black and white, it was blue and yellow orange, and looking textured.

"Yin and yang?" Shiloh asked.

"Fire and water," Harley replied, smiling softly.

Shiloh's hand touched the other tattoo on the right side of Harley's bikini line. It was done in the shades of the rainbow starting from red, going to orange, then yellow, green, blue and purple. The symbol itself was an almost cross shape, but the lines of the cross, looked like lizards with a circle in the very center.

"I have no idea what that is," Shiloh said.

"I got that one from Rayden actually. It's the Cherokee symbol for unity in diversity," Harley said.

Shiloh nodded, smiling. "Yeah that sounds like you too."

Shiloh's hand smoothed over Harley's skin, as Harley stepped closer to her again. She kissed her lips and pressed her back onto the bed, positioning her body over Shiloh's. Shiloh touched and caressed Harley's skin, mimicking what Harley had done to her and feeling Harley's breath quicken in response. Harley surprised her by laying on her back, pulling Shiloh over her, her hands holding Shiloh's body close.

Shiloh lowered her head, kissing Harley's skin and marveling at the lean muscle of Harley's body. She kissed Harley's neck and felt her jump and gasp in response, her hands burying themselves in Shiloh's hair, holding her head. In response, Shiloh continued her exploration of Harley's neck, kissing and sucking at her skin, even biting gently. She received a loud groan in response, spurring her on.

Within minutes, Harley was crying out in her release and Shiloh could not believe the feeling of power it gave her to know that she'd caused this in Harley. In the end they spent hours making love, exalting in exciting each other over and over again.

Finally, in the wee hours of the morning, they lay on the bed, their bodies intertwined. Shiloh rested her head against Harley's stomach facing her, who half sat up against the headboard.

"I think Devin might have been right…" Shiloh said languorously.

"About?" Harley asked grinning.

"She said that to have someone like you decide to make me their own is the most incredible thing in the world… I think she's probably right."

"Is that what you want?" Harley asked, looking inscrutable. "For me to make you my own?"

Shiloh sat up and touched Harley's cheek tenderly.

"More than anything in the world," she said softly.

Harley looked back at her, her look wondrous as she smiled. "Well, I think I just did."

Shiloh bit her lip. "Then I think you just made me the happiest woman alive."

"Good."

***

A month after Jazmine and Dakota got back together, Dakota finished the Craftsman house and gave Cassandra a final walk through. Cassandra had shocked Dakota by asking her to bring Jazmine with her. Jazmine had further shocked Dakota and accepted the invitation,

275

wanting to see what Dakota had been working on that she loved so much.

Jazmine was both stunned and impressed by the house that Dakota had worked so hard to make beautiful again.

"Dakota, this is amazing," Jazmine said, holding Dakota's hand, her green eyes sparkling in pride.

"I agree," Cassandra said, smiling as well.

"I'm glad you like it," Dakota said, nodding to Cassandra and smiling at Jazmine fondly.

They finished the tour and walked out to the front. Cassandra pulled an envelope out of her purse and handed it to Dakota.

"Final payment," Cassandra said in explanation.

Dakota looked confused, but opened the envelope. As she read the paperwork her eyes widened, and she looked at Cassandra.

"Are you kidding me?" Dakota asked.

Cassandra smiled, shaking her head. "Not at all," she said sincerely.

Dakota blinked a couple of times and looked over at Jazmine who was looking between them trying to figure out what was happening.

"This," Dakota said, holding up the paperwork, "is the deed to this house. See what it says there under owners?" Dakota said, pointing the line of the document she was referring to.

Jazmine read it and her mouth dropped open. She looked at Dakota then at Cassandra who smiled benevolently.

"You're giving us this house?" Jazmine asked Cassandra shocked.

"Yes," Cassandra said. "Dakota worked so hard on it, and I know that you two will love it and appreciate it in a way I never could."

"But why…" Jazmine asked.

"For the same reason I bought the house and wanted Dakota to restore it," Cassandra said. "To make amends."

"Cass…" Dakota said, shaking her head. "This is so much though…"

"You deserve more," Cassandra said, "but I know I'll be lucky if your pride will allow you to take this, so…" She shrugged.

Dakota looked at Jazmine wanting to know what Jazmine thought. Jazmine looked back at Dakota and then at Cassandra. She stepped forward and hugged Cassandra.

"I'm accepting it for both of us," she said.

Cassandra surprised them both by crying softly and whispering, "Thank you," to Jazmine.

"Now, I need to get going," Cassandra said, dabbing at her eyes with her handkerchief. "Salina and I are headed to New York…"

"Salina?" Dakota asked with a raised eyebrow. "Isn't that the artist you were working with on the mural for the Art Center?"

Cassandra bit her lip, smiling and nodding.

"Well, alright," Dakota said, smiling widely and nodding. "Run along then."

Cassandra reached over and hugged Dakota. "Thank you for everything."

"No, thank you," Dakota replied.

A few minutes later Cassandra left in her car and Dakota and Jazmine stood staring at each other.

"Holy hell… Now we have two houses…" Dakota said, grinning.

"Well, I hear you can never have too many," Jazmine said, grinning.

"I guess not," Dakota replied.

"Come on, let's go look at it again, now that we know it's ours," Jazmine said, smiling mysteriously.

Dakota found out why a little while later when Jazmine seduced her in the master bedroom on the newly refinished wood flooring.

"I love you," Dakota said, lying on the bare floor, trying to catch her breath.

"Just remember that," Jazmine replied grinning.

Epilogue

"So she just gave you two the house?" Quinn asked, not for the first time.

"Yeah," Dakota said, nodding. "Damndest thing I've ever seen."

"Not complaining though," Jazmine said, grinning. "Dakota did an amazing job so you're all going to have to come check it out."

For the first time in a long time, the entire group had made it out to the bar, including a rare appearance by Sebastian and Ashley, as well as Lyric and Savanna. They were there to celebrate Dakota's triumph with finishing the Craftsman. Everyone had heard all of the drama the project had caused between Jazmine and Dakota and they were relieved that the couple had made it through all of it.

There was a sudden flurry of excitement at the entrance to the bar, causing the group to look in that direction. As they did, Kashena and Sierra walked in and over to the grouping of tables, both grinning widely.

"Did you see what was going on there?" Jericho asked, always on guard.

"Oh yeah," Kashena said, grinning. "It's a friend of ours that we brought with us."

"Causing that kind of stir?" Jet queried, raising a black eyebrow.

"She causes a stir wherever she goes," Sierra said, smiling.

"So who is it?" Quinn asked, always one to get straight to the point.

"Remi LaRoché," Kashena said offhandedly.

"Are you fuckin' kidding me?" Quinn asked her tone shocked.

"Who is Remi LaRoché?" Xandy asked Quinn.

"Only one of the best MMA fighters on the planet!" Quinn said. She looked at Kashena. "How the hell do you know her?"

"Marines," Kashena said. "I was in basic with her at Pendleton."

"Holy shyte!" Quinn said looking like a kid at Christmas.

"She is pretty awesome," Tyler said. "I saw her fight in D.C., never seen such speed and agility before."

"I caught a fight in New York," Dakota said. "And yeah, she just beat the crap out of the girl before the chick could even think about fighting back. She's damned fast."

"Yeah there was a fight on Pay-Per-View a few months back, and I couldn't believe her jabs, just rabbit fast…" Jericho said, nodding.

"Didn't she retire recently?" Quinn asked.

"Yeah," Kashena said, nodding. "She's thinking about bodyguard work, so I'm hooking her up with Joe and Mackie."

"Good call," Quinn said, nodding.

Remington LaRoché walked up to the group then, having finally gotten through the crowd of women asking for her autograph. She stood at five foot nine, and weighed in at 135 pounds of solid muscle. It was evident in her arms, bare due to the red tank top she wore. She wore her brunette hair in cornrows that fell to her mid back, tipped with red on the top. Remington was of Creole descent and it showed in her milk chocolate colored skin and lighter colored hazel-gold eyes. There was no arguing that Remington was a beautiful woman, but also very intimidating with her size and obvious strength.

"Remi," Kashena said, "this is the group. You all can introduce yourselves to her. Guys this is Remi."

Remington surprised everyone putting her hands together prayer form, and bowed her head respectfully to the group.

"Onre," she said, her light eyes shining. "That's means 'honored' in Creole."

Quinn was the first to stand up and extend her hand to Remington. "It's an honor to meet you," she said. "You are the best damned MMA fighter I've ever had the pleasure of watching."

"Mesi, thank you," Remington said, smiling.

"This is Xandy," Quinn said, touching Xandy's shoulder.

"I like your music," Remington told Xandy. "Your recent work more so."

Xandy smiled, nodding. "Yeah, BJ Sparks has a way of getting better work out of everyone. I'm no exception."

"Remington," Jericho said, extending her hand to the other woman. "A pleasure, I've seen you fight as well, you're credit to the sport."

"Please call me Remi," Remington said. "And thank you, I appreciate your praise."

One by one, the group introduced themselves to Remington. Before long they were all drinking and enjoying themselves.

It was nearing midnight when there was a sudden jolt. The ground began swaying as a sound like a boulder rolling down the street began.

"Earthquake!" someone screamed, followed by many screams of other patrons.

"Take cover! Cover your heads!" Jericho yelled, pushing Grayson down under the table.

Others did the same. Various members of the group helped others to take cover as the shaking continued for what seemed like forever. There was crashing sounds as glasses and bottles fell from shelves. There was a louder crash and feedback as some of the larger speakers fell over. Screams and crying ensued as the shaking continued. Car horns and alarms went off, the screech of tires and yelling could be heard outside.

"Everybody just stay calm!" Sebastian yelled over the din, as he kept his body covering Ashley's.

Tables fell over, causing people to scramble for other cover. When the shaking finally ended it had only been a total of fifteen seconds, but it had seemed like forever. As soon as the shaking stopped, the group went into action. Quinn, Jericho, Rayden, Sebastian, and Remington started pulling debris off of people, while Lyric, Savanna, Cody, and McKenna started evacuating people from the bar, getting them to move toward the exit doors. Jet, Grayson, Jazmine, and Dakota moved to get people out of the back door through the patio. Raine, Natalia, and Fadiyah began checking on people who weren't moving, doing their best to help them.

"Ray, Quinn!" Raine yelled, kneeling by a woman who was trapped under a piece of roof.

Rayden and Quinn immediately moved to where Raine knelt.

"Okay, we're going to move this," Rayden said, nodding to Quinn. "Raine, just be ready to cover her if anything slips. Okay? Ready?"

"Yeah, go!" Raine said her hands at the ready.

The piece was moved, and Raine sheltered the woman's body with her own as smaller pieces of the ceiling broke away and dropped from the piece being moved.

"Raine, you okay?" Quinn asked, seeing the debris falling.

"Yeah, got it," Raine said, nodding. "Thanks guys!"

Rayden and Quinn moved off then, seeing that Sebastian and Jericho were struggling with one of the large speakers.

"Remi!" Quinn yelled, getting the other woman's attention and motioning to her.

The five of them were able to move the speaker. The woman who lay under it wasn't breathing. Quinn performed CPR and Xandy who stood near her, called out for someone with a cell phone to see if they could get through to 911. Sierra was already on her phone calling and nodded to Xandy, holding up her hand. After a few very tense moments, the woman started coughing. Xandy hugged Quinn for her quick action.

Within twenty minutes of the quake, the bar was cleared, and everyone was out on the street. The group got together and started talking about what they could do.

"We can work out of my house," Harley offered. "I'm like a mile away."

"Good, yeah, that'll work," Jericho said. Being the highest-ranking one out of the group, she naturally took charge. "Gray, you and Skyler should try to get to the locals and offer your assistance with rescue. Shenin, can you get ahold of the Air Force for aircraft and assistance?"

Shenin nodded. "Yeah, come on you two, let's go," she said, looking around to see what they could use for a vehicle.

"We've got the Jag, let's use that," Grayson said. Rayden tossed her the keys and the three moved off.

"Harley and I can work with the locals to make sure emergency systems up are up and running," Devin offered.

"Perfect," Jericho said, nodding. "Take Shiloh. Sierra you might be helpful to smooth things over with the locals on that."

Sierra nodded. "I think you're right, I'll get ahold of Midnight."

"We can take my Hummer," Devin said, seeing that the large white SUV was mostly unharmed by the quake.

"I think we should start with this area to help pull people out and whatever else heavy lifting there is," Jericho said, her eyes touching on Quinn, Jet, Rayden, Kashena, Jet, Sebastian, and Remington. They all nodded. "Cat, maybe take some of the girls to see what we can do to help out setting up shelters and stuff?"

"I think McKenna and I will go check in with the animal shelter to see what's happening there..." Cody said, thinking of all the animals that were likely to be affected.

"I like it," Jericho said, nodding and grinning. "Dakota and Ty, maybe you can help with some of the assessments for the buildings and security?"

Within three hours, the group doing dig outs were pulling people out of collapsed homes and wrecked cars in the West Hollywood area.

A shelter had been set up in a few high school gyms, and at the Hollywood Bowl which had been undamaged by the quake. Cat, Jovina, and Fadiyah helped at the Bowl, whilst Ashley, Zoey, Savanna, and Raine ended up at a high school. Xandy had been pulled in by BJ Sparks to work on fundraising efforts to help the victims.

BJ Sparks used the talent he had in town to put on an impromptu concert, using Xandy, Jordan Tate, and his own band, Sparks. He also pulled in a singer he'd just signed to his label, who was already a star in her own right, named Wynter Kincade. John Machiavelli and Joe Sinclair pulled in some of their bodyguards to act as security for the quickly planned concert, including Remington, if nothing else for her notoriety.

The concert was held at the Santa Monica Pier a few days later, and was quickly advertised to gain support. The stage was set up on the beach, and they'd set up tents for the stars of the show. Remington and Quinn were put by the tents to ensure no unauthorized people got through. Quinn was dealing with a couple of teenagers who thought they'd sneak a peek at the stars. Meanwhile, a woman wearing a white baseball cap with the words "Be Yourself" in rainbow colored letters jeans and a white T-shirt with the words 'lipstick lesbian' on it, stooped under the yellow tape.

She started walking toward one of the tents while texting on her phone. Remington stepped into her path. The woman continued to stride forward, and would have collided with Remington if she hadn't put her hands out to stop her. As it was, the woman walked right into Remington's hands, which touched her shoulders before she looked up stumbling backwards in the sand. Remington had to grab her shoulders to keep her from falling.

"Jesus!" the woman exclaimed, glancing up as she did.

"Ma'am, you can't be back here without a pass," Remington said, as she set the woman back on her feet and let go of her shoulders.

"I'm one of the stars," the woman replied.

Remington looked back at the woman, her look indicating disbelief.

"Jesus! I am!" she said, reaching up to pull off her baseball cap, releasing a fall of long dark hair and exposing ice blue eyes.

She looked vaguely familiar to Remington, but that didn't mean she was telling the truth.

"If that's the case, you should have a pass," Remington said evenly.

"Oh for God's fucking sake, are you kidding me right now?" the woman snapped.

Remington didn't answer. She merely looked back at the woman calmly. Neither of them was budging.

"And what if I just push past you?" the woman with the blue eyes asked.

"You're welcome to try."

"And you're going to what? Accost me again?" the woman snapped.

"I believe it's called saving you from falling, ma'am," Remington said her look completely serene.

"If you hadn't been standing in my way, I wouldn't have been in danger of falling!"

"If you'd had a pass I wouldn't have stood in your way."

"That again!" the woman snapped. "God damn it I'm Wynter Kincade. Do you live under a rock or something?"

"No, ma'am," Remington replied.

"Then you should recognize me and let me by!" Wynter yelled.

"Sorry, ma'am," Remington said, shrugging.

Wynter looked back at the dark-haired woman with the braids. Part of her was insanely attracted to the very butch, but extremely attractive woman. The other part was fit to be tied at that point. The star took over then.

"What's your name?" Wynter asked.

Remington looked back at her for a long moment. It was clear she wanted to ask why that mattered.

"Just tell me your name," Wynter said her tone even.

"Remington LaRoché, ma'am," Remington pronounced, her tone officious.

"LaRoché…" Wynter said, rolling the name around on her tongue. "That's very sexy," she said with a wink.

Remington simply looked back at her with no emotion on her face.

"Do people call you Remi?"

"Some do, yes," Remington replied, not giving an inch.

Wynter narrowed her eyes. It was rare that her charm didn't work for her, especially on the gays.

"Well, Remi," Wynter said, her tone at its most reasonable. "I didn't get a pass, but I assure you that if you Google my name, you'll see my picture and you'll know that I'm me, okay?"

Remington looked back at Wynter, and to Wynter's shock, she folded her arms in front of her, her stance wide.

"No pass, no pass," Remington said simply.

"Argh!" Wynter screamed in frustration. "You have got to be fucking kidding me! Get out of my way, I mean it!" she yelled, moving to shove at Remington.

She was actually surprised when Remington didn't budge, completely unaffected by all the strength that Wynter had. Part of her was impressed, but the impatient part wasn't having it. She went to kick Remington in the shins, but suddenly she wasn't where she had been a second before. Remi had taken one wide step back, leaning back as Wynter's foot kicked thin air. Giving a banshee yell of sheer frustration, Wynter attempted to dart past Remington. She was stopped by one extremely well muscled arm in front of her. Wynter pulled up short, just in time to keep from colliding with Remington's arm.

"Fuck!" she screamed. "Go fucking get BJ he'll tell you who I am!"

Remington pursed her lips, her eyes sparkling now with amusement as she shook her head slowly.

Wynter blew her breath out in an exasperated sigh, and then suddenly ducked under Remington's arm and started to run toward the tents. She was caught by a surprisingly gentle arm to the mid-section, lifted off her feet, and held aloft with Remington's hip at her backside.

"Put me down, Goddamnit!" she screamed, struggling against Remington's hold.

Remington made no reply, simply carrying her over to the barriers and setting her down her feet.

"Go get a pass, and you can come through here," Remington said simply, then turned and walked away without a backward glance.

Wynter stared at the woman's retreating back and could not believe what had just happened. She also couldn't help but respect the strength it had taken for Remington to not only lift her off the ground, but to carry her struggling a good thousand feet back to the barriers.

Ten minutes later with her pass in hand, she strolled up to Remington, her look rebellious. Remington simply waved her on as if she were just anyone else. Wynter was stunned and literally stood open-mouthed staring up at the other woman.

"That's all I get?" she asked.

"What else did you need?" Remington asked her tone completely businesslike.

"An apology would be nice," Wynter counted.

Remington looked back at her impassively, but made no reply.

"Of all the…" Wynter muttered as she marched off to her tent.

She didn't see the grin that curled Remington's lips after she'd passed.

The quake had been a 6.8 magnitude, with the epicenter southeast of Los Angeles near the Chino hills. There'd been plenty of damage and a few lives lost. The loss of life was lessoned by the volunteers who'd pitched in to help. It was duly noted that eleven members of the Department of Justice were key in helping out in the West Hollywood area, saving as many at ten lives. Skyler and Grayson flew rescue choppers to help take people to local hospitals. While other members helped to dig people out of their homes and other various locations, working tirelessly for hours on end. Cody and McKenna worked with the shelter to find families who'd been separated from their pets, or find temporary housing for pets whose family couldn't be located.

The concert at Santa Monica Pier raised over a million dollars to help the victims and their families. Remington watched Wynter perform on stage and found that she was rather impressed with the tiny little fireball, not that she'd ever tell the girl that. Xandy performed to a screaming crowd, and was even prompted to bring her girlfriend onstage. As always, Quinn was reluctant to comply, but eventually walked onstage, waved to the people at the show. She kissed Xandy sweetly, then walked back off stage. The crowd loved it! Jordan performed to screaming and adoring fans. Sparks was the last to perform, and they brought down the house. It was a success all around.

Harley and Devin became the heroes to local emergency units as they assisted in setting up a tracking system to keep track of calls and progress made. They were also able to troubleshoot issues with the systems power grid and help to get power back to thousands of people. They also helped local law enforcement by restoring the CLETS system that had been knocked offline by the quake.

The group gathered at Harley's house, using it as a command post of sorts, to keep track of each other. It took almost a week for things to return to normal. During that time, Harley and Shiloh played host to the entire group and their families, including Ana, as well as Sebastian and Ashely's baby, Gemma. As always, the group looked out for each other, pointing out when people needed to rest. Savanna and Grayson took up the role of mother hens and made sure everyone ate, slept, and rested as appropriate.

As things finally calmed down, the group met at Harley's house one more time to have a celebratory dinner. Xandy had invited BJ, Jordan, and Wynter as well. The house was alive with music and people. Everyone ate, drank, and had a good time.

Remington had taken refuge in the backyard near the outdoor fireplace. She was sitting with a beer in hand, staring into the flames. She didn't notice the person watching her.

"Wishing you hadn't moved here?" Wynter asked from behind her.

Remington glanced over her shoulder, standing as Wynter moved to stand by the fireplace, a glass of wine in hand.

"Disasters happen everywhere," Remington replied, still standing.

Wynter nodded, having noted the gallant gesture. "True," she agreed. "But one helluva a welcome, huh?"

Remington didn't reply, and Wynter's phone buzzed. Remington watched as she looked at her phone, and rolled her eyes heavenward.

"I swear to God…" she muttered in annoyance.

"Problems?" Remington asked.

"Just with my girlfriend," Wynter said her tone annoyed.

Remington nodded, her look unaffected.

"I swear, it's like she wants to be connected at the hip all the time, it's really annoying!" Wynter said.

Remington nodded again.

"I guess your girlfriend doesn't annoy you," Wynter said.

"I think that if she annoyed me, she wouldn't be my girlfriend," Remington said mildly.

"So you do have a girlfriend?" Wynter asked, not caring if she was completely transparent.

Remington didn't answer. She just looked back at Wynter, her eyes only flickering slightly at the question.

"And you're not going to answer," Wynter said.

A slight smile curved at Remington's lips.

"Careful, that was almost a smile," Wynter pointed out, with a wry grin.

Remington lifted her beer to her lips to avoid responding. Wynter watched, knowing that Remington was trying to put her off.

"I guess I'll get back in there," Wynter said. She canted her head slightly to Remington. "Would you be willing to escort me?" she asked, testing out a theory.

Again, Remington's look flickered, and Wynter read mild suspicion in her look. However, she took the two steps to close the distance between them. Without a word, Remington extended her arm to Wynter who took it, grinning as she did. Remington turned to walk toward the house. Wynter knew she had a good old-fashioned southern gentleman on her hands, and she found that thought absolutely fascinating!

You can find more information about the author and series here:

www.sherrylhancock.com

www.facebook.com/SherrylDHancock

Made in the USA
Middletown, DE
11 December 2017